BOOK SOLD
NO LONGER R.H.P.L.
PROPERTY

Riot Most Uncouth

Also by Daniel Friedman

Don't Ever Look Back

Don't Ever Get Old

Riot Most Uncouth

A Lord Byron Mystery

Daniel Friedman

Minotaur Books

A Thomas Dunne Book

New York

A THOMAS DUNNE BOOK FOR MINOTAUR BOOKS
An imprint of St. Martin's Publishing Group.

RIOT MOST UNCOUTH. Copyright © 2015 by Daniel Friedman. All rights reserved. Printed in the United States of America. For information, address St. Martin's Press, 175 Fifth Avenue, New York, N.Y. 10010.

www.thomasdunnebooks.com
www.minotaurbooks.com

Designed by Molly Rose Murphy

Library of Congress Cataloging-in-Publication Data

Friedman, Daniel, 1981–
    Riot most uncouth : a Lord Byron mystery / Daniel Friedman. —
First edition.
        pages ; cm
    ISBN 978-1-250-02759-7 (hardcover)
    ISBN 978-1-250-02758-0 (e-book)
  1. Private investigators—England—Fiction.   2. Murder—Investigation—
Fiction.   3. Cambridge (England)—Social life and customs—19th century—
Fiction.   I. Title.
    PS3606.R5566R56 2015
    813'.6—dc23
                                                                        2015033767

Our books may be purchased in bulk for promotional, educational, or business use. Please contact your local bookseller or the Macmillan Corporate and Premium Sales Department at (800) 221-7945, extension 5442, or by e-mail at MacmillanSpecialMarkets@macmillan.com.

First Edition: December 2015

10   9   8   7   6   5   4   3   2   1

In memory of Dr. David Friedman

Acknowledgments

I'd like to thank my agent, Victoria Skurnick, and foreign rights manager, Elizabeth Fisher at Levine Greenberg Rostan, for their continued dedication to the Buck Schatz books, and for helping me to sell this jarring deviation from what was expected of me. I'd also like to thank Lucy Stille at APA for selling the film rights to *Don't Ever Get Old*.

Thanks to my editor, Marcia Markland, her assistant, Quressa Robinson, publicity manager Hector DeJean, Thomas Dunne Books publisher Thomas Dunne, Minotaur Books publisher Andrew Martin, and associate editor Kat Brzozowski.

I'd also like to thank my mom, Elaine Friedman, my brother Jonathan Friedman, Grandma Margaret Friedman, and Bubbi Goldie Burson for all their love and support. Thanks as well to Rachel Friedman, baby Hannah Dove Friedman, Sheila and Steve Burkholz, Carole Burson, Skip and Susan Rossen, Stephen and Beth Rossen, David and Lindsey Rossen, Martin and Jenny Rossen, Scott Burkholz, Rachel Burkholz, Claire and Paul Putterman, Andrew Putterman and Matthew Putterman.

*My time has lately been much occupied with
very different pursuits. I have been . . . performing
in private theatricals; publishing a volume
of poems (at the request of my friends, for their
perusal); making love, and taking the physic. The
two last amusements have not had the best effect
in the world, for my attentions have been divided
amongst so many fair damsels and the drugs I
swallow are of such variety in their composition,
that between Venus and Aesculapius I am harassed
to death.*

—Lord Byron, *from an 1807
letter to the Earl of Clare*

*I would to Heaven that I were so much clay,
As I am blood, bone, marrow, passion, feeling—
Because at least the past were pass'd away—
And for the future—(but I write this reeling,
Having got drunk exceedingly to-day,
So that I seem to stand upon the ceiling)
I say—the future is a serious matter—
And so—for God's sake—hock and soda-water!*

—Lord Byron, *fragment of a poem
scrawled on the back of the
manuscript of* Don Juan

Chapter 1

Whilome in Albion's isle there dwelt a youth,
Who ne in virtue's ways did take delight;
But spent his days in riot most uncouth,
And vexed with mirth the drowsy ear of Night.
Ah, me! in sooth he was a shameless wight,
Sore given to revel and ungodly glee;
Few earthly things found favour in his sight
Save concubines and carnal companie,
And flaunting wassailers of high and low degree.

—Lord Byron, Childe Harold's
Pilgrimage, *canto 1*

A poet must have a keen eye for details and for feelings; for subtext and for innuendo. This same set of skills is also essential if one hopes to have any success at the pursuit and capture of murderers. The 1807 publication of *Hours of Idleness,* my first collection of verses, cemented my reputation as the greatest poet ever to have lived. It therefore stood to reason that I also was the world's greatest criminal investigator.

That autumn, I was bored with my studies at Trinity College and feeling quite restless. So I was intrigued and a little annoyed when my butler, Joe Murray, informed me as I enjoyed an otherwise-pleasant champagne breakfast that a young woman named Miss Felicity Whippleby had been butchered in her Cambridge rooms. She was said to have been a quiet and well-mannered girl, and nobody could fathom what she might have done to bring such a fate upon herself.

Murder was a rare thing in Cambridge, and mystery was unheard of. I had no doubt Felicity Whippleby's name would soon be upon the lips of every local gossip and rumormonger, people whose time would have been better spent talking about me. I resolved to put my first-rate intellect to work capturing her killer. Such a diversion would burnish my notoriety and provide a good excuse to avoid attending classes. Anyway, Cambridge was large enough to support the misdeeds of only one villain. I would not be upstaged on my own territory by a knife-wielding interloper.

So, I roused my cohabitant, the Professor, from his hibernatory slumber, and after finishing off two bottles of Veuve Clicquot, we began canvassing the neighborhood, looking for the murderer. The air was crisp and fresh, and a stiff wind was blowing through the narrow streets, a welcome respite from the summer's merciless heat. I would have found the weather invigorating, but I was animated that morning by something much more sinister than the apple-scented blush of early October in a leafy college town; I'd been awake for fifty hours, and I'd spent most of it drinking. I was, thus, in a state of near delirium. The Professor was better rested and had his wits about him, but grouchiness was intrinsic to his nature.

Our manhunt quickly turned up a suspect; as we wandered

about near the scene of the murder, I noticed a shabby fellow staring at us with crazed, bulging eyes. My keen senses could not be fooled; something was out of place with this character.

"Do you have a problem?" I asked. He was taller than I, and broader through the shoulders, but I was younger and had become a skilled brawler during my years at boarding school. Still, if this confrontation devolved into fisticuffs, he might have been able to get the better of me, as I was not fully in command of my faculties. Fortunately, I was accompanied by the Professor, whose presence was sufficient to deter most evildoers.

"Perhaps it's not my place to say," said the suspicious man. His jacket was ill fitting and threadbare around the elbows. Unless he was the killer, he was nobody important.

"Perhaps it's not," I agreed.

"It's just that there appears to be a rather large bear behind you." He shrank away from the Professor.

I scowled at him. "Don't you think I know that?"

He shuffled his feet and avoided meeting my accusatory gaze; a sign of guilt. Inconclusive, though. His behavior could merely indicate that he was intimidated by my estimable presence. Even if he didn't know who I was, he must have known by observing my dress, which was only fashionably disheveled, and my carriage, which was just a little wobbly, that I was a quality sort. I was also uncommonly handsome, and my raw sexual magnetism had a tendency to frighten or confuse lesser men.

"I don't mean to be impertinent, sir," he said, his voice quavering. "But why is there a large bear behind you?"

"He's shy," I said. "He doesn't like you." I had little patience for the suspicious man's hyperbole and histrionics. The Professor was of ordinary size for his genus. "I don't like you much myself," I added.

The man gurgled a little and tugged at his shirt collar. "I apologize, then, to the both of you. I'll be going now."

But I grabbed hold of his lapels to stop him. He had given himself away; for even a novice practitioner of the art of detection knows that murderers are terrified of bears.

"You're not going anywhere," I said. His clothes were stiff with filth and dried sweat, and when I shook him, I must have loosed the stink he held close to his body. It erupted forth, like a brown fog rolling off a rancid moor; a stench so powerful, it had a taste. I gagged and tried to hold my breath. I didn't quite manage it, but I did hold on to the killer. I'd always wondered if evil had an odor. As the murderer's filth laid siege to my poor nose, I knew it did.

The Professor growled and licked his paw, pleased with my display of prowess. He had the benefit of vast and subtle reasoning capacities as well as an ursine olfactory mechanism, a tool far more precise than the nose of a man. He must have long ago deduced that this miscreant slaughtered that poor girl.

"Why did you do it, you foul blackguard?" I wheezed. "Why did you kill her?"

The man's eyes jerked around in their sockets, looking for a route of egress. But he was stuck between me and the bear, and there would be no escape. "I've got no idea what you're talking about," he said.

Less able explorers of the dark corners of the human heart might have been convinced by the killer's display of confusion, but I didn't believe him, and the Professor didn't either. So I twisted the man's stinky arm. Hard. Behind his back. He started to struggle, but the Professor growled again, and the man went limp. I drew the pistol I carried in my waistcoat and pressed it against my captive's jaw, in case he had any ideas about resisting.

Thus threatened, he became quite docile and allowed me to lead him back to the rooming house where the volunteer constable of Cambridge was guarding the murder scene.

The officer's broad face swelled and reddened. "I still can't let you examine Miss Whippleby's room or the body, Lord Byron," he said, smoothing his homemade uniform over the expanse of his belly. "I don't care how important you think you are."

This place had, of course, been the first stop in our investigation, but the constable did not permit us to hunt for clues. The house matron had dispatched a rider to carry news of the tragedy to the girl's father in London, and Lord Whippleby would surely send a professional man hunter to run down the killer. The scene and the corpse would be preserved, untouched, awaiting such expert examination.

It would be waiting, however, for a while. It was an hour's ride on a fast horse to the nearest station on the semaphore line, and it would take at least another hour to transmit the message to London. If fog obscured visibility between stations, relay riders would have to carry the news instead, extending the journey.

Once word of the tragedy reached the girl's father, he'd need another hour, or perhaps even two, to make the necessary arrangements to get an investigator on the road. A fast rider could clear the fifty miles between London and Cambridge in under four hours, including a stop to change horses, but the investigator likely would not be an expert equestrian. Also, he'd be hauling his equipment or his belongings, so he'd hire a coach, which would take quite a bit longer. Meanwhile, the killer's trail would grow cold.

I'd tried to explain that I was the world's greatest poet and the Professor was a noted expert, but the constable, quite unmoved by our impressive credentials, was loath to permit a drunk and a bear to root around the premises. No matter. I'd solved the case regardless.

"I have captured your killer," I announced. "This man did it." I threw the culprit down at the constable's feet. "Take him away and hang him, or do whatever it is you people do."

"Please," said the murderer to the constable. "This gentleman is quite mad, and he reeks of drink."

"You're the one who reeks," I countered.

The constable scratched the stubble on his chin with a long, yellow fingernail. "This is no killer. He is only Mr. Collins, the wheelwright."

The Professor sighed. We had both grown accustomed to dealing with our intellectual inferiors, but idiocy was tiresome nonetheless. "He is Mr. Collins, the murderer," I said. "People are rarely only one thing. Wheelwrights can also be murderers."

The constable didn't look convinced. "But I've known Mr. Collins for near to twenty years. He goes to my church. Decent-enough fellow. Family man."

I nodded. "Very well. You can tax his children to pay for his hanging, then."

"I didn't do nothing, Angus," said Collins the Murderer.

"He'll confess easy enough when the Professor interrogates him," I said.

Collins wailed.

"That doesn't seem like a good idea at all," said the constable. "When Whippleby's man arrives, he'll sort everything out."

"What are you going to do, then, with this criminal?" I asked.

Angus gave my suspect a dismissive wave with his fleshy hand. "You move on along, Mr. Collins. Send me best to the missus."

Collins scurried off, probably to kill some more people.

"The mistake you've made today is very grave," I told Angus.

"I don't think Mr. Collins is the murderer. If I had to make a guess, I'd be inclined to blame Mr. Leif Sedgewyck."

The name was familiar. "Sedgewyck is a student at the College," I said. "What's he got to do with this?"

"He was a frequent companion of the dead girl's; a man who might have married her. I spoke to him earlier this morning."

"Why do you think he did it?"

Angus started to say something, and then stopped, and paused to rub the loose flesh beneath his chin. "I'm sorry for wagging my tongue; I oughtn't have. I'm only an amateur constable," he said. "I'm just fine at running off rowdies from a pub, and I can patrol the streets well enough, but unless it's pretty obvious, I really don't have any way of knowing who has done a murder. That's why a professional is coming."

"You're keeping something from me," I said.

"Nothing that's really any of your business, Lord Byron. Why don't you go home? I think I got things squared until the man from London gets here." He kept his voice low and soothing, but he was obviously relishing this rare opportunity to pretend to be a figure of some importance. I didn't appreciate his condescension. "You should head back to your rooms and write some more of them pretty poems. I quite enjoyed *Hours of Idleness*."

Maybe he was right, and I ought to have just gone home. But I rarely do the things I ought.

Chapter 2

Within this narrow cell reclines her clay,
That clay, where once such animation beam'd;
The King of Terrors seized her as his prey,
Not worth, nor beauty, have her life redeem'd.

—Lord Byron, *"On the Death of a Young Lady,*
Cousin to the Author, and Very Dear to Him"

Leif Sedgewyck was the son of a wealthy family, but his people were common, so he had rooms in one of the less prestigious residential buildings abutting Trinity's Great Court; accommodations of a quality that barely toed the threshold of being adequate to almost justify the egregious tuition the College demanded in exchange for admitting men of his sort.

A pretty housemaid let me into his quarters, and Sedgewyck received me in his sitting room, which was expensively appointed, but garishly so. His furniture was upholstered in purple velvet and fringed with gold. Bad art hung on his walls in heavy gilt frames, and his rugs were so thick and opulent that treading upon them felt like walking in mud. It was a room decorated by the sort of person who believed that wealth conferred credibility, and that the wanton display of wealth was an adequate proxy for good taste.

"The notorious Lord Byron!" he said as I entered. "Even on this blackest of days, it is very much an honor to receive you." He was drinking wine straight from a bottle and looked somewhat impaired. I was probably drunker than he; I had not been sober in days. But I knew how to carry it better, so I figured I had the advantage.

"I am so sorry to hear of your loss," I said. "I wish you my utmost sympathies." It was a meaningless thing to say; idle chatter masquerading as sentiment. But it seemed wise to stick to pleasantries and volunteer as little as possible of my own agenda until I could take measure of the man.

He did not rise to greet me, but he did raise the bottle toward me and, in doing so, spilt some on his plush velvet divan. I could tell from the yellowed label that his wine was of an excellent vintage and most likely the good French stuff, which had become difficult to obtain due to His Majesty's little quarrel with Napoleon. I envied Sedgewyck's furnishings, and particularly his cellar; though I'd been in high spirits of late, lavishing champagne on the bear, my resources were dwindling, and I knew I'd soon be back to drinking sour German hock.

"Can I offer you a drink?" he asked.

My loathing toward him abated slightly. "I'd never refuse such an offer, but I'll have mine from a fresh bottle," I said. "Yours looks somewhat unsanitary."

Sedgewyck flapped his arm at the maid, spilling wine all over his trousers and his sofa. "I am normally more hygienic," he said. "I am grieving for my murdered betrothed."

"Is this the fashionable manner of mourning, then?" I asked. "I'm a bit traditional myself. I favor tearing one's hair and rending one's garments."

"Heavens!" he said. "My attire is quite expensive, as I'm sure you've noticed. Father would be ever so disappointed if my clothing got rent. I suppose he will be disappointed regardless; he was so very keen on my match with Felicity."

He wore his grief like a coal miner wears a dinner jacket: with considerable discomfort and no small measure of irony. I couldn't tell if he was insincere, or if he was merely trying to impress me with his inelegant approximation of wit.

"You must send him my deepest condolences," I said.

The girl brought me a bottle and a glass, and then retreated from the room. I was peeved to have to pour it myself, but the wine was, indeed, of the highest quality. Being well mannered, I quickly began matching my host, drink for drink.

"Is that your bear you've brought with you?" he asked. "How terribly eccentric it is to keep such a creature. It is precisely the sort of weirdness one might expect you to engage in. You know, it's been my aspiration to join your glamorous circle of associates for some time, but you are always so contemptuous toward everyone, and I find you difficult to approach."

I decided to respond to only the least offensive of his various observations: "Yes," I said. "It is a bear."

"Christ." He seemed genuinely impressed, and he lifted himself into a seated position for a better look. "Is it safe to have him around?"

"There's an implicit limitation on how safe a live bear can be. But he's reasonably placid, so long as he's well fed."

"Should I feed him?"

"He'd also never refuse such an offer," I said.

Sedgewyck, seeing the wisdom in my words, summoned his girl to fetch some meat. She found a lamb shank in the cool part of the pantry; a fresh one, which the Professor preferred to salted varieties.

We watched as she approached the bear, holding the meat at arm's length and moving with small, halting steps. Sedgewyck laughed aloud. Her fear seemed to amuse him.

"What's your name?" I asked her.

"Noreen," she said.

"You needn't be afraid, Noreen," I told her. "The Professor is a civilized sort of beast, and he mauls people only on the rarest of occasions."

She threw the lamb at the bear and then scurried out of the room. The Professor settled down to gnaw his prize and sharpen his claws on the walls.

Sedgewyck waited just long enough for Noreen to get wherever she'd run off to, and then he began ringing a little bell to summon her back. As he did this, he grinned at me, as though the two of us shared some secret.

After a moment, she returned. It was really unusual that she was there at all; it was customary for a gentleman to staff his Cambridge residence with only a single manservant while studying at the College. I, for example, was attended by a wheezing seventy-year-old valet named Joe Murray, whom I had inherited from my great-uncle, the previous Lord Byron. A larger retinue would seem fussy, and would crowd even the most spacious student rooms. If young men were ordinarily allowed to keep nubile servant girls like Noreen in their quarters, nobody would ever get married.

"So, is it the murder that has finally made me worthy of your esteemed attention?" Sedgewyck asked.

I drained my wineglass and refilled it. "Do you desire attention?"

"I've got lots of desires, but my desire for attention is among the most urgent." He smiled at me again, as if he and I were engaged together in some sort of conspiracy.

I was starting to grow bored of the conversation, so I said: "Is that why you killed Felicity? Because you wanted to be noticed?"

Sedgewyck was so surprised at the accusation that he spat a mouthful of wine onto Noreen's apron. "You think I killed her? Why on earth would I do such a thing?"

"Perhaps you'd grown sick of making love to her, and wanted to be rid of her," I said. "I couldn't blame you for wanting to unencumber yourself, but there are other ways to break an engagement."

He laughed. "Don't be ridiculous. I never tasted Felicity's fruits. Nobody did. Her knees were tougher to pry open than the sturdiest of padlocks. Marriage was a precondition to rummaging that girl's nethers. I courted her chastely, and I was most gentle and proper in my pursuit. I'm disappointed to have missed my chance, and in any case, her death is injurious to my interests."

"And what interests are those?" I asked.

"I seek to improve my social standing, of course," Sedgewyck said. The dilated pupils of his eyes seemed to contract partway, and his brow knit with concentration. Other than the deliberate and self-evident care that he put into preventing himself from slurring his words, he seemed remarkably lucid for a drunk. "My grandfather was a Dutch sailor. He made a few lucrative voyages before he settled in London and left a small fortune to my father, who made it much larger through prudent business maneuvers. But wealth means little in England unless it is properly aged, and the Sedgewycks and their new money are unwelcome among London society. My father perceives this as a slight, and my mother finds it humiliating."

He tilted his body into a seated position on the damp sofa cushion and mopped at his purple-stained lips with the back of a hand. He was a tall, striking man with white-blond hair and high, sharp cheekbones. If his eyes weren't so red and his nose weren't so inflamed, he'd have been nearly dashing enough to pass for the sort of person he seemed to want to pretend to be.

"There are two ways to become respectable in England. The first is to befriend the King and get him to bestow an honor upon you. The second is to marry into a good family, which has become my parents' greatest aspiration for me. It's easier to do that than it used to be, since people like my parents have amassed great wealth while people like Lord Whippleby have squandered theirs. Felicity's father drank away his fortune. He needed our money, and we wanted his friends and his name. Felicity had only one older sister, a woman who has given her husband no children. With only a little luck; a fortuitous case of tuberculosis, perhaps, my own son might have been a baron. But now, Felicity is dead and my family's hopes are dashed."

I imagined what it might be like to punch him. I suspected it might hurt a little. He was thin and rangy, and his face was all angles, without flat or soft surfaces to properly accommodate a fist. "You've clearly suffered a great loss," I said.

"Felicity had a pretty laugh," Sedgewyck told me. "And sometimes, she played the piano." As he said this, he looked almost wistful, and I wondered if perhaps my suspicions were mistaken, and he might be innocent.

But then, he smiled at me again. "Tell me, Lord Byron, is it true you're about to be kicked out of school?" he asked. "I've heard the faculty has finally tired of your outrageous conduct."

I finished my wine, rose from my seat, and left him there without giving any further response.

Chapter 3

*It is very iniquitous to make me pay my debts—you
have no idea of the pain it gives one.*

—Lord Byron, *from an 1818 letter to Douglas
Kinnaird, his literary agent*

It was my intense displeasure upon returning to my residence
to find that cherished sanctum befouled by the uninvited presence one Frederick Burke, Esq., a solicitor retained by Banque
Crédit Française to correct his client's foolish decision to loan
me money.

Joe Murray, my manservant, apologized as he introduced the
guest. The lawyer, like most vermin, had refused to leave, despite
Murray's repeated, polite requests. Burke offered his hand, and
I made an elaborate show of not shaking it.

"I must say, whatever is cooking smells quite delicious," said
Burke, who seemed to be possessed of the fantastic notion that
I might invite him to join me at my table.

"I agree," I agreed. "I hope you will be kind enough to leave
before it gets cold."

"His preparations seem quite extensive for just one man's midday repast." Burke's hope was a hard weed to kill.

"I take lunch with my associate," I said, gesturing toward the bear, who sat down heavily upon his rear haunches and asserted himself by making a noise; a sort of rumbling honk. In doing so, he opened his mouth, giving Burke full view of his teeth, which were rather impressive. The Professor, in addition to his prestigious academic credentials, was outfitted with two pairs of enormous fangs; four teeth, each as long as a man's finger and thicker around the base than a candlestick. One could easily imagine such implements, driven by the mighty engine of the beast's well-muscled jaw, punching through flesh and crushing bone. This was, in fact, their purpose; when bears find they have occasion for intra-species negotiation over females or territory, they employ their teeth in much the same manner as men use lawyers.

"He's tame, is he?" Burke asked. His hands fluttered about his face as he spoke. The crisp, high-collared shirt he wore accentuated the unusual length of his neck. His nose, his chin, and his limbs were also quite long, giving him a fragile, birdlike appearance, though he was a fairly large brute. He had the kind of limp yellow hair that grows only from the scalps of men possessing little character or fortitude. I wanted to shoot him in the throat.

"He's hungry," I said, letting some slack into the bear's leash and making sure Burke saw me do it. "I would suggest you handle your business here with all possible haste."

The Professor growled again and shook his massive head.

"I certainly shall, Lord Byron." Burke shifted on his feet and fingered his cravat. "As you probably remember, you met Armand Lafitte at a social event over the summer. M. Lafitte is a senior banker for my client, and I am to understand he was quite impressed by you."

I had already guessed that Mr. Burke's visit was related to the recent fraud I'd committed against his client. M. Lafitte was a sodding drunk and a bloody imbecile. I'd talked him into giving me a loan in furtherance of some fabricated commercial endeavor, secured against a property that I failed to tell him was already thrice mortgaged. I'd like to say this fleecing was influenced by patriotic concerns, but the truth was, I enjoyed the French people and French cuisine, and I admired Napoleon. I just wanted the money.

As soon as the bank disbursed the cash, I ordered six cases of wine and three whores up to my hotel suite. I did not leave for several days, nor did I sleep during that period of sustained debauchery. Mr. Burke was calling on me because the bank had finally discovered my misconduct. They were quicker than I expected; I had not yet wasted all their money.

"It seems there was some error in the paperwork," Burke said. "Our interest does not appear to be properly collateralized. While we certainly don't mean to impugn your honor or suggest a lack of trust and good faith, it is nonetheless a very rigid policy of the bank not to expose itself to the risks associated with unsecured credit, even where the borrower is as esteemed and distinguished as yourself."

"I'm afraid you made the trip up from London unnecessarily," I said. "My counsel, Mr. John Hanson, has offices there, and it is with him that you should discuss this."

Hanson was under strict instructions to summon his most potent lawyerly tools of obfuscation and misdirection to foil the efforts of creditors to collect from me. On that condition, his bills alone would be paid on time.

"I did contact Mr. Hanson, and he strongly encouraged me to speak directly with you regarding this matter."

Hanson! Whoreson! I'd been betrayed by that backstabbing brigand! The two of us had an arrangement; I tolerated his harangues and missives about behaving responsibly, and he cleaned up my messes when I disregarded his advice. It was a perfectly serviceable system, and he had spoilt it. No doubt he was having a good chuckle at my expense.

"I do not wish to be impolite," Burke continued. "But your agreement contains a guarantee on your part that the bank's interest is secured, and our remedy in the event that we learn otherwise is to accelerate repayment of the loan and attempt to recover our capital."

"Is that a threat?"

"I was merely discussing the business options open to the bank under the terms of the agreement. M. Lafitte hopes that any defect in the collateralization of the loan can be corrected without adversarial dealings and that you might continue to have a genial and mutually beneficial relationship with the bank."

I stared at him as hard as I could, trying to use the sheer force of my will to make him burst into flame. "So, it's just a threat wrapped up in lots of weasely nonsense?"

Burke broke away from my gaze and shifted on his feet again. I noticed he had very fine shoes, and I wondered if I could convince him to give me the name of his cobbler so I could direct some of Banque Crédit Française's money in that noble craftsman's direction. "The bank will, of course, offer any assistance you require in assessing your holdings to identify appropriate collateral to secure the loan."

I was not fooled by his petty and devious attempts at helpfulness.

"Do you know what has just happened here in Cambridge?" I asked.

"I only just arrived last night," said Burke.

"A young lady has been murdered, Mr. Burke. She was a charming and lively girl; a beloved friend to all who encountered her. The killing was senseless and unprovoked and the perpetrator remains at large. Your attempts to raise the mundane, petty subject of business are crass and inappropriate beyond belief on this black and tragic day. What sort of gentleman comes calling with these trivialities upon a house of mourning?"

"I'd hardly call these matters trivial, Lord Byron, although I am deeply sorry for your loss. But I assure you, I would not trouble you if this matter were not urgent."

"What is urgent is burying my dear friend Felicity," I said. "What is urgent is finding her killer and rendering him unto justice. What is urgent is comforting her family; I can tell you, they are quite devastated. Anyone would be in such circumstances. Forms and paperwork are not urgent, however, and the great magnitude of my recent bereavement makes your business here seem entirely trifling."

"I'm sure we can dispose of this matter quickly, then, so I may leave you in peace."

"If you and the bank have conducted your proper diligence, or if Mr. Hanson was kind enough to warn you before you came to visit, you know I am never unarmed," I said. "I wear my pistols every day and sleep with them under my pillow at night. They are as necessary a component of dress to me as my trousers."

I removed my waistcoat so he could see the weapons strapped to my torso. He started to say something, but I cut him off. "I also keep a stiletto tucked into my boot. So you have made a decision to come into my home on a day of sadness to threaten me. Your weapon is the possibility of accelerating my obligation to repay a bank loan. Arrayed against you, I have two guns, one very sharp dagger, and a hungry bear. I am overwrought, Mr. Burke. I am a broken soul, do you understand?"

"I don't see how this pertains—"

"I am unreasonable, sir. My faculties of reason have abandoned me. I am awash, right now, with emotions. I am like a toy ship, thrown about by crashing tides of grief and rage and unfettered anguish. In such circumstances, I cannot be held responsible for my actions. Also, I am heavily armed. Do you understand now?"

"I think I do," said Burke. "And when you put it that way, I believe I shall be going, though I wish our business could have been handled more amicably, and I am sorry."

As Joe Murray showed him out, the Professor looked at me and let out a noise like distant thunder from someplace deep in his throat.

"I'm quite aware he will be back," I said.

The bear snorted.

"No, I'm not sure yet what I am going to do about him."

Chapter 4

I had a dream, which was not all a dream.
The bright sun was extinguish'd, and the stars
Did wander darkling in the eternal space,
Rayless, and pathless, and the icy earth
Swung blind and blackening in the moonless air

—Lord Byron, *"Darkness"*

"Financial prudence is the virtue of those who lack imagination."
That's something my father often said, usually punctuating the
statement with a violent gesture and spilling his drink in the process. "I pity the sad bastard who dies without any debt. He hasn't
really lived."

I was too small to understand most of his quips at the time,
but I remembered them, parroting his manner and his speech in
front of my bedroom mirror when I was alone. I wanted very
much to be like him; he was so self-assured, and other adults
seemed to take him very seriously. He was always surrounded by
a crowd of friends and associates, and they always roared with
approval when he told his stories. It seemed his personality itself

was a radiant and mysterious force that drew these people to him; it was only much later that I came to understand that his charisma was helped in no small measure by the fact that he paid for all the booze.

He was a great man, though. He had a voice like a church bell and a fist like a hammer, and he made frequent use of both these gifts. He continued our family's military tradition; a captain of the guard and the son of an admiral. The soldiers who'd served under him called him Mad Jack, and not just for his fury in battle.

If he was never affectionate, he was always boisterous, except when he was hungover, of course. While he dwelt at my mother's Scottish estate, the place bubbled with constant activity; an endless parade of visitors and servants. Mad Jack was surrounded by strangers, and I, a small boy, was generally left to my own devices, or else locked in my room. My mother cared for me when she could, but she spent a lot of time alone, weeping. She was weak, and she could never equal his wit or satisfy his appetites. But my father made sure he always had plenty of liquor and girls around. He said these things gave him what my mother couldn't.

I rarely knew sleep in my earliest years; every night, the house would writhe with activity and pulse with noise. I remember lying in the dark, in my room, and listening to the sound of revelry all around me: stumbling footsteps in the corridors as men chased girls into various unoccupied rooms; laughter and yelling; the thrumming of strings and the pounding of drums—my father always hired the best musicians. And above it all, I could always hear his voice reverberating, clear early in the night and slurred later, but always authoritative.

One June evening when I was five years old, I climbed out of bed and found my mother had forgotten to lock my door, so I ventured forth to see the party. In the hallway outside my bedroom, two men were pawing at an unconscious woman. I followed my father's voice out to the courtyard, moving slowly to keep the brace on my leg from squeaking. I was frightened a little, for the adults were staggering about the house and vomiting in chamber pots. It was dark, too; the only light in the courtyard was from torches mounted on poles. A string quartet was playing an Austrian waltz, and some of the guests were lurching around, making drunken attempts at dancing.

"Death is not an inevitability," my father was saying. "It is merely a likelihood." He had draped his lanky frame over a high-backed wooden chair, and his friends were seated on the grass at his feet, waving crystal glasses at him, which he refilled with sparkling wine from a large green bottle. A young woman sat on his lap and was licking at his neck.

"I have been to the East," he said. "There are men, or things like men, in that region who have conquered death. They taught me their secrets. Mortality is for the foolish and the poor. Decay is a consequence of individual failure. A man ought to control his destiny, and not be victim to circumstance."

The crowd at his feet raised their glasses. "'Ave at 'em, Mad Jack!" shouted one of the drunks.

"I am not a fool, so I submit that I will live forever." With this, my father grabbed the girl by the throat and kissed her, hard on the mouth. "The rest of you bastards can give my regards to the Devil." He pressed the champagne bottle between the girl's thighs, and she gasped at the touch of the cool glass.

I dodged among the crowd and grabbed at his hand. "I want to live forever, too, Father," I said.

He looked down at me, and his upper lip curled. "Who let you out of your room?" he asked. Then, with a violent wave of his hands, he summoned one of the nearby servants. "Fetch my stupid cow of a wife." He dismissed the girl on his lap with a slap to her rump and made a show of rolling up his shirtsleeves.

My mother appeared a few minutes later, clad in her nightgown, her hair disheveled. Unwelcome at my father's party, she had been asleep. "Why are you out of bed, little George?" she asked me.

"He is out of bed because you are so bloody worthless that you are incapable of putting him in his room and locking the door." He rose from the chair and struck her face with the back of his hand. She fell to the ground. The party guests burst into laughter and applause.

"You continually embarrass me with your inability to perform the simplest tasks," he said. "I ask so very little of you, and yet I get even less." He grabbed me roughly under my arms and carried me back into the house. My mother followed, sobbing, behind him.

"Father, you're hurting me," I said.

"I ought to put you in a sack and drown you in the river," he told me.

I wanted to cry, but I was too scared. He threw me on the floor of my room, and my bad leg twisted under me as I fell. The door slammed, I heard the key turn in the lock, and I was alone.

In the hallway, he was still yelling. I couldn't make out all the words, because the door was heavy and the guests had followed us down the hall, making noise and hooting. But among his shouts, I understood "deformed," "lame," and "disgrace."

Chapter 5

I have got a new friend, the finest in the world, a tame bear. *When I brought him here, they asked me what I meant to do with him, and my reply was, "he should* sit for a fellowship. . . ." *This answer delighted them not.*

—Lord Byron, *from an 1807 letter to Elizabeth Pigot*

Though Trinity College had failed me in many ways, the school had at least attempted to provide accommodations that were not totally insulting. My rooms were in Nevile's Court, by far the most prestigious residential building at Trinity, which was the most prestigious college in Cambridge. Sir Isaac Newton himself had dwelt in this very edifice, and had calculated the speed of sound by timing the echoes of his footsteps in the north cloister. I was close to the riverbank, where I could swim. The other building residents were gentle and well heeled. Except, of course, for the bear.

I was also relieved of the obligation to take meals in the

common hall, when I preferred to dine alone or entertain guests in a more intimate atmosphere, for my suite had a kitchen where my servant could work his alchemy, and a dining room that was adequate for the presentation and enjoyment of fine cuisine. My table was large and constructed with consummate skill from fine, even-grained hardwood. The linens and the silver were of exquisite quality. Were it not so, I would have been embarrassed to play host to so distinguished a personage as the Professor.

Despite the sumptuous feast Murray had prepared, our mood was not celebratory. The murder of Felicity Whippleby had irreparably ruined my morning, and Mr. Burke's arrival marked the start of something that was likely to become a serious problem and a public embarrassment for me. But even more immediately, the rumors Sedgewyck had heard about my position at the College were not untrue: I was obliged to appear that afternoon before a panel of the Arts faculty to discuss matters relating to my "recent erratic behavior" and a "disturbing trend in academic performance." The College had finally had enough of my notoriety, and the Fellows had decided to humble me. I didn't have time for this nonsense; I had a killer to catch.

"I see you, sitting there, eating my food and judging me," I said, glaring at the Professor. "If you want to say something, then, by all means, have out with it."

He said nothing and continued chewing, quietly and unappreciatively.

"You are like my mother," I said to the bear. "You disapprove of my use of credit, and would see me dwell in squalor out of pride and some demented refusal to mark a balance sheet with a bit of red ink. I experienced hardship and poverty as a child, and indebtedness is quite an improvement over those sorry circumstances."

I had inherited the title of Lord Byron and its lands and incomes when I was ten years old. At the time, my mother and I were living in shabby apartments in Aberdeen; she could afford nothing better on the pittance that was left to her after my father abandoned us.

The previous Lord Byron was my great-uncle William, a man known for his violent temper and his unforgiving nature. Some people called him the Wicked Lord, and the rest avoided calling on him at all.

William had undertaken a systematic endeavor to destroy the accumulated wealth of his title during his lifetime, to spite his estranged son. In furtherance of this end, he let Newstead fall into disrepair. He burned the forests on the estate and slaughtered some two thousand deer. Swarms of insects descended on the property to feast on the rotting timber and carcasses. The Wicked Lord also threw lavish parties and accrued enormous debts, habits that seemed to run in the family.

But William's son devised a clever maneuver to escape his father's vindictive schemes; he died. So, too, did my cousin, William's grandson, who went to Corsica and tried to catch a cannonball with his face. That's how I, who had never met any of these people, inherited the peerage upon the old man's death.

It seemed to my mother like God's justice; after Mad Jack had squandered her assets, she was restored to her appropriate social status by his neglected child's unlikely inheritance of the barony of Byron.

But the Wicked Lord had left the coffers drained, the properties decrepit, and many of the family's inalienable, fee tail holdings burdened by liens, leases, and other encumbrances. His own interest had merely been for life, and many of these devices were, thus, illegal. However, untangling his fraudulent dealings and expelling unlawful tenants would require years of litigation.

Though the title didn't come with a fortune, I was determined, from a very young age, to live in a manner befitting my exalted station. And I learned that bankers opened their purses when gentlemen of my class came calling. Mad Jack always said that only a man who lacked imagination died without debt. And since I was, after all, England's greatest living poet, I had no shortage of imagination.

As I contemplated my history of financial missteps, the Professor's fist-sized eyes met mine. The uncomfortable silence was my fault. Our camaraderie relied upon my ability to maintain conversational momentum, since the Professor, despite being a canny judge of character and a splendid dancer, lacked the power of speech.

"Before he disappeared, my father used to speak of immortal creatures who fed on the blood of the innocent," I said. "My father and I left some business unsettled, and now, just as I have arrived at the full flower of my manhood and have finally become equipped to settle things, a young woman's corpse has been butchered like a sow's only a few hundred yards from my own residence and drained of blood. I will not assume this is coincidental, and therefore, investigating the murder must be my first concern. My debts and academic problems are insignificant by comparison."

The bear just watched me, chewing and looking slightly perturbed.

"Well, if you do not intend to assist me, I have no need of you," I told him. "I will unravel the mystery of Felicity Whippleby's death myself."

The Professor blew a disdainful burp toward me. I ignored

this; he was being rude, but there was no reason to start a fight. I did not speak to him again, and after a while, he retired to his chambers for an afternoon nap. I would not be able to join him in repose; my serious meeting with the faculty was only an hour hence. I called for Joe Murray to decant the remainder of the wine. The appointed time for my hearing drew close, so continuing to drink claret would be imprudent and possibly detrimental.

It was time for whisky.

Chapter 6

This place is the Devil, *or at least his principal residence. They call it the University, but any other appellation would have suited it much better, for Study is the last pursuit of the Society; the Master eats, drinks, and sleeps, the Fellows drink, dispute and pun; the Employment of the Under graduates you will probably conjecture without my description.*

—Lord Byron, *from an 1805 letter to John Hanson, his attorney*

"We hope you'll understand, Lord Byron, that our purpose here today is to ascertain whether you are having problems and to offer our assistance to you." As he said this, the bearded professor pressed his thin lips into an approximation of a grin. "We have known you for some time. We've watched you grow, and we feel quite affectionate toward you. We're concerned about your academic progress and your personal growth. But this is not an inquisition."

"Then why are your chairs so much bigger than mine?" I asked.

The three concerned faculty members were seated in ornate, high-backed thrones behind a heavy oak table in a big, drafty lecture hall lit only by a couple of those flickering oil lamps and located in the bowels of one of the imposing buildings that made up the College's Great Court. To get to the place, I'd had to pass through the massive Great Gate and under a huge, dour-looking statue of Henry VIII, who had founded the College. I wondered how old Henry would feel about my behavior, and what he'd think of the disposition of Felicity Whippleby.

The old dons had provided me a humble three-legged stool to squat upon in the near darkness. The entire arrangement seemed orchestrated to make me feel small. Their plan had failed, however. Marble floors and Corinthian columns had no capacity to intimidate me, and I was not the sort of subservient youth who would prostrate himself before anyone with sallow flesh, colorless lips, and a craggy countenance. I was Lord Byron, and I could expand to fill any space.

"I assure you, little thought was given to furniture in scheduling this meeting."

"Would you mind, then, if I took one of the big chairs?"

A long pause, and then: "Of course. It was not our intention that you should be uncomfortable."

The professor on the left rose from his seat, and I took his position at the oak table while he situated himself upon the stool. I had taken courses from each of these men, but I had a poor attendance record, and even when I was present in class, I generally whiled away those hours of instruction in various states of reverie, inebriation, and slumber and had never bothered to learn my teachers' names. Doing so seemed an unnecessary exertion.

The dominant authority among them, to whom I'd been

speaking, I just thought of as Old Beardy, on account of the long tangle of dingy, yellow-gray hair that sprouted from his chin and neck and wound its way downward to come to rest in a matted point upon the protrusion of his belly.

The gentleman to his right, being quite rotund, was known to me as Fat Cheeks, and the man who had taken the penitent's stool was Shar-Pei, because he looked like one of those wrinkly, jowly dogs. I suspected his name was actually Professor Sharp, and my nickname for him had originally been a play on that, but I had not been to his class in months, and I could no longer remember.

"The volunteer constable complained to us earlier this afternoon," said Beardy, who was the senior Fellow or the department head or something like that. "He said you accosted him with your bear and tried to trespass upon the scene of a murder. When you were denied entrance, you began harassing passersby. Is this true?"

"I thought my assistance could be of use in catching the killer," I said.

"Well, that is certainly a disrespectful and inappropriate way to indulge one's fascination with the macabre. And there's no reason to search for horrible things to look at. I suspect you'll see more death than you wish to, before long."

"What is disrespectful and inappropriate is your preoccupation with my minor eccentricities on a day when a murderer is stalking the campus. What efforts have you made to bring this monster to justice? What measures have you taken to ensure our safety?"

"When last I checked, this College did not admit women, and the safety of individuals who are not affiliated with this institution is not a matter which falls within the purview of our faculty. In any event, I understand the dead girl's family has hired a criminal investigator from London whose arrival, I'm sure, is imminent. A brutal murder in our small community is of concern to everyone, but there is no meaningful action we can take toward solving that problem right now, and we produce no benefit to anyone by milling about the murder house and generally being underfoot as qualified investigators pursue the killer."

"I cannot stand by and do nothing," I said. "I was not born with a passive nature."

"If you're looking for something to occupy your time, maybe you should consider going to class once in a while," said Fat Cheeks.

"Why?" I asked. "What possible good could that do?"

"That's what we've scheduled this meeting to discuss," said Beardy. "We'd like to help you to take advantage of the resources available here and to have a better College experience."

My title carried with it certain privileges. In addition to my superexcellent suite of rooms in Nevile Court, I was also essentially assured a degree at the conclusion of my tenure in Cambridge, without any regard to whether or not I committed to my studies or passed the examinations required of other students. This was England, and I was nobility. That was still important, perhaps more important than ever, in this tumultuous era of revolution. Failure, for me, was impossible by definition. These professors were merely vexed that I had refused to pay homage to their wisdom by appearing at their lectures; that I'd refused to pretend that their instruction was of any value.

"Your time would perhaps be better spent holding a hearing of this sort for Mr. Leif Sedgewyck. He's the worst kind of bootlicking social aspirant and a shameless drunkard. Also, I think he killed Felicity Whippleby."

"In my experience, Mr. Sedgewyck is a decent young man and a dedicated student," said Fat Cheeks.

"And, regardless, we would not discuss another student's situation in your presence, nor would we discuss your circumstances with him," Beardy added. "This meeting is to assess your progress, Lord Byron."

"Then, by all means, proceed," I said.

"We'd first like to discuss your living arrangements," croaked Fat Cheeks. The area around his mouth always looked very wet, and I wondered what sort of ailment caused such a symptom.

"Thank you for your concern," I said. "I find them tolerable, although a baron should be afforded more space for his possessions and his retinue. Perhaps we can work together to correct this."

His shiny pink jowls shook with annoyance. "You've got one of the finest residential suites on our campus, and it's more than adequate for your needs. What is unsatisfactory is your insistence on keeping dangerous animals in student housing. You amble drunkenly about the streets of Cambridge with that horrible bear, terrifying everyone you encounter. It's only a matter of time before some unfortunate person is mauled."

My pet had long been a contentious subject among the faculty; his very presence in Cambridge was an assault on the rules and restrictions passed down by the College. Prior to my matriculation at Trinity, I'd often embarked upon on my various adventures in the company of a noble and imperious bulldog named Smut. I intended to bring him with me to Cambridge, but the College forbade dogs of any kind in the residence and refused to make an exception for mine, even when I attempted to leverage my title. Frustrated, I obtained a written copy of the rules governing student housing and studied it with the assistance of my legal counsel. Prohibited to students were dogs, cats, trained birds, swine, and other livestock. As to the keeping of bears, these documents were silent.

Thus, the Professor.

"My companion is quite docile," I said. "And both of us find that long walks in the evening aid in the processes of digestion and contemplation. Moreover, that animal happens to be a noted naturalist and esteemed Professor, and if I've anything to say about it, he'll soon be joining you on the College faculty and enjoying these lovely chairs. You should have brought a fourth, for your associate." Here, I pointed toward Shar-Pei. "He looks rather forlorn on his stool."

Fat Cheeks was beginning to turn red. "Your applications for fellowships on behalf of that animal and your continued overtures to the administration to grant it tenure are both annoying and detrimental to your standing here at the College. And your boasts that you plan to endow a position for the bear only embarrass you, as everyone knows you are not financially situated to do so."

"Perhaps you should join the Professor and me for a run or a swim sometime," I suggested to Fat Cheeks. "You look rather gassy and bloated, and I suspect a bit of moderate exercise would improve your humors and overall disposition."

"Stop calling that beast a professor." His voice was high and shrill.

"I see little basis for making a distinction between him and one such as yourself," I said. One certainly could not do so on the basis of relative body mass.

"Where did he study?" Fat Cheeks shouted. "What has he published?"

I stared at him but didn't say anything. Old Beardy looked at Fat Cheeks, then at me, and then back. Shar-Pei avoided looking at anyone and, instead, picked at a hangnail on his left index finger.

I let the room settle into uneasy silence until I was certain nothing I might say would rescue Fat Cheeks from his embarrassment. When all risk of that had passed, I said: "Contrary to your previous statements, I don't feel that this gentleman is affectionate toward me at all. Nor does he seem concerned about my personal growth."

"Well, our affection has become tempered with frustration at your erratic behavior," Old Beardy conceded.

"So, this is an inquisition, after all."

"Of course not, Lord Byron. But we do intend to give voice to our concerns. Your class attendance has shown a marked decline this period. Your instructors feel you have become contemptuous toward them and toward your studies since the publication of your book."

I nodded. "In light of my recent accomplishment, I do find the classroom to be small and provincial and an impediment to my artistic development. My great talent carries with it a moral duty to experience the world; to live, to love, to never deny any impulse."

Fat Cheeks snorted.

Old Beardy leaned forward and placed a hand on mine. "There will be time for all of that. But the academy has value you've been rash to discount. We provide the frame of reference through which you may filter your future experience. We provide the tools to examine the pleasures of life and to find meaning in them."

"What use have I for your frame of reference, when my own is already so refined?" I asked. "I am, after all, the finest romantic poet in the history of the world."

"Mr. Shakespeare would dispute that contention," said Fat Cheeks.

"Seeing how Mr. Shakespeare is quite dead, I'd be extremely

surprised if he did," I told him. "And, anyway, Shakespeare was a man of no imagination who cribbed all his stories from old novels. He was also a limp-wristed cross-dresser who probably spent his evenings getting buggered in alleyways."

Fat Cheeks's eyes narrowed. "We've heard unsettling rumors of your own immoral predilections, especially in regard to your relationship with young Mr. Edleston."

My fingers twisted around the thin silver ring I wore on my left small finger. "Mr. Edleston did not return to Cambridge this term." Little needs to be said about John Edleston, except that he was my protégé, and I loved him. His voice was honey-sweet, his features were pleasing to look upon, and by the fall of 1807, he had been ejected from Trinity, which was part of the reason I, too, wished to take leave of Cambridge.

Edleston was an orphan of modest means, brought to the College to sing soprano in the choir. When his voice changed, the College revoked his scholarship. Thus, we parted. I could not draw enough credit against my holdings to fund his education as well as my own, and he never would have taken my charity. Love blooms in the spring and dies in the fall. My fallow period would not last. My ardor was rarely dormant, and some new infatuation would soon quench my heart's grief and rage. But none had yet.

"That's not what I asked you," said the fat man.

My burning gaze locked with his. Old Beardy, stuck between us, squirmed a bit. "Like many gentlemen of my class, I went to boarding school at Harrow," I said. "A boy there, especially one of small stature and clear complexion, must learn to fight with his fists and feet and teeth, or else he must learn to savor whatever dubious pleasures are foisted upon him."

"I hope you're telling us you learned to fight, Lord Byron." His voice was low and his jaw was clenched, and his shiny pinched features squished together from the sheer force of his contempt toward me.

"I shall happily punch you in the face, if doing so will alleviate your concerns," I suggested.

"I'm sure that won't be necessary," said Beardy.

"You still haven't answered my questions."

I bit my lower lip. "If you and I were to meet in one of Mr. Shakespeare's alleyways, it would not be I who would end up buggered."

He rose from his big chair. "Is that a threat, Lord Byron?" The tension of confrontation set his whole body jiggling.

"Think of it as a compliment," I said. "You have very lovely skin. Has anyone ever told you that? You are like a ripe piece of fruit."

Fat Cheeks remained standing but turned his rage upon Beardy. "I don't need to hear any more of this. My recommendation regarding this matter remains unchanged." He pivoted on his heel and turned to Shar-Pei, who had not spoken at all. "And you've been thoroughly useless today, Sharp, so, congratulations."

Then he heaved himself out of the room, the aged floorboards complaining about his ponderousness each time he brought a stumpy foot down upon them. When, at last, the oak door at the far end of the hall slammed closed, Shar-Pei turned on his stool to make sure Fat Cheeks was indeed gone.

"What a colossal twat," he said.

Silence shrouded the three of us, until Beardy cleared his throat.

"Lord Byron," he said, resting a patrician hand on my shoulder. "You are one of the most brilliant boys any of us has ever encountered, but you are also intemperate and arrogant and disrespectful. You have the potential within you to be a great man. It is our mission to help you, if you are willing to pursue a righteous path. The question we must address is whether you really wish to be here at the College."

"I think I do not," I said.

"To leave would be a rash decision, and a regrettable one," Beardy said. "Take some time to think about your future, and we will speak again at the end of the term."

He stood and departed. Shar-Pei trotted out after his master, leaving me alone in that dim, cavernous space.

I waited a few minutes, and then I stole one of the chairs.

Chapter 7

My father threw a china plate straight up. Its gilt edges glinted in the sunlight, and its painted pattern, pale pinks and greens, swirled as it spun near the top of its arc. Mad Jack drew his pistol and fired at it, but he was too drunk to aim properly, and the shot was far to the right of its mark. The plate fell to the ground and shattered. I covered my face with my arms to protect my eyes from errant shards.

He rose and flung the spent weapon as far as he could. Then

he staggered backward a step and collapsed into his high-backed chair.

"In the East, little George, the dead are not content to remain in their graves," my father said. "They rise, and they walk, and they hunt and feed upon the living." His church bell voice was rusty and jagged, like he'd swallowed a fistful of gravel.

I was six years old and delighted by his attention, but he was talking to me only because he required an audience and his friends had deserted him. The money was almost gone. Men had been coming into the house over the last several days to carry things away. They'd taken all the paintings off the walls. They took away my mother's jewelry, the pretty things she told me had once belonged to her own mother and would one day be my wife's. My father, having finally exhausted all the credit he could draw, was powerless to protect himself from such indignities. The significance of these events quite escaped my comprehension.

"Tell me about them, Father."

He was drinking whisky from a crystal glass. The bottle sat open next to his chair, along with the china, which he was entertaining himself by destroying. He had taken to imbibing in the daytime lately, as well as at night. He had hauled his chair, the last of the heavy high-backed ones, onto the lawn so he could look out at the garden. It had been weeks since he let the grounds-keeper go, and the landscape was turning wild again. The shrubbery had grown tangled from lack of pruning, its carefully maintained shapes dissolving into chaotic messes of brambles. The beds of flowers were choked with weeds, and the once-manicured carpet of grass had grown long and uneven.

"The gypsies pin corpses into coffins with wooden stakes, through the heart and the mouth so they will stay where they are put. If they are improperly secured, those who make a bargain with the Devil can arise as *vrykolakas,* as vampire. And the vampire would dearly enjoy the blood of a plump boy like you, if you weren't so damaged."

My father, too, had grown unkempt and wild in those last dire weeks. His beard was shaggy and mottled with patches of white, though he had yet to reach his thirty-fifth year. His hair was lank and dirty, and his clothing was tattered and stained. He had not been sober in days.

"Mother believes I can get better," I said. "I am going to see a doctor."

I'd been to lots of doctors, in fact. As my father's health and the family finances deteriorated, my mother had become increasingly preoccupied with fixing my clubfoot. The treatments hurt. The braces the doctors screwed onto my leg caused constant pain. But I tried not to cry; I wanted to be better, to be worthy in my father's estimation. I wanted to be a soldier one day, to follow in Mad Jack's path; to thrive in the family business of war-making.

"The doctor is a charlatan," he said. "Your mother is stupid, and so are you. Nothing can fix you; you're a physical manifestation of my failings and inadequacies, a curse from God. He wants me to stare at your misshapen form every day as punishment for my sins."

My mother, overhearing this, swept me up and lifted me away from him with her plump round arms. "Why are you so cruel to him, Jack? He's only a child."

"His flesh isn't worth the price of what I feed him. If I could swap him for a cask of low-end whisky, I would. But nobody wants a defective child, not even the *vrykolakas.* He's thick and stupid, like you, Catherine, and so is his damned gimpy blood. He would offend the tastes of even the most ravenous ghoul."

Just then, four men carried a heavy armoire out of the house to load it on the back of a cart drawn by two big draft horses. Mad Jack winged a plate at them but missed. One of the men swore loudly, but my father ignored this and just swirled his whisky glass. "Me da' was an admiral," he said. "He had to earn his rank in the Navy because his no-good brother got Newstead. Foul-weather Jack, they called my old man. He knew how to keep his keel level through twenty-foot swells. And look at me. I had to marry a disgusting cow like you to get the funds to keep myself soaked in spirits. And the son you gave me: he's worthless, ain't he?"

My mother braced my weight against her ample hip and pouted at my father. "I don't see why you're so horrible to me and the boy, so bent on destroying yourself. We had everything we needed to be happy, before things started falling apart."

"Nothing fell apart," he said. "I ruined it, intentionally and out of spite. None of it was worth preserving in the first place."

"You ruined us, Jack." She brandished me at my father. "What sort of future will there be for him?"

"There isn't any future, not for him or anyone else." He caught a glimpse of his reflection in the side of his glass; his nose webbed with broken red veins, his brown teeth protruding like desiccated stumps from the infertile clay of his purple-gray gums. "Ruin comes whether we court it or whether we cower. Might as well drink while we can afford a bottle. We're all just staggering toward death."

"Not you, Papa," I said. "You're going to live forever. You know the gypsy secrets. You know about the vampires."

One of the workmen approached. "We've got to take the chair, too, Mr. Gordon," he said.

"Mr. Gordon," my father repeated, and he laughed. "I wasn't born Gordon; I was Byron. Gordon is hers." Here he pointed an accusing finger at my mother. "I had to take her surname to get her money. And now, of course, the money's gone, and I'm left with nothing but a fat wife, a crippled son, and somebody else's name."

The man rubbed his hands across the front of his canvas trousers as he tried to decide what to say. He came up with: "Your name ain't no concern of mine, sir. I just need the furniture."

My father stood, his motion remarkably smooth and deliberate, considering his drunkenness. He drew his second pistol and fired it at the chair. The ball struck the place where the back met the seat, sending an explosion of slivers and cushion fluff into the air. My mother was hit by shrapnel in several places, and I got a thick chunk of wood stuck in my forearm, and another in my side. I began to cry.

"Have the sodding thing, with my blessing," said my father to the workman, and he threw his crystal glass against the side of the house. Then, to my mother: "Take the child away. I can't stand to look at it any longer, or listen to the sound of its mewling."

At sunset, she brought my supper to my bedroom, and I ate it alone, as the governess had left several weeks earlier for want of pay. I did not see my father again that night, and when I awoke the next morning, he'd left us and fled the country. Had he stayed, he would have been imprisoned for his unpaid debts.

The castle at Gight, which had been Catherine's inheritance, went to my father's creditors. When she met Mad Jack, she was a wealthy heiress with a substantial income. Now, all that was gone. My mother was willing to give up everything for love, so love found her a match who was willing to take everything from her. My father, despite his other flaws, was not lacking in imagination, and he put his creative faculties to good use, devising new ways to spend money and accumulate debt. Once he'd stripped away her assets, my mother was no longer of any value to him.

Soon after he left, I heard he had died. There were rumors that he was murdered by the husband of his mistress. I never believed it, though. My father always said that only foolish men die. Whatever else he was, Mad Jack was no fool.

Chapter 8

I loved—but those I loved are gone;
Had friends—my early friends are fled:
How cheerless feels the heart alone,
When all its former hopes are dead!
Though gay companions o'er the bowl
Dispel awhile the sense of ill;
Though pleasure stirs the maddening soul,
The heart—the heart—is lonely still.

—Lord Byron, *"I Would I Were a Careless Child"*

When I returned to my residence, the man from London was waiting there for me.

"I am Sir Archibald Knifing," said my new friend as I entered. Joe Murray looked irritated; it was his customary duty to introduce guests, and it was rude of Knifing to dispense with proper etiquette. But Knifing didn't seem like a man with much respect for protocol or much tolerance for inanities. He didn't seem like the kind of man one wants to meet when one has just lugged a heavy wooden chair up several flights of stairs after stealing it, either.

I shrugged off my greatcoat, which Joe Murray retrieved from the floor, and I pushed the throne against a wall in the parlor. I draped my body over the seat, trying to look as impressive as I could under the circumstances. My clothes and hair were damp and clingy.

Knifing remained almost unnaturally still as he watched me arrange myself. He had a sallow and waxy complexion; skin like that of an embalmed corpse, except for a puckered pink scar that sliced diagonally across his face, from the middle of his forehead, through his milky left eye, and down the side of his cheek. His clothing bore the hallmarks of the finest London tailors, but his suit was black, which was out of fashion for social calls during daylight hours, and so snug around his emaciated, cadaverous form that I was surprised the man could draw breath. In his hands, he held a wide-brimmed black rabbit-felt hat, and a long-handled umbrella hung by its curved handle from his forearm, though it had not been raining. Joe Murray would certainly have offered to take charge of such objects upon a guest's arrival. I assumed Knifing had refused to relinquish his accouterments, which was curious.

"Where did you get that?" he asked.

"Get what?" I asked in as nonchalant a manner as I could.

"The chair."

"Oh," I said. "I got it at the store."

"What store?"

I knit my brow and let my mouth hang slack, in an expression of baffled innocence. "Well, the chair store. Obviously."

He stared at me with his dead eye. "You don't have the furniture you purchase delivered to your residence?"

I paused. I should have recognized the flaw in my explanation. But I was a poet, and possessed of uncommon mental agility. "Vigorous exercise is beneficial to a gentleman's health," I said.

He frowned and didn't say anything.

"So, Mr. Knifing, that's a fascinating name you've got," I said, trying to control my heavy, ragged breathing. "Where does that come from? Is it Welsh?"

"I am here from London, at Lord Whippleby's considerable expense, to investigate the murder of his beloved daughter, Felicity," he said, curtly ignoring my question.

"Is it ordinary for knights to be engaged in the investigation of crimes?"

The corner of his mouth twitched with irritation. "I don't concern myself with the ordinary," he said.

"What should I call you, then? Sir Archie?"

"Mr. Knifing suits my purposes."

"Very good, Mr. Knifing. You may refer to me as the Honorable George Gordon, Sixth Lord Byron."

"I'd like to ask you some questions about the murder."

"Leif Sedgewyck sent you, didn't he?" I asked. "He's the one who you should arrest."

"I've spoken to Mr. Sedgewyck, and he told me about your strange preoccupation with this matter. I'm also aware of his interest in the decedent; an interest in her continuing to be alive. Angus the Constable mentioned you as well, and I'd like to know why you were loitering around my murder scene this morning."

"I was feeling heroic, and thought I might catch the killer."

"You don't catch killers," Knifing said. "I catch killers." As he said this, he pointed, for emphasis, at his concave chest.

"I see." I decided not to explain to this gentleman that I was the world's most gifted poet and, thusly, skilled at nearly every intellectual pursuit. He'd learn this for himself, soon enough.

"Your intrusion into this matter is unwelcome. Now the task

has fallen upon me to figure out whether you are merely a dilettante, or something more sinister."

"I quite hope it's the latter," I said.

"If it is, you'll have a date with the noose."

I stuck a finger in my shirt collar. "That would be unpleasant."

"Not for me," he said. A tight-lipped smile creased Knifing's sepulchral features.

I leaned back against the velvet upholstery of the big chair. "Surely, you don't think I killed the girl?"

"You're as good a suspect as any. People tell me you made a crass and explicit sexual proposition to Felicity a couple of months ago, and responded with anger when she rejected you. Is that true?"

I rubbed my fingers across a carved armrest. "I don't recall."

"Lying to me is a futile enterprise, Lord Byron. I'm difficult to deceive, and I'm smarter than you."

I shifted my weight, and crossed my legs in what I thought was a rakish manner. "No, I mean, that probably happened. But I don't recall. I make crass sexual advances toward almost every woman I encounter, you see. Usually, when I've had a lot to drink."

"You're often drunk?" His eyebrow arched, stretching that long, wicked scar as he regarded me with distaste.

I shook my finger at him. "I'm drunk right now, as it happens."

"It's the middle of the afternoon, on a Tuesday."

"Time is of little concern to me. I haven't slept in days." For some reason, I was proud of this. "May I offer you some whisky?"

"Certainly not." The furrows beneath his cheeks seemed to deepen.

"Very good." I produced a silver flask from my waistcoat pocket and tipped it back. "More for me."

"Are you telling me, then, that you had no particular animus toward this victim?"

"Until you told me, I was unaware I had ever met her. And I've no particular animus toward anyone. I'm quite peaceful." I adjusted my position on the chair, because my gun was poking me in the back.

"If you're lying, I'll find out," Knifing said.

I indulged in another nip from the flask. "You don't really believe I could have done this, do you?"

He rubbed his chin, pretending to think about it. "I'll tell you one thing. You've earned a fine reputation as a villain. There are plenty of thieftakers and bounty hunters I know who would send you up and collect the fee. It's a right good day's work."

"You'd see me hanged to save yourself the trouble of doing your job?"

He smiled again, and I worried his face would crack from the strain. "I'd rather enjoy seeing you hanged, even if I had to keep the trouble."

"But you won't accuse me of the crime?"

"For the moment, I don't intend to. You should understand, though, that I'm not sparing you because of any admirable qualities you possess, Lord Byron. As best I can tell, you have none. Your poetry is shit and your morals are abhorrent. And I'm not sparing you because I am especially ethical or fastidious about my work. I am satisfied with the arrest of a plausible suspect, in most cases. That's generally the best anyone can expect from men in my profession, and there's little profit in raising people's expectations."

He took a couple of steps forward, so he was standing very close to me.

"You might think that men like me are in the business of uncovering truth or delivering justice," he said. "We are not. The people who hire me have had their perception of safety upset by intrusion upon their rights, often by violence. They seek from me a catharsis; they want the disorder repaired. My job is to reaffirm the security of their position at the top of the roiling mass of civilization so that they can continue to live as they did before the disruption. My clients don't want me to deliver them further uncertainty, and I never disappoint the people who pay me. I don't think it's likely that you killed Felicity Whippleby, but I've got nobody better to accuse yet."

"What about Sedgewyck?"

Knifing knew, of course, that I was pressing him for information. He considered the implications of bestowing some upon me, and seemed to decide that I presented no threat that required him to hold his tongue. "Angus the Constable likes him for the killer," he said.

"What do you think?"

"Whatever Angus likes, I am inclined to take the opposite viewpoint," Knifing said. "Angus is the sort of fellow who couldn't deduce the existence of his own arse-hole if he took off his trousers and sniffed at the brown stain in the seat of them. And I've other reasons to doubt Sedgewyck's guilt. Based on my investigation of the murder scene, I believe the culprit gained access to Felicity's dormitory through an open second-floor window, not a typical mode of entry for an invited guest. If the killer was not someone she knew, he may well be impossible to conclusively identify."

"Well, what does it matter if Sedgewyck didn't kill her?" I said. "I didn't kill her either."

"I don't care," Knifing told me. "Sedgewyck has an influential father and a fortune to back his defense. You've got your family's name, which isn't as good as it once was, and the scant funds you can borrow. I will not return empty-handed to London, and if

I arrest you, you will have great difficulty clearing yourself of the charges. Though your guilt seems unlikely, judges and juries prefer to see disorder corrected, just like my clients, and they'll convince themselves of an unlikelihood before they will tolerate an uncertainty. You are protected, for now, only by the fact that this killer is particular and identifiable in his method, and seems apt to strike again."

"You mean that the killer's rumored blood-draining is an unusual hallmark?" I said.

"Yes. And if I were to accuse a prominent nobleman of this crime, and later on, another bloodless corpse turned up, there is a small chance my professional reputation might suffer some damage." He straightened his cravat as he said this, tightening it until it crimped the flesh of his neck, letting me know he was a man who valued his honor.

"If you don't mind my saying so, I'd rather enjoy seeing you embarrassed," I said. I took the opportunity to return his nasty leer.

"You'd have a fine view of my shame, while dangling from the gallows."

Chapter 9

And thou art dead, as young and fair
As aught of mortal birth;
And form so soft, and charms so rare,
Too soon return'd to Earth!

—Lord Byron, *"And thou art dead,*
as young and fair"

Distraught by my exchange with Archibald Knifing, I decided to return at once to the murder house. I found Angus the volunteer watchman still guarding the front door.

"What do you want, Lord Byron?" he asked.

"I have spoken to Archibald Knifing," I said. "I am concerned he may intend to wrongfully accuse me of this crime. Therefore, I must catch the killer so that I may exonerate myself."

"That's very interesting." He adjusted his bulk slightly, pushing the protrusion of his belly down into his trousers. "Let me know how that goes for you."

"I must see the murder scene."

"You know I can't let you do that."

"Why not? Knifing has already inspected the place for clues."

"It's disrespectful, nonetheless, to admit passersby to a place like this, merely to satisfy their curiosity. Death is a private affair, I've always believed. I suppose I am obliged to help preserve whatever I can of the poor girl's dignity."

I felt my face and throat flush hot with rage. I wished that I'd brought the bear. Then I became very conscious of the fact that I was armed and Angus was not. "What use have the dead for dignity?"

"What else have the dead got?" Angus said, letting a glop of emotion squish through the cracks in his absurd façade of official nonchalance.

"I need to see that body," I said, sensing vulnerability and inching closer to the constable. "What possible harm could it do to let me in?"

"What possible good could it do you?" he asked. "There's nothing in there for you to learn. You are not an expert criminal investigator. If Knifing missed some clue to the killer's identity, you won't find it either."

"Do you think I could have committed this crime?" I asked. I loomed even closer, putting my face near enough to the constable's that he could feel my breath on his cheeks. My strategy was to unman him with my overbearing youth and masculinity.

He did not back away. "I can't be certain. You seem mentally unbalanced, and very angry, especially for a gentleman of such privilege. But, no. I don't think you did it."

"Then let me try to exculpate myself while I still have a chance. The undertaker will surely arrive soon to take away the body, and my opportunity will be irrevocably lost."

His features pinched and his mouth curled sourly downward. He spat some thick gray phlegm into the grass. "You really want to see what's in there, Lord Byron?"

"I asked, did I not?"

Angus turned on his boot heel in a crisp, assured motion; his muscles perhaps recalling some long-past, slimmer time when he was a soldier. I followed the constable into the house, past the house matron's parlor, and up a narrow stairwell. I could hear the sound of muffled weeping coming from some of the other girls' quarters.

Angus led me down a dim hallway and stopped in front of the third entryway on the left. He removed a key from a metal ring he had looped through his belt, worked it in the lock, and cracked open the door. The windows were covered with heavy curtains, so Angus took an oil lamp down from a fixture on the wall and held it so the light cut in through the doorway.

The corpse of Felicity Whippleby was bound about the feet with knotted bedsheets and hung upside down from a chandelier-hook on the ceiling. Her open eyes had dried and begun to shrivel in the sockets, exposing pink connective tissue around the milky, discolored orbs. Her lips hung slack and loose; her cheeks were purple-white.

"She might have been beautiful," I said.

Angus shrugged. "She's not anymore, though."

Her neck was slashed open, and blood pooled on the rug beneath the dangling form. The half-dried puddle was thick and brown around the edges, on the way to turning black. I noticed that there was much less of it than one might expect to find in a human body, and there was a mashed-down spot the rug beneath the corpse, which might have been left by a heavy washbasin or some similar vessel. The killer had collected her blood and taken it with him. He'd also slit her torso open from the throat to the navel, and gray coils of swollen viscera, shiny in the low light, protruded from the ragged wound.

I tried to hide my shock at the sight of the body. It was necessary for me to demonstrate my brilliance here; to find something Knifing had missed. "If the killer took the blood with him, how did he get it out of here?" I asked.

Angus was unimpressed by my observation. "He hung up the body with rope. He probably used rope to lower his bucket out the window. It would have weighed maybe fifteen pounds; plus the weight of the container. No great feat for a healthy man; easier than lifting the corpse. Knifing found a bit of spillage below, on the street. We canvassed all the houses with views of the window, but nobody saw anything."

All I could think to say was: "Spillage?"

"Have you anything else to contribute, Lord Byron? Does your keen poet's eye spot some subtle clue that escaped Mr. Knifing?"

"Nothing," I said. "I've got nothing else right now."

"I thought not. Have you a joke or a quip? Have you a clever bit of wordplay?"

"None springs to mind." My voice cracked a little.

"Personally, I will sleep worse tonight for having looked upon this sorry tableau," said Angus. "I've got a daughter, and I fear for her. Frightens me deep down to know this kind of thing is out there in the world."

I nodded, staring transfixed at the corpse, which swung in little circles, moved by the slight breeze from the doorway.

"You didn't need to see this," he told me. "I don't know what you think you're doing here, but I've got no patience for it. This isn't a game. This isn't some lark. This isn't for your drunken amusement."

He drew away the lamp, put it back on the wall. Felicity Whippleby fell back into shadow as he closed the door.

Chapter 10

Say, what dire penance can atone
For such an outrage, done to thee?
Arraign'd before thy beauty's throne,
What punishment wilt thou decree?

—Lord Byron, *"Lines Addressed to*
a Young Lady"

Angus pivoted on his heel and descended the staircase. I was about to follow him, when I heard the sound of someone moving around in the quarters opposite Felicity's. I felt I would be remiss in my investigative duties if I failed to question a potential witness, so I knocked on the door.

A young woman about my age, wearing an informal housedress, opened the door.

"Oh my goodness," she said. "You are not supposed to be here."

Her appearance was really quite striking; her skin was pale and clear, and her lips sensuous. And though her figure was quite trim, her bosoms were sufficiently ample. It was immediately evident that she was a subject of great interest, and not only to my investigation.

I smiled at her, and stepped through the door and into her small, clean room. "I find the best things happen when one ventures where one is not supposed to be."

She retreated from the doorway, so that her bed was between us. "But men are not permitted entrance to this residence, and certainly not without a chaperone. Your presence here could cause quite a scandal."

"I came in with Angus, the constable. We were inspecting the scene of last night's tragedy."

"And what has that got to do with you?" she asked.

"You know who I am?"

"Yes. Everybody knows who you are."

I was already aware of that, but was pleased to hear her say it, nonetheless. "Then you know I am one of the finest and most famous young poets in all of England."

"What has that got to do with anything? Why would someone like you need to examine a murder scene?"

"The poet's skills can be constructively applied to a wide range of problems and circumstances. I believe my expertise may be vital to capturing Felicity's killer."

"The logic of that escapes me," she said.

I nodded. "That does not surprise me. The workings of a mind as subtle and intricate as my own baffle the mind of normal folk. And though it is no fault of your own, you are doubly disadvantaged in matters of comprehension, due to your sex."

She frowned at me. "You overstate my disadvantages, I think. Informal though my education has been, I have spent a significant amount of time and a considerable sum of money under the tutelage of faculty members here. In fact, I have probably devoted more hours to study than you, Lord Byron. You are notorious for your poor record of class attendance."

"I'm notorious for a lot of things," I said.

"Yes, I'm quite aware." It was clear my notoriety was less delightful to her than it was to me. "I cannot understand why someone admitted to Trinity would squander such an opportunity."

"A chance to listen to a bunch of blathering professional mediocrities is hardly an opportunity," I said.

"It is when you're denied it," she told me. "There are thirty colleges in Cambridge, and none of them has ever admitted a woman. Despite calls for reform, the only chance I've got to obtain some semblance of an education in mathematics and the Arts is to take a squalid room in a Cambridge boardinghouse and hire those mediocrities for private tutoring at obscene rates."

I thought about this. "You know who I am," I said, "but who are you?"

Her eyes narrowed, their delicate lashes fluttering with her irritation. "It took you a long time to ask. I'd wondered if you cared."

"All facts are relevant, and all facts will be uncovered," I said. "The processes of the skilled investigator are deliberate and methodical."

She seemed to consider making some further comment about my investigative skills, but decided against it. "I am Olivia Wright," she told me.

Wright. It was a common name; a laborer's name. But private tutoring from Cambridge faculty was no small expense, so she was new money, like Leif Sedgewyck. I thought of what I'd told Angus that morning; that wheelwrights can also be murderers, and I performed a series of calculations. Knifing had assumed the killer accessed Felicity's room through the window, but her neighbor in the rooming house could also have gotten in. But I had no reason to suspect this woman, and anyway, the killer must have been a man, for a woman could not have inflicted those wounds or hung the corpse from the chandelier.

I continued my line of inquiry: "And Felicity was, like you, a thwarted scholar?"

She paused. "Not as much," she said. "I think her tutoring sessions were a bit of a pretense."

"Yes, of course," I said. "She came to Cambridge in a spirit of reform, and in defiance of social norms. If she could not be admitted to college, she'd hire the professors to educate her. And she'd live in a rooming house without a chaperone, despite whatever gossips may say about her. Of course, it would merely be a joyous and unexpected accident if she happened, by chance, to encounter a wealthy and wellborn young undergraduate one fateful morning while she meandered across the warm and dewy expanse of the Great Lawn. And it would be completely unanticipated if a marriage were to result from such a meeting."

"She met someone," said Olivia. "And something resulted."

Silence between us.

"But unlike her, you're here to get an education, not to find a man?" I asked. "Have you already got a man?"

"Why should I need one?"

"All the usual reasons, I expect." I gave her a lascivious smile, but she did not return it.

"I knew her, a little, before we were neighbors in this place," she admitted. "We both attended the seasonal events in London for two years. Neither of us found a reasonable suitor. Her father's wealth was insufficiently vast, and my father's name was insufficiently respectable. After two failed seasons, there's little point in attempting a third. The attention of the gentlemen will be focused on fresher goods."

"The ordinary course of action would be to host a series of balls or formal events on one's estate to introduce one's daughters to eligible men."

She nodded. "And we attempted this. But my father had little standing among the social set he hoped to marry me into. His invitations were politely declined, or impolitely ignored. And Felicity's father had his money problems."

"Yes," I said. "Lord Whippleby could hardly be expected to throw a ball to find a husband for his second daughter. He was probably far too busy shuttering wings of his country house and letting go of servants he could no longer afford to keep."

She allowed herself a bitter laugh at this. I was making progress.

"What do you know of Leif Sedgewyck?" I asked.

"He's quite nice," Olivia said. "Good manners. Soft hands. His family's money would have rescued Felicity's father from his difficulties."

"Did he love her?"

"I don't think love was a prerequisite for their arrangement." A flicker of genuine contempt flickered across her face, and she started to say something further. But then she caught herself. "I really think I've told you too much about this. It feels wrong to speak ill of the dead, and it's wrong for you to be here at all. I really think you ought to go."

I tried to ask another question, but she shut her door in my face, and did not respond to my subsequent knocks. I was shocked by her abruptness; she did not even kiss me good-bye.

Chapter 11

The dew of the morning
Sunk chill on my brow—
It felt like the warning
Of what I feel now.
Thy vows are all broken,
And light is thy fame:
I hear thy name spoken,
And share in its shame.

—Lord Byron, *"When We Two Parted"*

When a man finds himself in low spirits and at the mercy of his enemies, it is natural that he will seek the most readily available source of comfort. So, stung by my failure to learn anything of use at the murder scene, or in my subsequent interrogation of Olivia Wright, I called upon Mrs. Jerome Tower.

Violet was a matronly twenty-eight years of age, but she was slight in the places a woman ought to be slight and ample in all the places a woman ought to be ample. Her husband was a Fellow at Trinity, and an instructor in literature. He'd given me poor marks in a class my first year, complaining that my writing was self-centered and lacking in worldly knowledge. I took his criticism to heart; seeking to expand my experience and better myself, I obtained knowledge of the gentleman's wife by the end of that week. It was indeed a rewarding pursuit, and I enjoyed it thoroughly. I subsequently continued to follow Professor Tower's advice and advanced my education at every opportunity.

Seducing maidens is a fraught and challenging enterprise; they're overly concerned with their marriage prospects. I was largely able to avoid becoming a target of anyone's matrimonial designs, due to rumors about my financial circumstances and my well-earned reputation for promiscuity, but my endeavors were substantially harmed by the belief among girls that involvement with me diminished their chance to ensnare other desirable men. I had, thusly, begun to direct my seductive efforts toward married women; they had already realized whatever value their virtue might have had, and were free to engage in philandering, a favorite sport of England's idle classes, second only to foxhunting.

I found Violet in her home, with only her children, which she locked in a back room upon my arrival. We stripped and fell into her bed, saving the conversation until our lust was spent.

"You taste strange," she said, panting, as we lay tangled in the sheets.

"Perhaps it's because I had food this afternoon. But I expect I taste mostly of wine and whisky; on miserable days like this, I must rely upon the nourishing and medicinal qualities of those edifying tonics."

"I'm glad you're eating again," she said. "I was growing concerned for your health."

I'd recently completed a three-week weight-loss regimen during which I had engaged in regular, violent exercise and subsisted on bread alone, with nothing to drink but brine and strong spirits. This diet caused frequent vomiting, but liberal allowances of laudanum dulled the pain and buoyed my mood. I'd come through it with a fashionable paleness of skin and I cut a rather svelte silhouette.

"I'm down to twelve stone, a loss of twenty-seven pounds in the last few months," I said.

"Your bouts of asceticism seem to conflict with your hedonistic tendencies."

"If the hedonist fails to care for his body, it will serve him but poorly in his future hedonistic endeavors."

"Well, given your tendencies toward self-annihilation, I am pleased to hear that you're considering the future at all. You've certainly been neglecting your studies. My husband said all the Fellows at the College have been gossiping about your meeting today with the senior faculty. Were you expelled?"

"Would I be here with you now if I had been?" I asked.

"I really don't know," she said. "It's hard to discern, these days, why you do the things you do. I like to think I know you better than most, but lately, I find you opaque. Your behavior is not driven by motivations I can understand."

"And yet, despite the inadequacies of your own faculties of reason, your utmost concern is *my* educational standing," I said.

"I can't tell if you're trying to be clever, or if you're evading the question."

"No, Violet, I was not expelled. When one is possessed of my potent charm and noble birth, one gets a lot of second chances."

"Not so many chances as you might think. The Fellows are concerned about you. Your manner has become steadily more erratic since Edleston left, and since those poor reviews came in for *Hours of Idleness*."

I swore so loudly that Violet recoiled a bit. I needed no reminder that my emergence into the pantheon of great Western poets had been met with less than universal acclaim. *The Edinburgh Review,* a periodical unfit for use as arse-wipe, had published a vicious attack upon my person disguised as a criticism of my poetry. They had dismissed my precocity by noting that it was unsurprising and unimpressive "that very poor verses were written by a youth," and suggested that I "forthwith abandon poetry, and turn [my] talents . . . to better account."

"My poetry has elevated me to literary celebrity, to immortality, despite the barbed quips and puerile protests of that syphilitic crowd of ewe-fuckers who call themselves the critical establishment," I said. "They'll get theirs soon enough; I'm working on an answer, a satire. I will eviscerate them."

"Do you really think you should be talking about eviscerating people in light of recent local events?" she asked. Everyone in town had heard about the murder by now.

Instead of responding, I crossed my arms and sank into the pillows.

She reached for me and caressed my neck. "I worry about you. You've become so thin, and you appear frail and sickly to me sometimes."

"And yet I find that few women complain."

She sighed and rolled onto her back. Even with my carnal needs thoroughly sated, I couldn't help staring at her breasts or, indeed, at any breasts available to be gazed upon at any time, ever. "It vexes me that I must share you with others," she said.

"And, I suspect, if you asked your husband, he'd express similar sentiments."

"You're suddenly a moralist as well as an ascetic, Byron. I am not sure your charms benefit from your embrace of puritanical impulses."

For some reason, I decided then to tell her about my visit to the women's rooming house, and what I'd seen there. I told her about the smell of the ripening corpse, and about how the fingers of the girl's bloodless hands had been slightly curled, on account of their tendons drying and tightening.

As I spoke, Violet drew herself up from her post-coital sprawl and gathered the sheets around her body.

"I'd always thought your preoccupation with the macabre was a hobby or some kind of affectation," she said. "You drink your opiates and write your poems, and you collect those grotesque trinkets, and you traipse about in monk's robes in that grand, ruined church you own. I've come to enjoy the way your postures become your identity. But you're taking this too far. To walk into that room with that corpse is a choice I cannot comprehend. This is a family's very real tragedy. It's not a story for you to tell about yourself. Darling, I fear you are descending into madness."

"Murderers ought to be punished for their crimes."

"But they are punished routinely, all over Europe, without your participation. Why does this demand your involvement? What is at stake for you here?"

"How can you ask what is at stake?"

"I have heard that the body was drained of its blood. Is that what drew your interest? You can't seriously believe that this crime is somehow connected to those vampires you're always talking about?"

That was exactly what I believed, but I was ashamed to admit it. I said: "I believe a woman is dead and a killer is loose. I cannot tolerate the idea that something like this can happen arbitrarily and that it might not be set right. How can we believe anything has meaning in a world so disordered that fathers leave their sons and never return, and girls are slaughtered for whimsy and sick pleasure? How can anyone bear to witness such injustice?"

"That's an interesting question to ask while you lie with a married woman in another man's bed."

"I commit no injustice; I'm merely a fornicator. You, however, are an adulteress."

If she was piqued by the insult, she didn't show it. Her voice remained even. "But our sins violate society's order and flout its strictures, just as the murder does. And we sin arbitrarily, for no reason, and against an undeserving victim."

"Who says your husband is undeserving? He made the mortal error of marrying you. I would not have." I thought this was funny, but I suppose I should not have been surprised that she didn't share my amusement.

"You like to hide behind your quips when your delicate vanity is wounded, and you try to use your humor to lighten the weight of the wrongs you commit," she said. "But you know better, and so do I. My husband is quite affectionate. He adores me. He cares for his students and he dotes upon his children. He is a fine man. We commit acts that would surely harm him, were they discovered. Our conduct is in no way justified. And why do we do it? Fleeting pleasure. There's no man alive better suited than you to carrying the banner for selfishness and indifference, for social disorder. I'd think you'd tear the world down to sate your own appetites."

"I don't need to hear these things. This is not why I come here. This is not what I need from you."

"I care about you, Byron, and I am concerned. Your personality has grown inconsistent and erratic." Perhaps she cared, but she didn't know me. My personality had always been inconsistent and erratic; it was one of the few ways in which I resembled my mother.

"If what happened to Felicity Whippleby was arbitrary, then the things that happen to me are likely arbitrary as well," I said. "That is an unacceptable premise, and one I cannot abide. Events must be animated by purpose. There must be a reason why I spent my childhood in poverty. There must be a reason my mother sank into despondency and failed to protect me. There must be a reason my father left me alone. There must be a reason for this." I pulled the sheets off my naked, shriveled leg, and then, ashamed of the way it looked, I covered it again. "Either the indignities of my past were preparing me for the special destiny I've always believed I was meant for, or they are just a bunch of things that happened."

Violet crawled across the bed to touch my shoulder. "Byron, I don't know what to say."

"That's all right," I told her. "I didn't come here to listen to you talk." Then, because my lust and vigor had returned, I flipped her over and took her from behind.

Chapter 12

And vain was each effort to raise and recall
The brightness of old to illumine our Hall;
And vain was the hope to avert our decline,
And the fate of my fathers had faded to mine.
And theirs was the wealth and the fulness of Fame,
And mine to inherit too haughty a name;
And theirs were the times and the triumphs of yore,
And mine to regret, but renew them no more.
And Ruin is fixed on my tower and my wall,
Too hoary to fade, and too massy to fall;
It tells not of Time's or the tempest's decay,
But the wreck of the line that have held it in sway.

—Lord Byron, *"Newstead Abbey"*

"This place is like something out of a fairy story," said my mother. She flexed her fat ankles and then lifted her bulk into a sort of clumsy pirouette. She spread her arms and wiggled her thick fingers, and tried to spin around but stumbled halfway through her rotation.

"Come dance with me, George!" The sleeves of her dress slid back, so I could see her white, dimpled elbows. The flesh of her arms was like raw bread dough.

"I am not your little George anymore," I said. "I'm Lord Byron." I stretched my back, trying to look taller. I was nine years old.

"Dance with me, Lord Byron," said my mother. I had a great, unwieldy iron brace on my leg, and no intention of trying to dance in it, but she lifted me off my feet and twirled me in the air.

Newstead was a decrepit ruin. The great drawing room had an inch of dirt on the floor, and mold growing up the walls. Shafts of sunlight poked through fissures in the ceiling, for the roof above was mostly blown away. The room was otherwise fairly dark; most of the lamps along the walls were unlit, and many of them were broken.

"There's no music, Mother."

Most days, Catherine was beset by melancholia and consigned herself to isolation, and she wept ceaselessly for her dead parents and her lost castle at Gight, and for Mad Jack. On such occasions, I was left mostly to my own devices, and to the depredations and abuses of whatever unsavory sorts I encountered. But when my mother was boisterous, she was inescapable.

"I hear music! The most wonderful music. An elegant chamber quartet; oh, waltz with me, Lord Byron. Do me the honor."

In the dark recesses of the great long hall, I saw the stooped figure of Joe Murray appear in a shaded doorway. His pale face seemed to glow in the dim light.

Joe Murray had come with the house. He'd been a longtime servant of my great-uncle, and funding had been set aside in the old man's will to provide a salary for him, as long as he wished to serve whoever was Lord Byron. This was more likely a scheme of some sort rather than an act of generosity, for William Byron was always a schemer and never a benefactor. I suspect that Joe Murray would have been a malevolent presence in the house if the Wicked Lord's hated son had inherited Newstead, as expected. But the old Byron had borne no particular animus toward me, and so Joe Murray was mostly benign; a servile wraith always hovering at the edge of my perception.

My gaze met his, and he cocked an eyebrow as if to ask if I needed assistance. I waved him off, and he vanished. Catherine never saw him; she was too busy dragging me across the floor, my brace squeaking and scraping through the thick layer of rot and filth caked on the swollen floorboards.

"I had a castle," she said. "And I lost it unjustly, and my man went away. And I was left all on my lonesome. I was a pretty, pretty princess, consigned to filthy, squalid exile. But my own, only laddie love turned out to be a secret heir to a magnificent fairy palace, and now we will live happily ever after together and never be lonely."

"You know I must go away soon. To school. I cannot stay here."

"But today, we dance! And when your father returns, he'll be so happy to see what we've got that he'll take us both in his arms and never leave again."

"Father is dead. Everyone says so."

"Of course he isn't. He's traveling on business. You mustn't believe every naughty thing you hear."

I was willing to cling to whatever hope my mother gave me, though I'd learned of my father's death, indirectly, from Catherine. While we were still in Aberdeen, she received a black-bordered letter and retreated into her room to weep for weeks. Concerned by this deep and extended fit of hysteria, I crept into her chambers while she slept, and read the bad news. But I didn't want to believe it, and looked for any excuse not to.

So my mother and I denied it, and we danced in the dim and cavernous hall of our ruined fairy castle to music only she could hear.

The next day, she was morose again, and wouldn't leave her bed, so I took my little shovel and went treasure-hunting in the graveyard. Other than the occasional glimpse of Joe Murray peering at me through one of the dirty windows of the house, no adult interrupted my activities until I returned to the house at nightfall, for supper.

I was lucky to have had the stern, corrective influence of my lawyer, Mr. Hanson, in those days, or I might have grown up to become some kind of degenerate.

Chapter 13

Where once my wit, perchance, hath shone,
In aid of others' let me shine;
And when, alas! our brains are gone,
What nobler substitute than wine?

—Lord Byron, *"Lines Inscribed upon a*
Cup Formed from a Skull"

If I learned one thing from Catherine and her maudlin tendencies, it is this: One must never respond to adversity by retreating into solitude. Others may make untoward imputations; they may think one is ashamed of oneself. Like my father before me, I am proud of my every sin, excess, and abomination, and I respond to rebuke in the only appropriate way: I fling myself headlong into hedonism. It is incumbent upon the unrepentant sinner to flaunt his debauchery.

So, as a means of throwing off the humiliation of my disciplinary hearing and my shabby treatment by Mr. Knifing, I resolved to do precisely that.

I was also emboldened by my congress with Professor Tower's wife, and I was primed for more ambitious pursuits. Specifically, I had devious designs upon Olivia Wright. I wanted to see if she might tell me more about what had happened to Felicity Whippleby, and I wanted to know what she looked like naked. As the world's greatest poet, lover, and practitioner of the deductive art, I was amply qualified to solve the mystery of that woman.

And I had acquired a lovely and unexpected piece of furniture. The feet of it were carved like eagle talons, and the armrests were lions' heads. The upholstery was velvet. This was an object worthy of cradling my noble and talented arse. Such a thing deserved to be celebrated.

Moreover, I'd learned by virtue of painful experience, when I was taken by one of my black moods, I had the most urgent medical need to surround myself with laughter and music and clinking glasses. Otherwise, the whispers inside my head would poison my thoughts and drag me into the abyss, from which I could emerge only with great difficulty and after a prolonged period of convalescence.

For all these reasons, it was requisite upon me to throw a bacchanal.

Since the invitees had barely an afternoon's forenotice of the hastily planned party, only about thirty people showed up, a smallish crowd by my standards, but the celebration was commensurate to my reputation for excess. I'd hired laborers who carefully disassembled and removed the dining table from my banquet room, and they'd rolled up the rug to reveal the polished hardwood floors.

The curtains and linens and window dressings were replaced

with velvet and satin, all black, to signify the unhappy course of recent events, as well as my own dark mood and current state of disreputability. I was clad similarly; wearing a crisp, high-collared bespoke black shirt, a deliberate affront to conventional tastes, beneath my evening jacket. I disdained the customary cravat and waistcoat, choosing instead to wear a black silk scarf over my shoulders.

I wore the shirt open at the throat to expose the dramatic concavity of my clavicle, and my jutting collarbones. I was proud of my starved physique, and intended to display it at every opportunity until it softened and swelled from indulgence. When that happened, I would have to quit eating again for a while.

I'd brought in some passable musicians, and the cleared room was a fine space for dancing. Cooks had been busy in my kitchen all afternoon, preparing French and Continental delicacies under the watchful eye of Joe Murray, who was quite competent with a saucepan in his own right. My rooms were bedecked with fresh flowers to an even greater extent than usual.

Preparing an event like this on such an abbreviated schedule was costly, but money was no object to me. Whatever funds I left unspent would be reclaimed by the gentleman from Banque Crédit Française in short order. I considered it my moral duty to waste as much of the bank's money as humanly possible before Mr. Burke managed to claw anything back.

The Professor was uncomfortable in social situations, so he retired early. I opened a couple of cases of the better vintages from my reserves, and greeted attendees from my new magisterial seat while drinking champagne from my most special and macabre of goblets, a thing I call the Jolly Friar.

The Jolly Friar is made from a human skull, less the lower jaw, mounted upon a silver stem. The interior of the cranium is polished to a high sheen, like tortoiseshell. It is an excellent vessel for wine, burgundy, champagne, or any other fine quaffable, and the appearance of the thing shocks and scandalizes many of my acquaintances, which is really the whole point of the thing.

I noted Olivia's arrival, but I ignored her for more than an hour, until she'd had time to get appropriately drunk and mellow. When I figured her thirst for my attention must have grown unquenchable, I shooed my friends from my side and beckoned her over; it was time to overwhelm her defenses.

The first thing she asked was the first thing everybody asks when they see me drinking wine out of the Jolly Friar:

"Where does one acquire such a chalice as that?" She reached out with her fingers as if to touch the bleached bone, but she changed her mind and drew them back.

"I have many such strange and delightful things," I said. "The silversmith in Nottingham has grown accustomed to my unique orders. I am a man of singular tastes, with access to credit."

"But where do you get—" Here she paused. "—a skull?"

I waggled the cup at her. "It's quite an easy thing to procure, in fact. There are skulls all around you. To retrieve them, one requires only a sturdy ax, a large pot of boiling water, and a strong stomach."

"Surely you didn't?"

"His death was for a worthy cause." I raised the goblet in a silent toast to the splendid fellow who'd given his head to produce such a marvelous object. Felicity Whippleby had been the subject of everyone's conversations all night, and many of my guests had heard about my visit to the murder scene. At the back of my mind, a small, raspy voice counseled me against openly joking about murder. I ignored it.

"I think you mock me, Lord Byron," said Olivia.

"Only with the greatest affection," I assured her.

"So tell me the truth?"

I touched my fingers to my lips as if I were swearing an oath. This was a trick, to get her to look at my mouth. "The Byron mansion at Newstead used to be a functioning abbey, and it is still full of relics of its previous, pious occupants," I said. "I had an idea that the monks had buried a great deal of money on the grounds, so I had the flagging pulled up in the cloisters."

The girl's eyes widened. "Did you find the treasure?"

I shook my head. "Not a single shilling. But I did find the monks, interred in great stone coffins."

"Oh my."

"This fellow's head was by far the largest, a distinction that earned him the right to join me thereafter as my regular companion in revelry and drink. Behold the only skull from which, unlike a living head, whatever flows is never dull." I tipped the Jolly Friar back, and drank deeply to demonstrate.

Her brow crinkled like lace. "It seems awfully disrespectful."

"On the contrary. Few of us will be invited to as many parties as the Jolly Friar when we are dead."

She laughed, and I knew that she'd be mine. Women always swooned at my swashbuckling tales of grave-robbery and corpse defilement. "The Reaper lurks near us, always," I said, "but there is no reason he oughtn't be pleasant company."

It might properly be called a sort of irony that Leif Sedgewyck chose that moment to glide into my dining room and approach me through the crowd.

"Lord Byron," he said. His voice was low and melodious, like an unreasonably self-satisfied cello. "I believe we've met before. My name is Leif Sedgewyck, if you don't remember. I must say that I adored *Hours of Idleness*, and ardently await your next volume."

Olivia broke her gaze from mine to inspect the interloper, and did not seem displeased by what she saw. Sedgewyck was sober and composed now. No trace remained of the wretched, grieving lover I'd spoken to earlier in the day. Scrubbed and dressed, he cut an impressive figure. His hair was straight and fine and white-blond. His skin was like Italian marble, and his imperious jaw jutted forth like a fjord or the prow of a Viking warship. His smiling mouth was a slash of red, a bloodstain on fresh snow. I locked my gaze with his, and he stared back with eyes like black mirrors that held within them twin reflections of my own clenched teeth. And when those eyes met mine, he looked down, for he was over six feet tall; a gargantuan freak of a man.

"Pardon me," he said. "I do hope I am not interrupting anything private."

"The lady and I were having a conversation," I told him.

"Oh, Byron." Her hand brushed my elbow. "Mingle with your guests. Don't be an ungracious host."

"I would never think of misbehaving," I said. "But Mr. Sedgewyck is not a guest. It is unseemly for him to attend such an event while he is in mourning, it would have been crass of me to disturb his grief with an invitation, and I would never be so rude as to force the coarse company of this disreputable Dutchman upon my distinguished friends."

Even as I was saying it, I think I was aware that I was making a mistake, and when Olivia's countenance hardened and her lips pressed together, I knew I'd spoiled my chances with her, at least for the night.

"My family earned its fortune in London trade, the same as

Mr. Sedgewyck's," Olivia said. "I'd hate to think I'd inadvertently been inflicting myself upon all these marvelous and cultured people you've gathered here tonight."

I could feel myself sweating beneath my clothes. Such social errors on my part were atypical, but my usual facility and glibness had been diminished somewhat by my days of sleeplessness and heavy drinking.

"I didn't mean to impugn your family," I said. "I only meant that Mr. Sedgewyck's decision to appear here unbidden was a coarse and unbecoming behavior."

At least I'd embarrassed Sedgewyck; spots of pink appeared on his sharp, white cheekbones. "You have me; I am here un-invited. When I learned of this event, I could scarce resist the chance to spend an evening in the presence of one of the great literary figures of our age."

I remained still, so as not to make any gesture that might be mistaken for an offer of absolution.

"I'm sure such minor errors in protocol will be forgiven by our magnanimous host," Olivia said. Her voice had a cold edge to it as she addressed me, but she was softly touching Sedgewyck's arm.

The fact that I'd fumbled my seduction and lost my grasp on the girl made my desire to conquer her all the more urgent, and my distaste for Sedgewyck was amplified by my awareness that I might have been able to get inside of her if that lumbering Dutch bastard had had the good sense to stay away from where he wasn't wanted. I had my pistols tucked inside my waistcoat, and I would have relished the opportunity to put them to use. But such action seemed unlikely to achieve my desired ends; Olivia wasn't the type to be aroused by a display of wanton violence.

He apologized again, and when I failed to absolve him, he

grabbed my hand and gave it a vigorous, friendly shake. His grip was dry and cool, like the skin of a reptile, but when he released me, I rubbed my palm with my handkerchief anyway. I held the soiled rag at arm's length, and Joe Murray appeared to carry the thing off to the furnace. He did not speak as he did this; unlike some people, my butler felt no need to interrupt the conversation.

"I must compliment you on your ambulation this evening," Sedgewyck said with a malicious nod. "You are quite spry for a cripple."

"I am not crippled," I said.

"But it's true you are—" He licked his lips. "—malformed." Sedgewyck let the word roll around on his tongue, and I was so infuriated that I nearly bashed him over the head with the Jolly Friar. I held back only because I didn't want to damage the skull or waste the wine it contained.

"Many brilliant men have secret vulnerabilities," Olivia said. The lovely corners of her mouth turned up slightly, and I decided this was mockery at my expense, which made me want to send all my guests home and throw her down on my bed.

Sedgewyck bent over and squinted at my weak left foot. "It isn't really much of a secret, though," he said.

"We do not discuss that," I told them both. "I am quite strong. Any of the Eton boys who had the misfortune of boxing against me can attest to that."

"And yet you look so very frail," Sedgewyck said. "Thin. Sickly, I daresay."

"You oughtn't dare, you son of a bitch." I stretched my spine to look taller, but I failed to match his height. "We can brawl right here, if you'd enjoy a demonstration of my fitness and haleness, right in your goddamn teeth. I will break you open and spill you in front of all my guests, and they shall know that you amply deserved such treatment."

Sedgewyck took a step back; he managed to conjure an expression that might have looked, to a bystander, like genuine shock. "I don't mean to be rude. I was only curious."

"Well, your curiosity has been indulged. I think you ought to leave," I told him.

"Don't be cross," Olivia said.

"Byron has been a gracious host, and has been most kind to an unbidden visitor in his home," Sedgewyck said. "Thank you, my friend, for your patience, and for the lovely poems."

"No thanks are required, now or hereafter," I assured him. "If you never speak to me again, I shall not think you impolite for it. Quite the contrary, in fact."

Sedgewyck turned back to Olivia. "The hour grows late, and I would be happy to see you home, if you require an escort."

"I'm sure I can find the way on my own," she said.

"But there are dangers in the night." He leaned toward her so she could better see his sensuous red lips. "And even if my protection is unnecessary, I'm sure my company will not be unpleasant."

Sweet Christ! I should have shot him! "I disagree," I said, which prompted an awkward pause in the conversation. When nobody spoke up to fill it, I added: "If she needs the assistance of a gentleman, I shall provide it."

Sedgewyck's eyes twinkled kindly. I wondered how he made them do that. "But you are already in your home," he said. "And the uneven cobblestones of the thoroughfare will be difficult for you to navigate in the dark, with your lameness."

I ground my teeth. "You shouldn't trouble yourself."

"No trouble at all." He patted the top of my head.

"I thank you, Mr. Sedgewyck, for being so thoughtful," Olivia said. "Good night, Lord Byron." And she left with him.

Earlier in the evening, a woman named Clarissa Something-or-other had made a point of apologizing to me on behalf of her husband, who had business out of town and was regrettably unable to attend. This was, of course, a signal that she was available, and so I availed myself of her.

After I finished, she made some indication that she might like to spend the night, so as not to risk anyone seeing her leave my residence in the scandalous hours of the morning. I told her I was happy to oblige, but Joe Murray released the Professor, who wandered into the bedroom. I let the bear climb up onto the bed, and the woman reconsidered her decision to stay over and vacated my premises shortly thereafter.

It was not until she'd left and I was lying in the dark, with my arms around the bear and a head full of liquor and laudanum, that I turned my thoughts back to Olivia. I had allowed her to walk out into the night with an amoral deviant. Sedgewyck was the murderer; it was obvious. And that sweet, unsuspecting girl would be his next victim.

Of course, I realized that if Sedgewyck was the murderer, then Felicity Whippleby could not have been killed by vampires. Unless Sedgewyck was himself a vampire. His mouth seemed very red, but red mouths weren't necessarily a quality of vampirism. I had read that vampires slept in the earth during daylight hours, and the smell of dirt clung to them. According to some legends, their flesh was hard, like stone, and could not be penetrated by mortal weapons. I tried to remember if Sedgewyck's handshake had felt stony, but my recollection was muddled by too much drink.

In many stories, vampires could not enter a dwelling uninvited, and Sedgewyck had clearly done that. So, perhaps he was not a vampire, but only a regular murderer. Or someone had granted him permission to cross my threshold; Joe Murray, or one of my guests. Or maybe he was just an ill-mannered piece of shit, and some other vampire had killed Felicity. I hoped so, for Olivia's sake. Why had she left with him, anyway? Had she fallen under some sort of sinister vampire charm or spell? Was she trying to make me jealous? Did she like him better than me?

Whatever the case, I decided the problem could wait until morning. I was far too drunk to sort out the particulars, and if Sedgewyck had been plotting to kill Olivia, it was probably too late to stop him. Anyway, I was already in my pajamas. So I drifted to sleep for the first time in days, listening to the Professor's rhythmic snores, and dreamt happy dreams of vengeance against tall, pale men.

Chapter 14

Slight are the outward signs of evil thought,
Within—within—'t was there the spirit wrought!
Love shows all changes—Hate, Ambition, Guile,
Betray no further than the bitter smile;
The lip's least curl, the lightest paleness thrown
Along the govern'd aspect, speak alone
Of deeper passions; and to judge their mien,
He, who would see, must be himself unseen.

—Lord Byron, The Corsair

Dawn found me struggling to shake off the after-effects of the previous evening's raucous festivities. I was nursing a snifter of brandy and trying to figure out what to do about Olivia when Joe Murray announced that another stranger had come around and was awaiting an audience with me in the parlor. I found this vexing, as the visitor was interrupting my breakfast and forcing me to break off a stimulating conversation with the Professor. I apologized to the bear as I refilled his silver bowl with champagne, and I left him to go greet the intruder in the parlor.

"Good morning," he said. "I am Fielding Dingle."

"I don't care," I told him. My head was throbbing, and my capacity for tolerance was exhausted. In the space of twenty-four hours, I'd been hounded by Mr. Burke the debt collector, bullied by the faculty, and threatened in my own home by the unsettling Archibald Knifing. Then, Leif Sedgewyck had arrived uninvited to my party to humiliate me. For reasons that quite escaped me, I'd become the wrong kind of popular.

I took the measure of my unwelcome guest. He wasn't from any of the banks I owed; their people dressed better. His suit was well kept but poorly made, hugging his girth in some places and bunching up with excess fabric in others. His mustache was bristly and had a greenish hue to it; stained, no doubt, by cheap pipe tobacco. His face was round and red, and his lips were thick and beige. He had the sort of mouth that never seemed to close all the way, as if his big pink gums interfered with the operation of his jaw. His breathing seemed slightly labored. If one was quiet, one could hear him wheeze a little each time he exhaled.

Whatever he wanted, I was unwilling to endure further imposition without complaint.

"I am a thieftaker in the employ of Lord Whippleby," he said. "I arrived this morning from London to investigate the death of that gentleman's daughter. Your interest in this matter is well known, and I am sure that you'll be unsurprised to learn you're a suspect in the estimation of some of the locals, and therefore of concern to me."

"You're Whippleby's man from London?" I asked.

"I am."

"You're quite sure?"

"Thoroughly."

I looked at Dingle again to make sure he was not, in fact,

Archibald Knifing. He was not. "Who are these locals who accuse me, and what is the basis for their suspicions?" I asked.

"Rumors," said Dingle. "Gossip and innuendo."

"Is that the craft of the criminal investigator?" I asked. "You catalog the inanities uttered by housewives and day laborers?"

"My methods are sound," Dingle said.

"I've no doubt of it," I replied. "I've no doubt, either, that the evidence you collect is as solid and substantial as your own impressive intellect."

"I've also heard about your affinity for wordplay," said Dingle. "I don't share it; I am a concrete thinker. A bit of a brick, if you'll pardon me. I hope you'll be kind enough to dispense with your games and talk straight, so as to avoid confusion in the investigation."

"It's already too late to avoid confusion," I said, still trying to figure out why someone who had retained the impressive Mr. Knifing would also hire a man like Dingle.

"I don't get your meaning."

"Never mind."

I could think of no reason why Whippleby would send two men to Cambridge. Something was amiss, and if I could figure out what it was, and how it related to my father, or to Mr. Sedgewyck, perhaps I might unravel the mystery. Then, I'd inevitably become a famous and beloved national celebrity. This would certainly give my creditors a reason to avoid suing me for fraud. Such notoriety might also increase sales of *Hours of Idleness*, potentially providing remuneration sufficient to stave off financial disaster. And I had never experienced the sexual possibilities that were available to men with reputations for being noble and good. I was curious.

Dingle stepped closer and stooped down, so his face was

inches from mine. He seemed to study me as the point of his tongue tickled the wet rim of his mouth. "Have you ever participated in a dark ritual, Lord Byron?"

"I beg your pardon?"

"Ever worship the Devil? Ever conjure a demon? Ever take part in any kind of pagan or magical ceremony?"

"You are asking if I am a witch? Are you mad?"

"Witchcraft has been associated with ritualistic murder since ancient times." Dingle spoke with the authority of a man who had once read a book on this subject, which increased my estimation of him measurably, since I had presumed him illiterate. He seemed to gather his bulk as he leaned toward me. "Tell me the truth."

"I once attended a party where we attempted to conduct a séance. But it was done in a spirit of jest."

"This is a joke to you?"

"Many things are jokes to me, but I'm not certain to which 'this' you refer. Your attempts at communicating are somewhat thwarted by your imprecision with the English language."

His florid face surprised and delighted me by turning an even deeper shade of crimson. "I speak of the murder. Of the horrible death of young Felicity."

"Oh. No, I don't think that's a joke. The séance was a joke. You are a joke, Mr. Dingle. But the murder is not a joke." My hand curled into a fist. "I might add that, as jokes go, you are a bad one. And the longer I have to look at you, the less amusing you become."

"Witches have been known to perform rituals that involve drinking blood out of a human skull. Does that sound familiar to you, Lord Byron?"

"Certainly not."

"But you have been known to use a skull as a drinking cup."

The only chair in the room was the high-backed throne I'd stolen from the College. I sank into it and let Dingle stand.

"Here's what I see," said Dingle. "Witches and demon-cultists drink blood out of skulls. I've got a girl missing her blood, and I am looking at a gentleman who drinks from a skull-cup. Now, maybe this murder has to do with witchcraft. Maybe it doesn't. The evidence is circumstantial. Maybe it's even coincidental. Except that this skull-drinking gentleman is also connected to the second victim."

My throat felt dry. I swallowed, hard. "Second victim?"

"I've just come from examining a fresh corpse, Lord Byron. A corpse drained of blood."

A bead of sweat ran down my forehead, and then I felt damp all over. "Olivia?"

Dingle's brow furrowed. "Who?"

"Olivia Wright. She has been murdered?"

He shook his head. "Cyrus Pendleton, Lord Byron. Cyrus Pendleton is dead."

"I don't know who that is," I said.

Dingle bared his teeth at me. They were small and sharp, like the needle-fangs of a carnivorous deep-sea fish. I was briefly mesmerized by the way his lips slid over his gums as he spoke. His mouth bore a remarkable and improbable resemblance to a terrifying *vagina dentata* that featured prominently in one of my more baroque recurring nightmares. "I keep telling you not to lie to me," the vagina said. "I already know you earned poor marks in his course. I already know about the argument you had with him yesterday."

"Professor Fat Cheeks?" I asked.

"I don't know what that means," Dingle said. "The gentleman was quite rotund, if that's what you're asking."

"Oh. Yes, I did know him." My voice was tight, as if the words were squeezing out of my throat. "I had not heard of his death."

"You're going to learn that you cannot conceal things from me," Dingle said. "I am not susceptible to lies or misdirection. You can cooperate, or you can attempt to obstruct me. The result will be the same." At least his threats reminded me of Knifing's, though Dingle's versions were far less elegant.

"I know him, I just didn't know his name," I said.

"You've been acquainted with the gentleman for more than a year."

"I didn't think him particularly important."

"And yet you threatened to forcibly sodomize him in an alley, did you not?"

"I'd characterize our little discussion as a genial exchange of pleasantries."

"You threatened to forcibly sodomize him in an alley." Dingle wasn't really asking. He was letting me know he didn't need to ask. He'd spoken already with members of the faculty.

"I only threatened him in the nicest possible way," I said.

"His body was left in an alley." Dingle let that hang in the air like a wet fart.

"Sodomized?" I asked, trying without success to wring the fear out of the word before he heard it.

Much to my relief, he shook his head. "Not that I'm aware. Lucky happenstance for you."

"I wouldn't characterize it as such," I said. "The whole affair is quite unfortunate."

"Did you kill him?" Dingle asked.

"Of course not. I've not left my rooms since early yesterday evening. I threw a party here last night, and guests lingered until the early hours of this morning, when I retired to bed. I can give you the names of witnesses."

"That will not be necessary," Dingle said. "I've already spoken to several of your guests. They told me that you talked loudly about eviscerating a critic who wrote a poor review of your poems, and that you told a gentlemen that you would like to, in your words, break him open and spill him."

"Well," I said. "My innocence is proved, then. I could not very well have been two places at once."

He didn't seem convinced of this. "Have you any knowledge about who the killer might be?"

"You're asking me if I know who the killer is?"

"Yes. I apologize if I wasn't clear. I am hobbled by a certain imprecision with the English language."

"Mr. Dingle, I am awed by the subtly and sophistication with which you practice the art of criminal detection," I said.

Dingle scratched at his chin. "The point of your sarcasm evades me, I'm afraid."

I turned my back to him and walked to the nearest open window.

"If I could have your attention, gentlemen!" I shouted down at the students milling about on the lawn of Trinity's Great Court. "We are thieftakers, on the hunt for a killer. Have any of you murdered anyone? Any murderers, please, identify yourselves." A few men turned to glance up at me and then continued about their business. I pulled the window closed and turned back to Dingle. "Well, nonetheless, I'm sure this investigative tactic is effective when applied rigorously," I said.

"I don't think you are very funny, Lord Byron," he said.

"That's understandable," I replied. "You seem rather slow-witted."

"And you have not answered my question."

"What question?"

"Do you know who killed the girl?"

"If I did, don't you think I might have told someone?"

"I am unsure of your motives, but your poking about this matter has aroused curiosity."

"When I poke about, I assure you, I arouse much more than curiosity."

"And still, you give me no answers!" Dingle turned very red and balled his meaty fists.

"There is a deeply suspicious and shadowy man by the name of Leif Sedgewyck skulking about Cambridge. He was a suitor to Felicity, but I've no evidence yet that conclusively links him to her murder," I said. "Angus Something-or-other is the local volunteer constable, and may possess useful information. I'd not accuse him of corruption or complicity in the murder, but neither would I trust him."

"Thank you," said Dingle. "And I'll have you know, I am not slow-witted. I am deliberate. Methodical. I am a professional dedicated to the advancement of a burgeoning field, and though people like you may not respect what I do, I am sincere and diligent in the practice of it. And whatever you might think, I am effective."

"I'm sure you are," I said. "Now, methodically remove yourself from my premises."

Chapter 15

It seemed to me that criminality must be rooted in peculiarity, and I was surrounded by the strange. But the weirdest detail of all was the arrival of the second investigator. I decided to confront Archibald Knifing and see what he had to say about his new colleague. Perhaps he would let slip some useful fact. So, as soon as I got rid of Mr. Dingle, the Professor and I set out with resolve to interrogate the one-eyed man hunter.

We made it halfway across the Great Lawn before we got distracted. You see, although I was quite interested in untangling the mystery, I also had girls on my mind, and girls must always take precedence over all other concerns, even very urgent ones. So the Professor and I marched with purpose to the women's rooming house to see Olivia.

If one did not know the horrors that had occurred in there, one would think the house to be a peaceful place. It was a three-story white-columned structure on a rather quiet side street, close to the College but far enough removed that the noise and stink from the horse traffic along the main drag would not impose upon the young ladies' tender ears or delicate noses during their hours of repose. Indeed, the smooth, warm cobblestones were so spotless, they looked as though no horse had ever trod or shat upon them, and I imagined that they bore the footfalls of a disheveled, rakish young lord and his trusty bear with some measure of disdain.

My frenzied knocking upon the front door was met by the house matron, a dour and joyless spinster who served as the girls' chaperone. Her task was protecting the virtues of her charges from my sort of contamination, so she was naturally loath to permit me to enter upon the premises.

I was certainly not about to be cowed by this glorified nanny; the house matron was a mere servant, an unimportant person with no official capacity and no authority to prevent me from doing whatever I wanted. She was merely someone concerned parents had hired to keep men out of the girls' rooms. And better guard dogs than this one had failed to protect henhouses from bears. All that was required to gain entrance to the house was the invocation of my noble title and a threat to inform various respected friends of my displeasure at the matron's conduct if she refused me.

"I can't allow that animal inside, though," she said. "He's a danger."

I shrugged. "That's fine. He can wait with you. You'll find he is excellent company." I offered her the end of the Professor's chain leash.

She hesitated while the Professor busied himself by scraping his four-inch claws against the doorframe.

"Maybe you can take him in with you, after all," she said.

Olivia had not been awake for long when I banged on her door; she answered my knock clad in a sheer dressing gown that was falling off one shoulder. The girls shared a kitchen and the services of a couple of cooks among them, and the rooming houses didn't offer parlors or sitting rooms, so Olivia had only the single chamber. I noticed, however, that the room was immaculate, even though this house had no maids or servants. Like Archibald Knifing's clients, Olivia Wright would not tolerate disorder. Her bed was already made, the sheets carefully tucked and the coverlet pulled smooth. Books were stacked on her desk, alphabetized by subject, and none of the clothing or papers that typically littered the floors of collegiate residences were in evidence. Her mode of décor was antithetical to the chaos and grand decay that defined my own brooding aesthetic, and her room was precisely the kind of place where one might expect not to see a bear. Olivia took one look at the Professor and screamed.

"Do try to control yourself," I said. "You will hurt his feelings."

"What is that?"

"*Ursus arctos arctos.* The European brown bear. You may refer to him as Professor, or, if you do not like the honorary, you may call him Earl Honeycoat. He's not really an earl. That's just a name."

"Why are you here, Lord Byron? You're drunk."

"Usually. But there's a murderer about, and I feared you might be in mortal danger. My gallant friend and I rode to your rescue, because we are heroes."

She gasped a couple of deep breaths, recoiling from the bear and trying to recompose herself. "That's why you brought that animal to my home?"

"That's the most honorable reason."

"No one poses any danger to me, excepting you, and possibly your pet," she told me. "Your presence here is a scandal, especially after your visit yesterday with the constable. I fear this will be the subject of much gossip among the other girls, and may harm my prospects."

"Your prospects?" I asked. "But why should you need a man?"

"We've already had this conversation," she said. "You don't have to tell me what I need."

"If what you need is a respectable marriage you do yourself injury by wandering unsupervised in the dubious company of Leif Sedgewyck," I said. "I am convinced he's responsible for the plague of violence that has torn Cambridge asunder."

"Mr. Sedgewyck? A murderer? That's absurd. Mr. Sedgewyck is the portrait of propriety. Nobody would accuse you of being anything similar, Lord Byron."

"I should hope not."

"Mr. Sedgewyck took his leave at the front door, so as not to allow others to cast aspersions," she said. "But they will certainly be cast in the wake of your arrival."

"Let them. I enjoy aspersions."

"Not everyone shares your appetite for notoriety."

I grabbed her around the waist. "I have appetites for all sorts of things."

"You ought to have stayed away, Lord Byron." Her white skin flushed red up from her chest to her cheeks. Her breathing was rapid, and I could hear her heart pounding as I pressed her against me.

"I couldn't stay away. You're so beautiful." I moved my face close to her neck and took in the scent of her skin and her hair.

"Why do men always tell girls that they're pretty?" she said. "Why don't you ever say a woman is bright or talented or witty?"

"We do say that," I said. "We say it all the time. To the ugly girls. We tell them they have charming personalities and remarkable senses of humor, and we avoid looking directly at them; we fix our gaze on a point behind them, or off someplace to the side, to see if a prettier one is just beyond the periphery of our vision."

"You must let go of me."

"I don't believe you want me to," I said.

"I do. I think you should. I know you're a kind of trouble I don't need."

"You say that. But your eyes are pleading me to stay."

She hesitated. "I cannot deny that I have sometimes admired you, from a safe distance."

I knew it!

"Desire for me is a common affliction of your sex," I assured her as I exhaled onto her neck. "I'm afraid I only know of one cure for it."

"I never thought my distant affection put me in danger, because I didn't imagine that it might someday be noticed, let alone reciprocated. You are so very dashing, and yet you're such a very awful person."

"The two qualities are not unrelated."

She pressed a pale hand against my chest. "Lord Byron, I really think you ought to leave, before we make some irreversible mistake."

"You're probably right." I pulled her body against mine. "But I rarely do the things I ought."

She stamped her bare foot on the rug. "Why do you insist upon being so impertinent?"

I touched my lips to hers. She didn't pull away. "Because I know what's best," I said. "And I know your prudent impulses cannot stand for long against the force of unreasoning desire."

"You're mad," she said. But her voice was scarcely a whisper; and her protest was weak.

"Probably. I'm also right." I pressed my mouth hard against hers and briefly lost track of time, place, and several of my senses as I explored. I carried no watch, but when she finally decided to resist my embrace and pry my roving hand off her ass, the sunlight was streaming in the window from a slightly different angle.

I tried to shove her down onto the bed, but she grabbed my arm and pushed me back, toward the door.

"You must leave at once," she said. "Even with this killer on the loose, you're still the worst and most dangerous man in Cambridge."

I relented, hoping for both our sakes that she was right, and I set out to find Leif Sedgewyck, who was obviously probably the murderer. I would vent my fury and disappointment upon him, and perhaps, if I was really piqued, I'd turn loose the Professor and give the bastard what he really deserved.

Chapter 16

Am I a villain? Am I a madman? The reader will inevitably ask himself this, and it's a question I've given much consideration to. One fact that may prove relevant: some months prior to the death of Felicity Whippleby, I told my mistress Violet Tower a secret, one so closely held that no soul knew it, save my loyal Joe Murray and, of course, the Professor. I was drunk, which was not unusual, and I was speaking a bit too freely about Mad Jack and my desire to hunt him down and hold him to account for his treatment of me and my mother.

"Your father is dead," she said as we lounged after an athletic lovemaking session in my rooms at Nevile Court. "He pressed a gun to his head while riding the French harlot he'd spent his last shilling upon."

I'd never spoken to her of this particular myth about my father, though I'd heard it before. Her knowledge of it surprised me. Perhaps it should not have; I was the subject of much gossip, as Mad Jack was before me. Both of us did everything possible to make ourselves objects of popular fascination.

"Lies and misdirection," I said. "I will reveal to you the truth. But you must promise to share nothing of what you learn here with any soul."

She teased my hair with her fingers. "Byron, you're frightening me."

"And you should be frightened. I've discovered things that are truly terrifying; things that will upset your understanding of the nature of life and death."

She smoothed my tangled hair and wiped sweat from my pale brow. "You know, when people say you're mad, I defend you. But I am beginning to think you need some kind of help, perhaps a tonic, or treatment in a sanitarium."

"Swear to keep my secret."

"This is ridiculous."

"Very well. Forget I ever mentioned it."

"Oh, come now! You cannot dangle the possibility of such exclusive knowledge and then withhold it."

"Then swear."

"You're being dramatic."

"Swear it."

"Fine." She crossed her arms. "I swear that I'll never betray your secret, Lord Byron."

I rose from the bed, and she followed me down my hallway, where I unlocked the door of the Professor's study, a window-less interior room that made a nice lounge for a gentleman or a suitable lair for a medium-sized mammalian predator. I cracked the door slowly, to avoid surprising the occupant, and ushered Violet inside. The bear stirred from slumber upon the pile of rugs and skins he used for a bed, and regarded the woman with a rumbling growl.

"That creature makes me uneasy," she said.

"The Professor is perfectly harmless," I assured her. "In any case, our concern is over here." I pointed toward a large, heavy piece of furniture, a thing like a wardrobe. It would have been sleek and black, but the Professor had scored the wood with his claws. It had come from Newstead; part of my inheritance from William, the Wicked Lord. Joe Murray told me my great-uncle had liked to lock his whores inside the cabinet when they dis-pleased him, hence the heavy doors and sturdy lock. The use I'd found for it was arguably more disturbing. I unbolted the doors on the front of the chest with an iron key.

"This contains treasures and truths from across the world, obtained at great effort and expense over a period of years," I said.

"But you never have any money." I wondered if I'd spoken too freely of my financial difficulties in front of this woman. Perhaps it was a mistake to reveal my treasures to her. I wondered if she ever betrayed my secrets to her husband, as she betrayed her vows to him with me.

"I find credit whenever it's available," I said. "And I employ my borrowed funds toward the pursuit of this." I opened the cabinet to reveal several rows of ancient heavy tomes.

"Why, it's a bookshelf," Violet remarked. "But who locks a bookshelf?"

"There is some knowledge that is valuable and dangerous. Some knowledge must be shielded behind locked doors and guarded by bears," I said. "You are looking at the most comprehensive library in all of Britain on the subject of immortal creatures, and on vampires in particular."

"Vampires?"

"The undying dead," I told her. "They rise from their graves to feed on the blood of the chaste. Stealing life allows them to stave away death. They do not age, they cannot be hurt, and they never die."

"I've never heard of any such thing," she said. "This sounds like a fairy story."

"It's true that there have been no documented sightings of these creatures in England," I said. "But they are quite common in the East."

Violet was examining an ancient heavy tome and rubbing with a pink thumbnail at a small, dark spot on the cover.

"That won't come off," I said. "It's a mole, I think, or a freckle."

She looked at me with confusion.

"That book is bound with human skin," I explained, to clarify.

Violet turned very pale, which I thought was attractive. But she looked like she might drop the precious volume, so I took it from her and opened it to show her a lithograph printed onto one of the parchment pages, depicting a fanged wraith sucking at the throat of a young woman.

"My father told me stories about these creatures when I was a child. He said they possessed the secret of eternal life, and that, with their knowledge, he would live forever. I was very young when he disappeared. There are two possibilities: either my father deserted my mother and me and he died someplace, destitute and alone, or he went to the East to take his place among the vampires. The second scenario seems unlikely, but I would submit that the first is impossible. My father loved me."

"Men are imperfect, Byron," she said. "They are weak and flawed. Your father was incapable of being what you needed him to be. You do yourself no service by mythologizing him."

"In 1676, stoneworkers in Cornwall discovered a hunk of calcified bone in a quarry," I said. "A professor of chemistry at Oxford deduced that this bone was the base of a femur, but no known animal has a leg-bone of comparable size. This creature, you must understand, would have easily exceeded the bulk of the African elephant by several orders of magnitude, and it dwelt in England at some point in the past. Fanciful creatures are realer than you think. The natural world exceeds and outpaces man's ability to document and catalog it."

"I'm sure your father loved you as best he could."

I ignored her. "Six years ago, a gentleman named Schneider discovered the estuarine crocodile, an eighteen-foot reptile with jaws that can tear a horse in half. If a thing like that can exist in the saltwater swamps of the Indochine, why can't vampires dwell in the sparsely populated mountains and caves of Rumania?"

"If such a thing existed, there would be documentation. There would be proof."

"What do you think is collected in these volumes? Vampires are real enough for the mountain Gypsies to drape their doors and windows with strings of garlic in hopes of warding the things off, and to nail the dead into their coffins with wooden stakes."

"You're talking about superstitions and folktales."

"Like the tales of giant reptiles, with teeth like knives, which we have only recently verified?"

"I don't think we're talking about the same thing."

"It would have seemed impossible that the American colonies would revolt and throw off the rule of the Crown, and yet they did. Nobody would have believed that the French would haul their royal family out of Versailles and execute them upon the guillotine, and yet it happened. Who would have imagined the mechanized textile-factory or the steam-powered mine were things that could exist, until they did? Who can say what is possible, when we live in an age in which the inconceivable happens with regularity?"

"The progress of the practical sciences does not justify your credulity regarding the existence of the fanciful and mythical. I see no relationship between the one thing and the other."

I put the ancient book back on the shelf. "The estuarine crocodile is the relationship," I said. "It's a verified, documented dragon."

"No, it's not. It's just a crocodile," she said. "When your father left, you were a small child, and it was no fault of your own. But you're a man now, and your father is gone. You only do yourself harm with these elaborate fantasies."

I kept a green-glass bottle of absinthe on the shelf next to my vampire texts. I pulled the cork stopper out with my teeth and took a long pull of the burning-sweet liqueur.

"You are frantic and crazed some days, and sullen and brooding on others," Violet said. "And you're always drunk lately. You have friends who care about you, but not so many as you used to. People will not stand by and watch you destroy yourself, Byron. I won't."

"You're welcome, then, to go away," I said, and I tipped the green bottle back a second time.

Chapter 17

*Every day confirms my opinion on the superiority of
a vicious life—and if Virtue is not its own reward I
don't know any other stipend annexed to it.*

—Lord Byron, *from an 1813
letter to Henry Drury*

As I figured it, the best way to establish Sedgewyck's guilt was to
search his rooms and find some proof. The killer had taken Felicity Whippleby's blood with him, so if Sedgewyck had done the
deed, the blood might be stashed away in his residence, or at least
I'd find the dirty bucket, if he'd already drunk the contents of his
gruesome haul. Perhaps he also had a vampire coffin. Regardless,
my nemesis would be exposed, and I'd be a hero. It went without
saying that I would claim Olivia as the spoils of my victory.

The Professor and I skulked past Sedgewyck's building. He
lived on the second story, but I caught a glimpse of him through
a window. He appeared to be dressing, and if he was dressing,
he might soon be leaving. I retreated about fifty yards down the
road and crouched behind a stout tree to wait for him.

It may seem ridiculous to the reader that I would employ a bear as my partner in stealth and skullduggery, but bears are, in fact, among the sneakiest of the predatory mammals. You may point out that you've never seen a bear sneaking up on anyone, but my response to that is: "Exactly!" Bears are masters of subterfuge.

I had to wait only a few minutes before I spotted Sedgewyck leaving his building by the front door. Evidently, traditional dark mourning garb was too plain for him; he was wearing a light gray greatcoat with brass buttons and a bright blue silk scarf. I didn't think he looked particularly vampiric, but perhaps monsters don't look monstrous when they're incognito.

According to some texts, vampires cannot bear daylight; and several mythological traditions hold that the creatures will burst into flame if the light of dawn catches them still prowling. Most experts, however, believe it patently ridiculous that an ostensibly immortal creature could be so fragile, although it is commonly held that vampires prefer to sleep by day.

However, if Sedgewyck was a vampire, the daylight must have dulled his preternatural senses, for he seemed to be preoccupied with something, and he did not spot me and the Professor lurking in the foliage. As soon as he'd rounded the corner, we bolted for the front door of his apartment house, vaulted the common stairwell, and I began frantically pounding with the knocker. When Sedgewyck's pretty housemaid opened the door a crack to see who was calling, I threw my shoulder against it, knocking her to the floor. Having thus secured my entry, I rushed past the girl, through the sitting room where Sedgewyck had received me the previous day, and into his quarters, where I began rifling cupboards and searching rooms.

All the suspicious cooking vessels in the kitchen were clean and empty, and looked as if they had not been used in days. Most undergraduates did not maintain full-time cooks on staff in the College residences even if they had the means to do so, as even the better residences had quarters for only one servant. Sedgewyck likely took his lunches at the College and had a town woman come in to cook for him sometimes in the evenings. I inspected his collection of cutlery. The knives were completely appropriate for kitchen use, but also suitable for throat-slashing. So nothing conclusively pointed to his guilt.

I checked the pantry and was disappointed when I found no buckets of blood. No ropes in evidence, either. The Professor discovered a ham that he believed might contain some promising clue, so I left him to investigate it while I checked Sedgewyck's private chambers.

Within, I found, to my disappointment, an ordinary feather mattress instead of a coffin. I spotted a large chamber pot next to the bed and my pulse hastened, but when I opened it up and looked inside, I found nothing but a fresh turd.

"I haven't emptied that yet," said the maid, who had recovered and followed me into the bedroom.

"I noticed," I said, replacing the lid. I peered under the bed, but there was nothing hidden underneath, so I checked the closets.

"Have you come to kill me, like Felicity Whippleby?" the maid asked. She seemed more curious than frightened.

"Don't be ridiculous." The closet seemed innocuous at first, so I started pulling Sedgwyck's clothes off the shelves and racks and tossing them on the floor to see if he'd concealed anything behind or beneath.

"Well, if you've come to lie in wait to kill Mr. Sedgewyck, I shall have to warn him. He did give me a job, after all."

"What the hell?" I yanked open all the drawers in his armoire and emptied the contents into a large pile.

"Mr. Sedgewyck says he thinks you might have killed her, though his spirits seem to have recovered quickly from the shock of her death. I had a kitten once that died, and I was inconsolable for weeks. I guess refined sorts of people are quick to regain their composure."

"There's nothing refined about Mr. Sedgewyck," I said. His shoes and garments were thoroughly unremarkable. However, I found a scarf like the one I'd seen him wearing when he left, but in red. I liked it, so I stuffed it into my coat pocket.

"Are you going to ravish me?" the maid asked.

"I hadn't planned on it."

"I won't resist. I mean, if you want to."

I was barely listening to her, because I was busy rapping on the walls, looking for a hidden doorway or a hollow section. "I'm very busy this morning," I said.

"I only asked because I've just put clean sheets on the bed. But I suppose, if I have to, I could change them again."

I paused again and took a look at the girl. She wasn't pale like Olivia. She didn't have yellow hair or crimson lips. But she was shapely and graceful in a sort of uncultured way. She would certainly be good for an evening's entertainment. Or a morning's.

But I was also thinking that, if the evidence wasn't here, then Sedgewyck must have taken it with him. I needed to find out where he'd gone.

"What's your name?" I asked the maid.

"Noreen," she said.

"Be a darling, Noreen, and entertain the Professor for a bit while I dash out."

"What?"

"Don't worry. He's quite docile. Unless he's hungry!" I shouted this over my shoulder, for I was already out the door. I vaulted back down the common stairwell and raced back out the front door and dashed down the row of houses, turning left onto Sidney Street. Foot traffic was light; people were staying indoors after the second murder. My weak foot ached as it pounded against the cobbles, but it was a pain I'd learned to ignore. My legs would do what I told them to, and I could run until my lungs gave out.

I glanced down Green Street as I flew past, but I didn't think he'd have turned there; it would have taken him back to the College. Classes were canceled on account of Fat Cheeks' death, and nobody who mattered ever went to class anyway. Instead I headed toward Market Street and the Holy Trinity Church. But Sedgewyck didn't seem like the pious sort, and I knew where I would be heading in this neighborhood. I turned down an alley and caught sight of the blue scarf just as Sedgewyck slipped in the front door of my second-favorite local brothel.

I waited outside for ten minutes. My plan was to burst into the room and catch him in the act, and then draw my pistol on him while he was naked, and search his belongings for proof of his guilt.

I caught my breath, composed myself, and knocked the secret knock that indicated I was a customer in good standing. I heard the madam inside working the bar-locks, and then the door swung open.

"Lord Byron," she said. "It's a pleasure to see you, as always. Which of the girls would you like?"

"Which of them are available?" I asked, tempted. I almost never forgo an opportunity for a roll with a whore. Life is harsh, volatile, and of indeterminate length. It thus seems irrational not to spend every moment mired in depravity.

"We don't entertain many visitors in the mornings. You can have whichever girl you like."

This particular brothel employed: a dishwater blonde, two brunettes, a redhead who wasn't so saucy and spirited as I might have hoped, and the only black African prostitute in Cambridge, a girl I sometimes visited when I was in the mood for something exotic. Also, a boy whom I'd tried once but found uninteresting. Still, someone must have patronized him regularly; the lad had to earn his keep. I made a quick calculation about Leif Sedgewyck.

"Is Clyde around?" I asked.

"I'm sorry," said the madam. "He's not, today. But any of the girls would be delighted to see you."

"You know, I think I've changed my mind," I said. "Please give them all my fond regards, though, won't you?"

I turned on the heel of my good foot and went back out onto the street. Mr. Sedgewyck, Olivia had said, was the portrait of propriety. I wished she had been present to see this. But she wouldn't have been pleased to have me return to her rooms, and I couldn't think of a good way to inform her of her new beau's predilections without explaining my own.

Anyway, I needed to retrieve the Professor from Sedgewyck's quarters. Also, for purposes of my investigation, it was imperative that I debrief Noreen, thoroughly and at once.

Chapter 18

Ah! since thy angel form is gone,
My heart no more can rest with any;
But what it sought in thee alone,
Attempts, alas! to find in many.
Then, fare thee well, deceitful maid!
'T were vain and fruitless to regret thee;
Nor Hope, nor Memory yield their aid,
But Pride may teach me to forget thee.

—Lord Byron, *"To a Lady"*

I've always been touched and a little mystified by the extent of female generosity. Women look at boys like me; fatherless and badly mothered; despairing, depressive, debauched, and drunk; and they see only the possibility of redemption.

They offer their love generously, in hopes that I'll be moved and transformed by their outpouring of affection. But they're wrong about redemption. Women have a habit of adopting emotional narratives that directly contradict observable facts.

Their love can't redeem me. I won't let it. I'm uninterested in being redeemed.

Women feel the heat and see the light, and they recognize that love is a kind of flame. But they don't know which kind. They think love is a votive candle, and it isn't. Love is a wildfire. It's bigger than they comprehend, and more chaotic. It dances against the sky and sucks all the moisture from the air and earth, and leaves everything charred and desiccated. Love doesn't redeem. Love consumes. Like *vrykolakas*. Like my father.

And the fire goes out when there's nothing left for it to burn.

But there's not really much of a reason for me to try to explain this to them, especially not when I've got an opportunity to fornicate, as I did with Noreen.

"Does Sedgewyck ever fuck you like this?" I swirled my hips and she gasped.

"Mr. Sedgewyck doesn't touch me at all. He's quite—Oh!"

"Is he the portrait of propriety? Is that what he is?" I pressed into her hard enough to hurt her a little bit.

"Mr. Sedgwyck never paid me that kind of attention," Noreen said.

"I'll bet he didn't," I said, thinking of Clyde with his angular jaw and pimpled arse. He was what piqued Sedgewyck's interest. But Sedgewyck also seemed interested in Olivia Wright. Why?

"What's that supposed to mean?" Noreen asked.

"Shut up. Never mind." I pulled out of her and spun her around. "Bend over, and put your hands on the floor. No. Flat. Yes, like that."

"My God!"

"Indeed, I am. And you will worship me."

"My mother told me when I came to work for him to watch

out for myself. She said rich men didn't know what it was like to be told they couldn't have something. She said he'd take advantage. But he never did."

"It was me she was warning you about. I'm what all mothers warn their daughters about. Here, put your arms around my neck and your ankles on my shoulders."

"Can you support me?" I still had my boots on, but I knew she was talking about my clubfoot. Sedgewyck must have told her about it.

"I can, if I want to," I said. But I braced my leg against the bedpost.

"Ooh. How did you learn to do this?"

"I'm a Trinity man; a recipient of a world-class education. If you want to have it better, you'll have to go to Oxford. Did you know Felicity Whippleby?"

"She came around sometimes. Mr. Sedgewyck's affections always seemed polite rather than passionate. She seemed to like him very much, or at least I think she hoped he'd marry her. When Mr. Sedgewyck's parents came to visit, they seemed very keen on the match as well."

"Would he have killed her to avoid being pushed into the marriage?"

"You'd know better than I. He told me yesterday that he expects he'll just be pushed into another marriage, though."

"Have you seen him carrying any strange buckets or pots? Perhaps at night?"

"I don't think so."

If Sedgewyck was guilty, there was nothing in his rooms that appeared to link him to the murder. I'd pretty well torn the place apart, and the Professor had done quite a bit of damage as well.

And despite a thorough examination, Noreen had revealed no evidence of her employer's guilt.

I flipped her over, put her on the bed, and climbed on top of her to finish off my line of inquiry.

"Is he the killer?"

"I don't think so. He thinks you are."

Did he really think that? Or was he just clever enough to lie to his servant? No way to tell. But there was no evidence here to corroborate my suspicions, and my theory regarding Sedgewyck's guilt was looking weak. I supposed I would have to go find Knifing and see if I could pry information out of him. I didn't expect that would be fun. I was of the opinion that all the witnesses should look like Noreen, and that they should all be susceptible to the same interrogation tactics.

"It was some stranger, probably," Noreen said. "A vagrant. A drifter. Some lunatic who came out of the woods and climbed into her window."

"Stop talking. I'm trying to concentrate."

"Concentrate on what? Oh—Oh!"

"Yes. Exactly."

Chapter 19

The languages, especially the dead;
The sciences, and most of all the abstruse;
The arts, at least all such as could be said
To be the most remote from common use,
In all these he was much and deeply read;
But not a page of anything that's loose

—Lord Byron, Don Juan, *canto 1*

Members of the Trinity faculty made a habit of convening after hours at a tavern near the College called the Modest Proposal, an establishment known for above-average ale and a rather dubious stew. The service alley next to the bar was wide enough for a horse-cart to enter, and curved around the back of the building. This was where the local brewer delivered kegs twice a week. It was also where Cyrus Pendleton—Professor Fat Cheeks—had met his end. Angus the volunteer constable guarded the wrought iron gate at the mouth of the alley to keep curious types away from the scene.

"Hello, Angus," I said. "You look civilized today."

He was wearing a new uniform; one that was not frayed at the elbows and did not strain around his belly. Someone had taken the time to comb the tangles and gnarls from his hair. He even appeared to have bathed, for he had no smudges on his cheeks and no dirt caked beneath his fingernails. To Angus, involvement in this investigation was a source of pride and accomplishment, a chance to socialize with knights and to scold impudent young lords. I was not one to judge him for this, however, since my own reasons for interjecting myself into these matters were difficult to explain.

"Thank you, Lord Byron. You look drunk." Angus didn't miss a step.

"Looks can be deceiving," I said.

"But, I think, not in this case." He pushed a finger at his red-webbed nose. "I lack Sir Archibald's sort of knowledge, but I ain't one to miss the stink of booze."

The Professor grunted assent; Angus was right.

"A bit of brandy serves as a fine lubricant for the creative processes," I said.

"Well, being so well lubricated, why don't you go ahead and slide off down the street." His lower lip twitched as he spoke, and I could tell that one had taken some effort for him to think up.

"Will you deny me entry to this alley?" I asked him.

"I'll warn you away, because I think you should leave," he said. "But if you persist, I'll let you pass, as was Sir Archibald's instruction."

It was my turn to fall silent as I digested this new bit of information and tried not to take offense at Angus's unconcealed amusement at my speechlessness. "He told you I would be coming?" I asked.

"Yes," he said, and then he lowered his voice so Knifing, who was behind the building, could not hear. "And that's as good a reason as any to flee. The gentleman is not somebody you ought to trifle with. I doubt you committed these crimes, but you're getting yourself into trouble here, nonetheless. I've encountered a lot of the fellows and a fair few of the old dons in my rounds here in Cambridge, and none of them ever seemed so quick as Mr. Knifing. I know you take a measure of pride in your own cleverness, Lord Byron, but you can't think your way around a man like this. I don't know what he can see, with that white eye he's got."

Angus had a point. Knifing had anticipated my arrival at this murder scene, even as he'd warned me to stay away from the investigation. We might both be playing the same game, but I had to concede that he was several moves ahead of me, and I could not figure out what sort of strategy he was unfolding.

How had he known I would come here? Perhaps he'd sensed the curiosity or morbid fascination that had drawn me to Felicity Whippleby and guessed that it had not been fully satisfied. I had no problems with being morbid or curious; these were traits I'd come to embrace. But I didn't like being predictable, and I didn't like being manipulated.

"Let me pass," I told Angus. "I will see Mr. Knifing."

"I can't see how this turns out well for you," he replied as he shifted his bulk away from the gate. "Consider yourself warned."

I left the bear with the constable, who took the chain leash without hesitation and rubbed the animal behind its ears. The Professor settled upon his haunches and yawned, contented. It was unusual to see him warm so quickly to a stranger, and my estimation of Angus improved somewhat. Bears are excellent judges of character.

The iron gate groaned in protest as it closed behind me, and

I followed the alleyway around the side of the building, stepping carefully on the uneven stones for fear of turning my weak foot. Behind the tavern, Knifing paced in tight circles around the corpse of Professor Fat Cheeks, which was flayed open and spread across the alley like jam on a slice of bread. The killer had not, this time, collected much of his victim's blood, for the body was surrounded by a huge, gummy pool of the stuff, with more splattered on the back wall of the building.

The investigator touched the wide brim of his black rabbit-felt hat with two fingers as a manner of greeting me. When I had seen the hat gripped in his gnarled fingers the previous day, I had assumed it was the sort of austere headwear commonly favored by ministers, but now that it was on his head, I saw it was a queer thing, a sort of slouch hat or bush hat, like one might expect to see on the head of an ex-soldier turned sheep rancher in some far-flung, hot-weather colony. Regardless of its style, it would have been appropriate for him to uncover his head in my presence, as I was his social better, but Knifing seemed to be unabashedly indifferent to protocol. I found this disrespectful but decided not to make an issue of his boorishness.

"I had not known one man could contain so much gore," I said.

"Yes," Knifing agreed. "But as containers go, he was a rather large one."

I suspected that was some sort of joke, but Knifing wasn't smiling, so I kept my face blank. "Angus the Constable said you had expected me."

He glanced up from a coil of purple viscera he'd been poking at with the tip of his black umbrella. "Like the common maggot, you can be found wherever there is putrefying flesh."

Perhaps this was what passed for wit in the world of Archibald

Knifing, but it was sour stuff. "What has your investigation uncovered?" I asked.

He opened his arms as if to draw my attention to our grisly surroundings. "It appears that there is a dead man here."

Evidently, Knifing was auditioning to be the jester in the royal court of Hades. "And will you use the science of detection to render his killer unto justice?" I asked.

Knifing sighed and drew himself to full height. He seemed to become even thinner and more wraithlike, which I would have thought was impossible. Whatever flicker of mirth had animated his features vanished, and he seemed to grow colder and grayer. "I don't enjoy being here or doing this, you know," he said. "It's a dirty business, mucking about with corpses. And far beneath my station; I did not distinguish myself in four wars on three continents so I could get a job as an undertaker in Cambridge. I'd be quite pleased to see an end to the science of detection, and return to an era when justice was served by inquisitors and confessors who extracted God's truth from the guilty before rendering them unto the gallows."

"Such methods have fallen into disfavor among England's educated classes," I said.

"Not with me." Knifing noticed a spot of Pendleton's blood on the toe of his calfskin boot. He rubbed it on an unsullied cobblestone. "That was clean justice. That was certain justice. A confession certified by a clergyman and swiftly followed by a public execution. The matter was resolved without doubt or ambiguity, and everyone could go home satisfied that right had been vindicated."

I sensed he was trying to lead me into some sort of rhetorical trap. "Confessions extracted through torturous interrogation cannot be relied upon."

"How could a sworn confession be unreliable? How could injustice be perpetrated in the name of the Lord? He would not allow such a thing. God is justice, and there is no justice but God's."

"A man in torment will say whatever is necessary to be granted respite, even the respite of death."

Knifing tapped his soiled boot against the wall of the alleyway, trying to shake the blood off it. "Your supposition is that a man exposed to the mild discomfort associated with traditional inquisitive methods is likely to admit to a crime of which he is innocent, with full knowledge that such an admission will result in his own execution?"

Traditional inquisitive methods included sleep deprivation, beatings, flaying and scourging of the skin, and chaining accused individuals in painful positions for hours, or even for days. "I'd take issue with your assumption that the discomfort caused by torture is mild," I said.

Knifing spat upon the ground, and his thick, yellow-gray wad of phlegm landed with a little splash in the wide, deep pool of blood surrounding Pendleton's corpse. "It is the amount of discomfort that learned and moral members of the clergy believed was appropriate to apply in pursuit of the truth," he said. "By suggesting differently, you are putting your assessment of their methods ahead of their own, though you are a child and know nothing of God or of justice or of morality."

I started to say something, but he wasn't really looking for a conversation, and he raised his voice and talked over me.

"We've replaced sanctified truth with the justice of man, and look at where it has gotten us. We stand in a dirty alley, speculating upon events that may have occurred, using methods adapted from the hunting tactics of savage American Indians and the heathen tribesmen of Africa. Do you think we can fashion from these crude materials a better truth than God's? Why disdain a clergymen's words while credulously accepting extrapolations drawn by a secular shaman about the direction of a spray of blood or the size and depth of a footprint? Why distrust a confession yet uncritically accept an ex-thief's divinations about a bit of discarded pipe-ash?"

"If you've such contempt for your employment, why do you continue in it?"

"I serve at His Majesty's direction. England has spent years at war, and London is rife with lawlessness. The populace demands safety, and perhaps His Majesty hopes a few high-profile investigators employing fashionable methods can forestall the need for the Crown to make a more comprehensive investment in stopping crime. If His Majesty says there must be scientific inquiry into a few murders, then so there will be. Indeed, because it is my duty to serve the King, I have become the foremost practitioner of this so-called science. I can read a murder scene as well as any Comanche can read a buffalo trail. But the alleged quality of my application of these methods is aided in no small amount by my lack of reverence toward them. I'm not here engaged in a search for anything like the truth. I'm performing a ritual; I'm here as a priest of man's godless justice, though I fear this ridiculous blasphemy might be the seed of England's downfall."

"I hardly see the nation's ruin in the science of detection," I said. "I am, indeed, baffled at how the two things could be related."

His brows pulled together and his face became a collection of shadowy triangles. "I suspect you spend a lot of time being baffled, Lord Byron. You certainly seem to spend a lot of time drunk."

I couldn't help noticing that he parried my rhetorical jabs with the same sort of bored insouciance that I'd employed in insulting Fielding Dingle. Everything about Archibald Knifing was scary, but the scariest thing about him was how brilliant he was. I suspected, for the first time, that my assumption that I was the world's greatest criminal investigator might have been mistaken. I wondered if Knifing had ever written verse, and I rather hoped he had not. He'd probably have been spectacular at it.

I replied: "I am a poet, and I am thusly endowed, at least, with a finely honed sense of truth."

"A finely honed sense of the truth?" His clenched features lifted and spread apart, and his lips peeled off his teeth. I was terrified that I was about to find out what it sounded like when he laughed, but he restrained himself.

"It is not a thing for your mockery, Sir Archie. It's the most sacred and exquisite tool in an artist's repertoire."

He tucked his hands into his waistcoat pockets and rocked back and forth on his heels, stretching his legs as he did so. Finally, he spoke: "I just want to make sure I understand this," he said. "Your finely honed sense of the truth is an exquisite tool?"

"I do not appreciate your tone," I said.

He relinquished his self-control and cackled. The evil sound reverberated off the blood-spattered stone walls. "I must say, I am thoroughly enjoying your ridiculous presence. You add no small amount of levity to these grim and routine proceedings."

"I spread joy wherever I go," I said. Contrary to rumor, I am capable of embarrassment, and I was, then, embarrassed.

"Do you use the whole repertoire to spread the joy, or do you merely require the exquisite tool?"

"You're very funny yourself."

"Perhaps, my dear Poet, you'd like to engage your tool upon

the matter at hand. Do your finely honed senses lend you any insight into what has befallen our poor Professor Pendleton?"

He was baiting me, but I wanted very badly to humiliate him by demonstrating that my talents eclipsed his own, even in the narrow field of his supposed expertise. I scratched my chin and wobbled a little bit on my feet. "Well," I said. "Professor Fat—er, Pendleton wouldn't have climbed over the gate. He probably couldn't have, for he was quite heavy. I'd assume the killer either possessed a key to the padlock, or he was strong and agile enough to carry his victim over seven feet of wrought iron."

"My God, I must retract and apologize for all my previous mockery; your reasoning is wondrous to behold," said Knifing. "We elderly fellows often forget that we have much to gain by availing ourselves of the cleverness of youths. Were it not for you, I might have overlooked the significance of the gate."

I should have perceived his sarcasm; which would have been obvious to even the least savvy of observers. But I did not. It is possible, I will admit, that my perception was impeded by drink, for I was already about six fingers deep into a bottle. I was also considering whether Fielding Dingle could have heaved Pendleton over the gate. It seemed unlikely; Dingle didn't seem much of an athlete. Knifing couldn't have done it either, for the victim matched his weight, plus half of it again.

Sedgewyck, perhaps, could have managed it; the Dutchman was large, and such a feat was, perhaps, within his abilities. But the timing was also difficult to work out; he'd been at my party, and then he'd walked Olivia home. So when could he have committed this murder? And how could any of them have known Fat Cheeks? There was only one suspect in these killings who had feuded with the dead man: me.

What I said to Knifing was: "It's wise of you to acknowledge your deficiency."

Knifing glanced downward, ashamed, and seemed to notice something on the ground.

"Have a look at this," he said, pointing to one of the cobblestones. "See, there, how it's scuffed in the middle, how its coloration is dull, while the others around it are damp and shiny? Suppose I said that I could deduce from my scientific methods that this scuff mark was made by the boot of the perpetrator of this crime, and suppose I could tell you that based on the angle of the marking and my scientific knowledge of the force necessary to scuff such a stone, that the killer had a foot-length of roughly ten and one-half inches, a weight of at least two hundred and ten pounds, and was likely taller than six feet, but no taller than six feet and three inches."

"Why, that's remarkable," I said, mentally calculating Sedgewyck's height and weight. "I believe you've nearly solved the thing, for there could only be a handful of men in Cambridge matching that description."

"Perhaps I could determine the guilty party by deduction and intuition," Knifing agreed. "I could round those men up, interview them, and see who has reasons to want this man dead. I could examine their boots to see whose match the cobblestone. Indeed, that would be convenient, except that everything I just told you is utter fabrication."

"Pardon?"

"Fabrication. Horseshit. I made it up."

"You made it up?"

"Entirely."

"But there really is a scuff."

His good eye gave me a blank stare. His bad eye always looked blank. "So?"

"So what, then, does that scuff mean?"

He laughed again. "It means nothing at all. It was probably like that before the murder. And yet, you were ready to believe me, and ready to place criminal suspicion on a small group of men based upon that assessment. How is the employment of such easily manipulated scientific methods more reliable than a sworn confession by the accused? How can judges and jurors assess the veracity of statements by professed experts regarding these obscure forms of evidence?"

"Perhaps such observations are reliable if they are the legitimate deductions of qualified men acting in good faith," I retorted.

"The legitimate deductions of good faith experts such as yourself?" Knifing asked.

"Precisely," I said.

He smiled his thin gravedigger's smile. "Well, let's explore, then, your little theory about the gate, shall we?

"I'd be delighted to hear your thoughts."

He seemed delighted as well. "Tell me what you smell in this alley."

The air was heavy and stank of copper. "Blood," I said. "And also, shit."

"Yes, that happens when murderers kill by disemboweling. He must have slashed open the lower intestine whilst digging with his knife in Professor Pendleton's guts."

I shuddered. "That is a fact I could have lived without knowing."

Knifing puffed up his narrow chest and pointed an emphatic finger at me. "You came here of your own volition, without any prompting or invitation. You appeared unbidden as well at the scene of Felicity Whippleby's murder. If, as you contend, you have no connection to these killings, then you have no reason for involving yourself with me or my investigation. Your presence here is an unseemly expression of your curiosity, so if you cannot endure the unpleasantness, you are welcome to leave me alone."

"I just don't see how the stink of Pendleton's blood and shit are at all relevant."

"Blood and shit are not relevant," Knifing said, making a steeple of his fingers and assuming a lector's pose. "The important fact here is that this alleyway smells like piss."

"You mock me," I said.

"Even a man of my assiduous discipline and impeccable manners could scarce resist such a ripe and easy target for ridicule, but on this matter I am utterly without pretense. The smell of urine, pungent though it may be, would not ordinarily be discernible over the stink of this corpse, or of all this blood, unless said urine was present in large quantities. Observe, also, the water stains upon the walls around this alley, suggesting that the buildings here are regularly leaked upon from waist-high spigots."

"I still fail to see the importance of this."

"Despite the benefit of your finely honed poet's sense, and despite the advantage of having twice as many eyes as I've got, your observational failure comes as no surprise to me. I have already learned that, though this establishment serves as many as twenty concurrent patrons on a busy night, it is equipped with only a single outhouse. It's evidently the custom among the bar's regulars to relieve themselves in this alleyway. That gate was not locked last night, nor was Pendleton carried over it. He most likely stepped out here, of his own volition, to see to his functions. The killer took that opportunity to empty out all the stuffing in the unfortunate gentleman's torso."

I thought about that. Knifing continued:

"Now, there are only a few taverns in Cambridge, and you've been a local resident and a drunkard for quite some time; certainly for long enough to become familiar with this place and its accommodations. Therefore, you should have known, and probably did know, that this alley is left open as a public urinal."

He was right. Only a few evenings earlier, my weak foot had rolled sidewise on one of the wet, slippery cobblestones in this very alley as I'd leaned against the wall. Staggering, I'd pissed all over the front of my trousers. How could I have believed the gate was locked? My mouth felt very dry, and I fumbled in my waistcoat for my flask. "I was not trying to mislead you," I said.

"I don't believe you were. I simply think your faculties as an observer are substandard, your deductive capabilities are undeveloped, and your alleged gifts as a poet are of limited applicability to the task of hunting killers. Among criminal investigators, Lord Byron, you're the worst I've ever seen."

I cast my eyes downward and noticed what looked like part of a sticky boot-print at the edge of the pool of blood.

"Well, here is a clue you missed, perhaps due to the disadvantage of having half as many eyes as me. Unlike your fake scuff mark, this may lead us to the killer."

"No," said Knifing. "The foot to match that print belongs to Fielding Dingle."

I shuddered as if I'd been struck; Knifing had disarmed me of the last advantage I held over him. "Oh, so you know already, of Mr. Dingle's arrival?"

"Yes. And let me revise my earlier statement. Now that he's in Cambridge, you are only the second-worst investigator in town."

Grasping for any form of solace, I decided this was a back-handed compliment. "Why is he here, anyway, if you're investigating the murders?" I asked.

Knifing shrugged. "The man who hired me mentioned no one else. I suppose he sent Dingle down so we could collaborate, or so we could each confirm the other's findings. Whatever the reason, it makes no difference. Dingle will second my conclusion. He has neither the professional credibility nor the intellectual capacity necessary to persuasively disagree with me."

"Even if you are wrong?"

Knifing laughed his wicked laugh again. "Especially if I'm wrong. When I am wrong, I am at my most compelling. You should keep that in mind, in the event I decide to accuse you of the murders."

As I tried to formulate a retort, Angus came charging down the alley with the Professor in tow. Both of them were panting loudly and clearly excited.

"Get that creature out of my crime scene!" Knifing shouted.

"There's been another one," Angus said.

"Another bear?" I asked.

"Another murder," Knifing said.

"More than a murder," Angus said, gulping mouthfuls of air, like a hairy grouper flopping upon the deck of a fishing boat. "There's been a massacre."

Chapter 20

Man, being reasonable, must get drunk;
The best of Life is but intoxication:
Glory, the Grape, Love, Gold, in these are sunk
The hopes of all men, and of every nation;
Without their sap, how branchless were the trunk
Of Life's strange tree, so fruitful on occasion!

—Lord Byron, Don Juan, *canto 2*

It was only when I began preparing this account of the Cambridge murders, nearly a decade after the relevant events occurred, that I finally arranged to meet with Lord Whippleby, the father of the first victim. His fortunes were in decline even before his daughter's death, which was why he had been trying to marry her to Leif Sedgewyck. After the murder, his finances had unraveled entirely; he'd become too despondent to tend to his affairs. I found him residing in cramped London apartments, having leased his lands and his ancestral manse to better-situated tenants.

"So," he said as I entered his parlor. "The poet has come, at last, to pay me a visit." His voice was like a sheet of sandpaper being drawn across a velvet curtain.

"I'm really surprised we haven't encountered one another before, at some function or other," I said.

His laugh was angry and hollow. "I don't attend many social events anymore, Lord Byron. People find my company unpleasant. They believe I am quite mad."

Whippleby's flesh sagged from his face in loose folds, and his rheumy eyes were set deep in dark-purple sockets. He scratched at the white rats' nest of hair upon his scalp with thin, spidery fingers. Everything about him seemed dried out, as if he'd wept away all his body's vital fluids.

"People believe you're mad as well, of course," he said. "But your kind of lunacy is so very entertaining, and mine is merely the madness of an old man racked by grief and loneliness."

"I am writing a book about the Cambridge murders, and I have come to ask if you have any thoughts to contribute."

"My daughter's death was a kind of entertainment to you, and now you've come to document my suffering so that you can share your depraved amusement with an adoring audience."

I didn't say anything. He smacked his lips a couple of times to work up enough saliva to spit at me. He failed to do so, and cursed with frustration. "I spent years and no small amount of money trying to establish your guilt or complicity in those crimes," he said.

"We captured your daughter's killer," I said. "His punishment was death." This was not a lie, exactly, but the statement contained a significant omission.

And Whippleby knew there was something wrong with the story; he always had. "I've never been satisfied with your explanation of the events in Cambridge, nor am I satisfied with the man you delivered up as the murderer," he said. "Even though I've been unable to prove you're a liar, you are a detestable man and I would like to see you dancing upon the air with a rope around your neck."

I let the insults pass without comment; I knew what had happened to my reputation. My fortunes were in such disarray that I had been forced to sell Newstead to stave off my creditors. The acrimonious dissolution of my brief marriage had left my reputation a shambles. People of all social classes gossiped openly about my affairs with chorus girls and spread the slanderous rumor that I had committed incest with my half sister, Augusta Leigh. This pained me greatly, for Augusta was my only living connection to my father.

"Your own hired man told you the same story," I said.

"The supposed perpetrator that you and that investigator accused was utterly ordinary; of so little consequence that his death brought me no catharsis or satisfaction. And yet, for years, you've been speaking in public of goblins and ghouls, and the involvement of mystical and supernatural elements in the Cambridge murders. How can you claim that mundane and fantastic explanations for my daughter's murder are simultaneously true? At least one of your stories must be a lie, and if one of them is, then the other might be as well."

My natural instinct was to be evasive about this subject, yet it seemed atrocious to lie to this bereaved old man. And why was I writing about the Cambridge murders, if not to finally tell the truth about them? I had no interest in continuing to preserve secrets that belonged to the dead.

In light of my own financial ruin and public shame, I was preparing to flee permanently to the Continent, to Switzerland, perhaps, and then to Italy or Greece. Or perhaps I'd go to the

East; to Greece, to Turkey, to Rumania, to Transylvania. I was not ashamed; I have never been ashamed. But I was leaving. I had no desire to live anymore among people with the audacity to question my moral character.

With no esteem or fortune left to risk, I was free to leave behind an unvarnished account of the truth about the Cambridge murders, a final volley of ordnance to blast the legs off my enemies and assure that, in my absence, England would not forget me. I had nothing to gain by lying anymore, and nothing to lose by telling the truth.

"During the brief period of my childhood in which I knew my father, he spoke often of the vampires he'd encountered in the East," I said. "I first involved myself with the murders in Cambridge because the killer's method of draining blood from his victims reminded me of those stories."

Whippleby's expression softened. "Yes, your father abandoned you when you were a small boy and died soon after, in France."

"It seems you know a lot about me, Lord Whippleby."

"You are inextricable from the events in Cambridge, which have, for years, preoccupied me. Yes. I know much about you. I have followed your antics; your rise to fame and your inevitable public shaming. I have studied your poetry. But I have never heard or read anything to suggest that your father was an important piece of the Cambridge puzzle. He left England years prior, did he not?"

"Even famous knaves are discreet about some things," I said, though I supposed I was done with discretion. "The deepest wounds are the ones we conceal."

"We are both preoccupied, then. We both grieve," he said. "A son grieves for a father, and a father grieves for a daughter. But my daughter and your father have nothing to do with one another."

"There are things I know and there are things I believe," I said. "Some of the things I know are things I cannot let myself believe, and some of the things I believe are difficult to reconcile with facts. This, I think, is a common human conundrum."

"You speak of God."

"No, I'm talking about Mad Jack. And about vampires."

"John Byron Gordon is dead."

"I know that," I said, "but I don't believe it. He cannot be dead. I'm not finished with him yet." Death was only for the poor and the foolish, Mad Jack said. And Mad Jack was no fool.

Whippleby licked his fingertip and contemplatively stroked it across his mustache. "They say both of us are insane, and perhaps they're right."

"A woman I once loved will proclaim to all who will listen that I am mad and bad and dangerous to know. I've also heard that I am a drunk and an addict and a sexual deviant. But madness and drunkenness seem to me the only reasonable responses to the desperate reality of the human condition. How else can one dull the pain of past sorrows and quiet the howling inevitability of future grief?"

When Whippleby spoke again, his voice was softer and gentler. His hands unclenched a little. After so many years of hatred, this man would never forgive me, but perhaps we had found a common cause. "If you truly mean to write a full account of the Cambridge murders, you must find out who hired the second private constable. This question has become, for me, an obsession. Both Fielding Dingle and Archibald Knifing claimed to have come to Cambridge on my behalf to catch my daughter's killer. But I swear on Felicity's grave that I hired only one man."

He waited for me to speak. When I did not, he resumed.

"People have, in the past, suggested that I gave duplicate instructions to two servants, and thus, through my agents, I hired both men inadvertently. For a time, I believed this myself. I was near delirious with grief in the hours and days after I learned of my daughter's death. But I could account for only one servant who had been dispatched on such a task. I consulted my bankers, and only one disbursement was made to compensate an investigator. One of those two men went to Cambridge at my behest. The second went there under false pretenses. The trouble is that I do not know which man I hired."

"Why don't you simply ask your servant whom he retained?" I said.

"He was killed only a few days after Felicity died, before I learned that a second investigator had gone to Cambridge, masquerading as my agent," Whippleby said. "My man was knocked down in the street by a speeding stagecoach. The driver was never identified, and I have come to believe my servant's death was not an accident."

"Does your bank not keep records?" I asked. "Can they not tell you who drew funds on your note?"

He shook his head, and a visible cloud of dust shook loose from his hair and danced in the dim sunlight streaming through his dirty window. The old man's skin was pale as milk, and blue veins rolled beneath the translucent surfaces of his neck as he spoke. Whippleby probably had not been outside in months. "My servant paid cash, so the bank could offer no assistance. I made inquiries into the backgrounds of both thief-catchers. Fielding Dingle was, at least, legitimate, known among the fraternity of professional investigators and respected for his doggedness, if not for his intellect. Knifing, of course, was among the profession's greatest lights. He was a war hero and a personal friend of the

King. His reputation was said to be unimpeachable, though I'd call that an overstatement."

Whippleby paused to pour himself a glass of warm, cloudy gin from a bottle with a crystal stopper. He didn't offer me any, but I took no offense. His stuff smelled like pine sap, and I had a flask of a finer spirit in my waistcoat pocket. I unscrewed the cap and indulged. It seemed rude to let Whippleby drink alone.

"Deceit and disreputability are the thieftaker's apprenticeship. These men are former spies and criminals, ostensibly reformed, but turned to a task only marginally more respectable. I told my man to find me the best one I could afford. I'd think, with my resources, I could have hired a better man than Dingle, but I doubt my coin was sufficient to employ someone of Knifing's eminence, unless he agreed to lower his rate for some reason. In any case, only one of the two went to Cambridge at my urging. The second was acting on behalf of other interests. Of this, I am certain, and for this reason, I have never been able to accept the claim that the killer was some deranged peasant of no particular consequence. Someone must have hired the second man. Something has been covered up, and if you mean to lay down a true account of these events, you must unravel that mystery. I've failed in all my attempts, but perhaps you will succeed where I could not."

I locked my gaze with Whippleby's; stared into the deep hollows around his eyes and at the pinched, mealy-white flesh of his face. This man was wrecked, and I was partly responsible. I'd told a lie I believed was insignificant; Felicity Whippleby and the other Cambridge victims had gotten a sort of justice. There seemed to be little harm in manipulating a few of the facts.

But this old man perceived the falsehood, and the lie had devoured him. He needed to know what had happened to his daughter, just as I needed to know what had happened to my father. And so, he'd ruined his mind and wasted his vitality trying to unravel a conspiracy I'd been a part of. We had offered the perception of justice, of certainty. And, as Knifing might have predicted, the others bereaved by the Cambridge murders had accepted it and found it comforting. But Knifing had been wrong about Whippleby. What the dead girl's father needed was the truth.

On one level, I had visited Whippleby to find an emotional center for my narrative of the murders. I didn't really know Felicity, and she was already dead when I entered the story. Thus, she was an abstraction within the narrative. The murders and the process of their resolution, to the reader, seemed to merely be sort of a puzzle, and this made everything that happened afterward seem unimportant. I'd gazed upon the corpses with my own eyes and I'd filled my nostrils with the stink of their decay, so the pursuit of justice, as I experienced it, had had an urgency that I failed to convey upon the page.

More than once, in the course of writing my polemic, I'd wished I'd spoken with Felicity's mourners in the days after she was killed instead of running around uselessly in a drunken frenzy. Archibald Knifing, with the assistance of Angus the volunteer constable, interviewed Felicity's close friends and her neighbors in the rooming house to try to reconstruct the events of her final hours. I will admit that it never occurred to me to do so. Just as, only a few years after the installation of gaslights, one can no longer imagine the streets of London dark and empty at night, it seems strange to recall that protocols of criminal detection have been only recently established, and to the extent they existed in 1807, they were certainly unfamiliar to those outside the fraternity of investigators. So, while readers of the mystery stories that now proliferate in the popular press may think it elementary to interview a victim's associates as a first step in investigating a murder, it was by no means the obvious course of action for me in Cambridge.

But there's no point in defending myself. Because of my investigative omission, I knew very little of Felicity Whippleby, and I needed more information to write about the events surrounding her death. I'd hoped the girl's father might provide me with some anecdote; some story about a sweet or precocious child that would become maudlin when placed opposite a depiction of the horrific details of her demise. If I could not fully convey my own visceral alarm on the page, perhaps I could instill in the reader some of Lord Whippleby's gnawing sense of loss.

But seeing the wreck that Whippleby became helped me realize that the story was never about his daughter, and I had portrayed her as unimportant because she never really had been important. The story I needed to tell about the Cambridge murders was about me and about my father, and about the choice I made.

My instinct that my narrative was incomplete had brought me to Whippleby, but the problem was not with the beginning of my tale, but rather, the ending. There was no new information for me to uncover in Whippleby's dirty London rooms. I'd come, instead, for some measure of redemption.

I'd spent years pondering the things I did over the course of those few days when I was nineteen, things I'd never spoken of to anyone. It was no coincidence that I had begun writing about what happened at Cambridge when my personal fortunes were at their nadir and my reputation was in tatters. I would not continue to lie, not to the world, not to Whippleby and not to myself. I would tell this man my secret and, thereby, atone for the wrongs I had committed and the scheme in which I had been a participant.

Doing so would endanger me, perhaps. And it certainly meant that my planned exile from England would no longer be voluntary. But that was fine. I was done with lies and I was done with the rainy, squalid islands of Britain and the small-minded people who dwelt on them. Redemption seemed a worthwhile goal, and there was a whole unspoiled Continent to explore.

"There's no mystery to unravel," I told Whippleby. "I know which investigator was false, and I know whose interests he served. And I know who really killed your daughter."

Whippleby wet his lips with his tongue and leaned toward me. His eyes bulged, and his hands quivered.

I told him everything.

Chapter 21

She walks in Beauty, like the night
Of cloudless climes and starry skies;
And all that's best of dark and bright
Meet in her aspect and her eyes:
Thus mellow'd to that tender light
Which Heaven to gaudy day denies.

—Lord Byron, *"She Walks in Beauty"*

After arranging to release the bear into Joe Murray's custody, I accompanied Angus and Knifing to the scene of the latest atrocity. The place was familiar to me; it was the residence of Professor Tower and his family. Indeed, Professor Tower was the first person I encountered upon our arrival there, though I did not immediately recognize him. I typically identify people by their faces, you see, and Tower was missing his.

"I didn't even know a face could come off like that," said Angus as he stared at the grinning skull, which was a wet yellowish-brown color with patches of red flesh still clinging to it. The rough and messy surface was quite unlike the smooth, polished interior of my Jolly Friar, but having drunk from that vessel on so many occasions, it turned my stomach to see a human skull in its natural state.

Angus had said there was not just one killing, but rather, "a massacre." This was not the only body here to be examined. Though I was feverishly trying to imagine some circumstance by which my paramour had escaped her husband's fate, I felt a near compulsion to fall to my knees and wail with anguish. I restrained myself, however, and maintained a bearing that suggested no emotion more intense than mild curiosity. Neither my interests nor her memory would be well served by the revelation of our indiscretions.

"The face is less than an eighth of an inch thick, and it's only stuck to the bone with soft, mobile tissues," Knifing was saying. "All you need to loosen it up and get underneath is an incision along the hairline or beneath the jaw. If you can work your fingers into that, the whole thing will rip away with a good pull, especially if you've practiced the movement."

"Why do you know this?" I asked. What I was thinking was: *One requires only a sturdy ax, a large pot of boiling water, and a strong stomach.*

"Knowledge of anatomy and other modern sciences are crucial to my profession," Knifing said. "I've participated in a number of autopsies. And in my former life as a soldier, I learned exactly how deep my own face went."

"You were cut all the way to the bone?" Angus asked.

"There is a notch, a groove in the skull beneath my scar. With only a bit more pressure, the wound would have been lethal."

"Mortality is for the foolish and the poor," I said, because the recitation had become almost a reflex. "Decay is a consequence of individual failure. A man ought to control his destiny, and not be victim to circumstance."

Knifing's dark eye narrowed, but his white one seemed to widen. "Those are the words of a man who has never experienced the horrors of modern warfare. Wedged into an infantry formation, there's no place to run when musket balls fall upon you like hailstones, and there's little one can do to evade a shot from a cannon. I've seen plenty cut down in battle; braver and better men than you. Their sacrifice was no failure, and nobody living has a right to call them fools."

"Can I feel it?" Angus asked.

"Feel what?" said Knifing.

"The groove in your face."

It was interesting to see Knifing's features register surprise. His dead eye seemed to bulge a little, and his mouth sort of dropped open, as if he intended to speak but had forgotten how to form words. Knifing's entire persona seemed to be structured around anticipating everything in advance, and he clearly hadn't expected Angus to want to palpate his face. Of course, whoever gave him the scar and took his eye probably also surprised him a little bit. "Is there something permissive about my manner or demeanor that might possibly make you think that's an appropriate thing to ask?"

"I don't know," said Angus. "I thought, perhaps, we were becoming friends."

"If I've said or done anything to cause you to believe that, you have my sincerest apologies," Knifing said.

The killer had not been very interested in the blood of Professor Tower, apparently; as most of it was smeared on the walls and emptied onto the floor around the body, which had been positioned at the head of the table in the dining room with a white cloth napkin folded in its lap.

"He was seated here at the table when he died?" Angus asked.

"I think not. Note the cuts and gashes across the left forearm and the knuckles of the right hand," Knifing said.

"He's ripped up so badly, I didn't think those were special," Angus said.

"Those happened when he tried to defend his vitals from a knife-wielding attacker," I said. "During the years before I inherited Newstead, my mother and I lived in Aberdeen, a city rife with drunks and brawlers. Knife fights are not uncommon when Scotsmen get to drinking, and I've seen such wounds before."

"Very good, Lord Byron," Knifing said. He bent forward, leaning on his umbrella, and squinted at a mashed-down bit of blood-soaked carpet next to the body. "The body was dragged in here, and posed in this seat."

"To what purpose?" Angus asked.

Knifing waved his hand; the kind of elegant gesture certain people can make to demonstrate that they don't know something, but don't really care. "Perhaps it's some private ritual of the killer's, or perhaps it's merely some sort of theatrical flourish, for the benefit of anyone who discovers these bodies," he said. "Or maybe it's some specific sort of message to me or to Dingle. Or even to Lord Byron."

"Why would it be a message to me?" I asked.

"Fielding Dingle can be relied upon to be the last person to learn of anything, so if he is aware that you have entangled yourself in this unpleasantness, you can be certain the killer knows, as well."

I stepped back and took a careful look at my surroundings.

I had walked through this room a number of times during my secret trysts with Violet, but I had never noticed that this dining table was virtually identical to the one in my residence. It seemed a shocking coincidence, until I remembered that I'd purchased my furniture locally. In a town as small as Cambridge, it was not unlikely that both Tower and I would patronize the same carpenter.

However, if Knifing was correct, and this scene was a message to me, then the killer must have been inside my home to have seen my furniture and learned of the coincidence. Leif Sedgewyck had seen my table, but how could he have connected me to the Towers? Another theory was gnawing at the back of my mind; the theory that had attracted me to the scene of Felicity Whippleby's murder in the first place: blood-draining was the mark of the vampire. And the suspect likeliest to have left me a message was Mad Jack.

My unease must have been plain upon my face, because Knifing said: "You're getting exactly what you wanted right now. You decided to involve yourself and I can see that you're only just realizing what it is in which you've become involved. I hope you're enjoying the experience."

He followed the trail of blood to the heavy door of the bedroom. He found it unlocked, and pushed it open.

"Oh dear," said Angus as we entered.

My sweet Violet had been killed and drained in the same manner as Felicity Whippleby. We found her naked body in the bedroom, hung by the feet from a knotted linen sheet, which was affixed to one of the four high posts of the canopy bed. I tried not to think about how I had cavorted there with her the previous afternoon, and instead concentrated on keeping my expression blank to prevent my face from betraying our affair to

Knifing. I wanted to take her down, to cover her, to offer her whatever protection I still could. But the revelation of our indiscretions together would only taint her memory, and it certainly wouldn't be the best thing in the world for me and my standing in the community. I did nothing.

But my heart pounded in my chest, and my pulse fluttered in my throat. Feverish sweat began to pour from my forehead and my armpits, though the room was quite cool. I mopped my brow with my shirtsleeve and hoped my reaction to the sight of the corpse had escaped Knifing's notice.

The idea that Violet could be ripped out of the world seemed a direct rebuttal to the sentiment I had shared with her the previous day. How could life be imbued with purpose if someone like Violet could be unceremoniously and arbitrarily unmade? My guts twisted within me, and I nearly swooned. This, I realized, was the intrusion of disorder Knifing had told me his clients hired him to rectify. He was right; looking at that still, dangling form, I wanted order and I wanted certainty and I wanted vengeance.

Knifing's stony expression didn't change when he saw the dead woman, and he did not seem to acknowledge her at all. He seemed more interested in a splatter of blood and bits of bone on the wall, near the doorway. He spotted a small hole bored into the plaster, and then, without commenting about Violet, returned to the dining room to look at her husband's corpse again.

Using the point of his umbrella, Knifing pushed Tower forward, so the corpse slumped onto the table. The back of the skull was a tangled mess of hair and bone and flesh and brains.

"A pistol shot, at close range," he said.

"He was shot in the back of the head?" I asked.

"Don't be preposterous," Knifing said with a dry chuckle.

He lifted Tower's mangled head up by the ears and tilted it

backward. Stinking red-and-gray pulp poured out of the gunshot wound, but Knifing paid no attention to it, except to make sure none got on his boots.

He pointed to a round, red wound beneath the jaw. "The bullet went in here, and out the back," he said. "Entrance wounds are typically smaller than exits. You'll find a pistol load embedded in the wall of the bedroom."

He went back into the bedroom and knelt down, grunting softly as he bent his aged knees. He found a tear in the rug and rubbed it with his fingers.

"With more luck, these poor people might have survived, and solved our mystery for us," he said. "Professor Tower struggled with the intruder, and had the better of him, for a while."

"How can you tell?" I asked.

"The same way the Comanche can read the trail to learn where the buffalo herd he's been tracking was attacked by wolves," Knifing said. "The brains on the wall are at a level with a man's chest, so Tower must not have been standing when he was shot. The track of the bullet is angled upward, and the entrance wound is beneath the chin. The killer must have fired the lethal shot while lying on his back, with Tower kneeling over him. The killer entered the bedchamber from the dining room with a knife or a dagger, and attempted to attack the victims. The husband resisted, and stripped away the weapon." He toed the rip in the carpeting with his boot, and I realized the blade must have fallen there. Knifing continued: "Tower wrestled the attacker to the floor, but the killer got a hand free, and drew a gun." He shook his head sadly at how close Tower had come to eluding his grisly fate.

Angus approached the wall and stuck his finger in the bullet hole to verify that it was, indeed, angled upward. "That all makes sense," he said. "And the evidence corroborates each supposition. It's really quite amazing, Mr. Knifing."

"I know I am," Knifing said, "but I wonder how the assailant gained access to the residence in the first place." He retraced his steps out of the bedroom, past Professor Tower's body in the dining room, and back to the front entryway. He scratched the loose, wrinkled flesh that connected his chin to his neck as he examined the bolt on the door, which looked ordinary. Then he opened an adjacent coat-closet, and the limp body of the Towers' domestic maid fell into his arms. Knifing examined her and showed us the dark purple bruises around her throat.

"He strangled her," Knifing said. "I doubt she even had a chance to scream."

"We don't have much violence here in Cambridge," Angus said. "The students and Fellows are from the better classes, and most of the townsfolk have been here for generations. We all know each other. But maybe people here trust too easy. Likely as not, the killer simply knocked on the door, and this poor girl opened it for him."

Knifing gently laid the body on the floor, and we went back to the bedroom to examine Violet's corpse.

"How did he hang her up like that?" Angus asked. "Did she not resist?"

"She was already dead," Knifing said.

"How can you possibly know that?"

"Imagine a wineskin filled with fluid, and suppose someone punctured it. The contents would drip or flow out, depending on the size of the hole, and if you held that pierced bag over a bucket, you could catch the fluid as it drained. But suppose you squeezed the wineskin."

"The fluid would spray out of the hole instead of flowing into the bucket," Angus said.

"Exactly. The beating of the human heart applies a force upon the veins and arteries not unlike that which you would apply upon the wineskin by squeezing the bag. For the killer to drain her into his pot or bucket, her heart must not have been beating when he cut her neck. If it had been, the mess would be evident."

Knifing grabbed Violet's head and peered into her glassy eyes.

"Cause of death is most likely asphyxia," he said, and having verified that fact, he seemed to lose interest in her. He wandered around the room twice, and then opened the door to the adjoining bedroom, where the Towers' children slept.

The older girl was also killed by smothering, Knifing told us. She was left in her bed, and looked as though she might only be asleep. I commented to this effect, and Knifing shrugged.

"Putrefaction will be quite noticeable in a matter of hours, if the body is left at room temperature," he said. If he felt any twinge of emotion at the child's death, his face did not betray it. I tried to mimic his stoicism. Angus didn't. He sniffled loudly and wiped his eyes. Then he began to turn very red, and he left the room.

The Towers' young son, only an infant in his crib, had been dashed to death against one of the walls. The baby had dark curls; hair like mine. I had inquired about this similarity, and Violet laughed at me. She had told me her father and two of her brothers had dark hair, as did her husband's aunt. She told me that she had foolproof methods to prevent conception during our illicit exchanges. And she told me that the timing of our affair made it impossible for me to have fathered the child. I believed her, because believing her was so much easier than considering the alternative. But the timing didn't seem impossible to me. As I looked at the tiny corpse, I tried not to think about this.

Knifing looked at me with a kindness that had not character-ized our interactions up to this point. "There's no weakness in reacting to the sight of a thing like this," he said. "It's an instinc-tive response, and a sensible one. I've grown used to such things. But sometimes I wish I had not."

I set my jaw and gripped the railing of the baby's crib with some measure of determination. "I can handle myself," I said.

"Normally, I'd call a situation like this a murder-suicide, and lay the blame upon the father. He seems unlikely to attempt to refute my findings."

Tower had been a decent gentleman, and I had humiliated him. If I had to be honest, I'd admit that the mangled corpse at the dinner table had been an enthusiastic and compassionate teacher, and one I might have become quite friendly with, if I were predisposed to taking instruction. "You don't plan to be-smirch poor Professor Tower's name, I hope."

"Unfortunately, I think I cannot," Knifing said. "I doubt I can credibly posit that he peeled his own face off. It's a pity he wasn't only shot. I could have pinned Felicity Whippleby to him, and been in London for supper."

I wondered if Knifing's constant boasts about his own dis-reputability and the moral bankruptcy of his profession were a kind of amusement for him. A man in his line of work might develop a black sense of humor.

"As it stands, I am hunting a maniac, which is a shame, because hunting maniacs requires a lot of work," Knifing said. He glanced toward the door through which Angus had fled. "These Indian techniques are just parlor tricks. The mechanical details of what happened here are of little value to our investigation. Their pri-mary application is theatrical; when I testify at trial, the details of the victims' deaths may cause an emotional reaction among the jurors. But nothing I've discerned here brings us closer to discovering the killer's identity. Most killers are motivated by cognizable desire; the desire for love or the desire for money. A typical murder investigation has a structure, like one of your poems." Here he paused, and chuckled a little to himself. "Pardon me. Your poems are scattershot and amateurish, and so, of course, that metaphor will not hold up. A typical murder investigation has a structure, like a *good* poem. I can work backward, in such cases, through the victim's associates to find someone with a motive and an opportunity. But I expect such exercises will prove futile here."

I thought of Mad Jack's stories, and I thought of the image in my ancient book; a lithograph of a vampire tearing at a woman's throat.

Knifing continued: "The constable seems to be a good man, though not an especially capable one. He reacts as good men do when they witness evil. He reacts with incomprehension. You're not a good man, Lord Byron. I think you like the idea of being good, so long as goodness comes easily. But decency is unnatural for you, at least when it requires sacrifice or self-restraint. You are callow and selfish."

Perhaps he was right. I had cuckolded the man who sat faceless and rotting at the dinner table in the next room. I'd loved the woman hanging from the bedpost, but I'd done nothing to keep her safe. There was a chance—I persuaded myself again that it was only a remote one—I may have fathered the dark-haired child, and I had not been around to protect it when a monster came into its nursery.

"Do you know why someone would do a thing like this to these people?" Knifing asked. "Comprehending such a man's motivation is quite beyond the abilities of our friend, the constable. But I think you might grasp the nuance."

I did understand. The killer did the things he did for the same reasons I did the things I did. "He did it because he wanted to," I said.

He nodded at me. "That's the whole of it. The act of killing rather than the identity of the victims carries significance. I will canvass the local innkeepers and see if any of them happened to see one of his guests hauling around buckets of blood, and I will send Angus to check the woods and fields around town for vagrant campsites. But I am pessimistic. Unless this killer pins some unmistakable proof of his identity to a murdered corpse, I feel that he may escape me. And if you're still underfoot when my talents are exhausted, I will arrest you. I am not returning to London empty-handed. You should leave Cambridge. Go spend some time at Newstead, while I hunt this monster. When he kills again, you ought to have an unimpeachable alibi."

I wondered how much he knew about me and Violet, but I didn't dare ask. "If I go, whom will you arrest?"

Knifing made a gesture with his hands that simulated the act of plucking an apple from a tree. "It doesn't matter. Sedgewyck, probably. Or maybe I'll arrest Angus. I find his earnestness annoying."

With that, Knifing walked out of the room and left me alone with the cold, still children. He had brought me to these crime scenes because he thought he could frighten me off. I thought it strange that he was so keen to be rid of me, especially since he seemed to think my arrest would make his work so much easier.

After a minute, I followed the sound of Angus's sobs back to the dining room, and found Knifing consoling the constable with soothing words that I would have thought were entirely un-characteristic of the man. He had figured me out entirely, but I really didn't know him at all.

Fielding Dingle showed up to investigate the scene just as we were preparing to leave. "It's a great honor to meet you, sir," he said to Knifing. "I've heard grand tales of your exploits and adventures."

"I've heard little enough about you, but more than I'd like," Knifing replied.

Dingle did not appear to comprehend the insult. "Perhaps you would like to confer with me on the evidence, as I reconstruct the events which transpired here?"

Knifing shook his head. "Our employer in London must have hired two of us for a reason," he said. "It's best we work independently. That way, when we reach the same conclusion, our testimony will be more persuasive at trial."

"Oh, quite right. Quite right, of course," Dingle stammered. Knifing turned on his heel and walked out the front door without paying any further attention to his colleague.

"Did he tell you if he knows who did it yet?" Dingle asked Angus.

"I asked him, and he said he didn't want to spoil the ending," Angus said.

"What do you think happened here?" I asked Dingle.

His small, beady eyes narrowed as he regarded me with undisguised suspicion. His fleshy mouth wriggled with distaste. He would never have brought me here or granted me entrance to this murder scene, I realized, and his mind must have been struggling to figure out what Knifing was doing with me.

His face slackened, and then he showed me a tight, cold smile. Since Knifing had decided to treat me politely, Dingle seemed to have concluded that he must as well. He scratched his chin and carefully inspected the corpse of Professor Tower, touching the wounds and examining the dead man's hair and fingers.

"It appears that this gentleman was murdered in his seat as he awaited his supper," he said.

"Why do you say that?" I asked.

"It's really quite elementary," Dingle said. He stuck a finger in his shirt collar, which was too small for his thick neck, and stained the fabric with a bit of Tower's congealed blood. "He remains where he fell, and his dishes are prepared for the service of the evening meal. You can see that the flatware is untouched. Thus, it is clear that he was caught unawares by his killer, and received violence where he expected sustenance."

Angus started to correct him, but I jabbed the constable with my elbow to shut him up. "It's really shocking when one realizes what sort of man one is dealing with," I said.

"Mortifying," Dingle agreed.

Chapter 22

Here's a sigh to those who love me,
And a smile to those who hate;
And, whatever sky's above me,
Here's a heart for every fate.

—Lord Byron, *"To Thomas Moore"*

Angus and I left Dingle to his explorations, and followed Knifing out onto the street, where I found the man hunter conversing with Frederick Burke, the lawyer from the Banque Crédit Française.

"Hello, Lord Byron," said Burke. "Joe Murray told me I might find you here."

I resolved to instruct Murray to stop informing people of my whereabouts. I was beginning to understand that I did not want to be found by the sort of people who might come looking for me.

"Mr. Burke has rooms next to mine at the inn by the College," said Archibald Knifing. "How is it that you two gentlemen are acquainted?" His expression was hard to read, but he had already demonstrated remarkably intuitive capacities, and I had no doubt that he perceived my discomfort with the situation.

"This gentleman is a representative from a bank I've had some dealings with," I said.

"Oh," Knifing said. "How very interesting." There was, of course, no reason he should be interested in this at all, except that he enjoyed seeing me humiliated.

"There has been a bit of confusion about some paperwork," I said. "Mr. Burke has come from London to assist me in correcting it."

"It seems Lord Byron may have committed a major criminal fraud against my client and has, thus far, frustrated my attempts to seek remediation," Burke said with a sweet smile. Evidently, he had taken my threats against him the previous day with some measure of personal umbrage.

"Mr. Burke has sought me out to trouble me over an internal clerical error committed by a drunken bank clerk," I countered. I was fully frothed and hungry for vengeance after seeing what the killer had done to Violet. I understood why Burke might be vexed, but I didn't care, and was fully prepared to engage him physically if he pushed me too far.

"So you're a solicitor?" Knifing asked Burke.

"I am," Burke said.

"And you work for a bank?" Knifing asked.

"A bank is my client," said Burke.

"A French bank," I added.

"Well, like I said, that is just terribly interesting," said Knifing. One of his arched eyebrows seemed to arch slightly higher. "I shall leave the two of you to your terribly interesting business."

"I believe I'll join you," said Angus.

"I'm sure I'll enjoy the company," Knifing growled. It was clear from his tone that he did not enjoy Angus's company much at all. Knifing walked down the street, taking long, deliberate strides; a proud old warhorse grown patchy and lean with age, his supple, London-cobbled hooves clopping with each step upon the paving stones. Angus bounded after him like a preposterously rotund puppy.

In a less harrowing situation, I'd have found this pairing quite amusing, and retrospectively, I cannot help but wonder what their conversation might have been like when they were alone together, without me around to bounce insults off of. At that moment, though, I was awash with emotions and unable to see any humor in the situation.

"Do you intend to threaten me again, here upon the public street?" Burke asked. "I see you are without your bear today."

He thought, perhaps, it was safer to confront me in the street than it had been in my residence, but Burke didn't know that, while my protestations of grief over Felicity Whippleby's death had been a convenient excuse to avoid dealing with him, I was truly anguished about the loss of Violet Tower. Burke didn't know that the bear was tame, whereas I was the danger.

"Why are you still in Cambridge?" I asked him, squeezing my right fist until the knuckles turned white, while adjusting my gun-belt with my left hand. "I told you that Mr. Hanson, in London, is the gentleman you need to speak to regarding any legal matters."

His Adam's apple seemed to recede slightly into his neck as his jaw clenched. "If I was satisfied to get run around by your lawyer, I would never have made the trip. In any case, you made the deal with Lafitte without consulting counsel, so I don't see why you need a lawyer to correct these defects."

"Well, first of all, I ought not concede that there are any defects in the agreement until my counsel has reviewed your allegations. And, second, if there are any defects, they are only innocent mistakes, consequences of M. Lafitte's incompetence as a banker, and perhaps attributable, in some small measure, to my own youthful inexperience in the norms of business."

"Be serious," said Burke. "After swindling our banker, you cannot really intend to play the naïf."

"You just accused me of serious criminal fraud, and this isn't the first time you have done so. I think I should have no further dealings or conversations with you or your client without Mr. Hanson present."

"You have our money, and are spending wantonly, by all reports. We lack proper collateral to secure our interest, due to your false representations. With each day that passes, you waste more of our funds, which we shall later be unable to recover. Only last night, I've learned, you and several dozen guests feasted on foie gras and champagne, though you'd refused to discuss business with me earlier the same day because you were overwhelmed with grief over the death of Felicity Whippleby."

"Are you upset because I didn't invite you to the party?" I asked. "I felt the adversarial tone of our dealings might have caused tension or awkwardness in a social setting. Also, I find your company unpleasant."

Burke leaned toward me. On the public street, without the Professor around, he was less frightened of me than he'd been the previous day in my residence. "If you need a lawyer, find one in Cambridge."

"Absolutely not." I would stand firm on this point. "I will not engage in dealings with you if I am to be deprived of my trusted advisor."

"This matter needs to be resolved at once."

I nodded. "I understand, Mr. Burke, and you can rest assured that Mr. Hanson and I will treat this with all due urgency.

His practice in London is, of course, quite busy, and I am deeply engaged with my studies here in Cambridge. However, I am confident that, with some effort, we can arrange to meet together within three months, assuming your availability coincides with ours."

Burke stared at me, aghast. I think, if I had struck him, he might have been less piqued. "In three months, you will have wasted all of my client's money," he said. "I must have either security or repayment, and I must have it immediately."

"Perhaps you should sue me. How much money do you think I can waste before a court rules on your petition?"

"I came here to seek your assistance in finding an amicable resolution to this problem. If proceedings become adversarial, you'll find I can be much less friendly. If we involve the courts in this matter, they'll rule for my client and order you to return the funds. If you cannot, you'll face debtors' prison." He poked his finger at me, and I slapped it away.

"Debtors' prison? Do you think I'm stupid? I'm shielded by the privileges of nobility, and your client is a foreign concern based in a nation that is presently at war with England. Given those facts, an English court is likely to rule that the defects in the agreement absolve me of all repayment obligations." I had no idea whether this was true, but my rage was fully stoked, and aggression seemed a necessity under the circumstances.

"Such an outcome would be unprecedented." He stammered as he spoke and he took a step back, away from me. All at once, his rage seemed to break open, exposing the impotence behind the threatening façade. I could see the fragility of his negotiating position in his downcast eyes and in the quivering corners of his mouth. And I lost all interest in his precedents or his threats. Really, I lost interest in the insignificant personage of Frederick Burke.

"It might be unprecedented, or it might not be. I really don't know, which is why I must rely on my lawyer."

Burke's hands clenched and unclenched. His Adam's apple seemed to crawl up and down his weird, long throat. A vein throbbed on his forehead. His whole body seemed poised for action. I wondered if he might try to hit me, or if he might flee in terror and humiliation.

He did neither; instead, he lowered his voice, nearly to a whisper. "Why on earth does a man of high birth defraud a bank? Why did you need the money so badly? Did you spend it on anything but women and drink?"

"I am not going to speak to you anymore without my lawyer."

"I've learned about you, Lord Byron, in performing my due diligence; my preparation to handle this matter. You delight in flouting rules and systems. You have treated your corrupt and dishonest dealings with Banque Crédit Française as a kind of game. You twist the rules of the College by keeping that awful bear. Even men who number you among their friends would not trust you alone with their daughters or wives. Nor with their sons, for that matter."

"I don't need your scolding, Mr. Burke. If we have business to conduct, you may contact Mr. Hanson."

Burke ignored me and continued speaking. His voice grew even softer, but the cords of his neck were tight with rage, constricting his Adam's apple so tightly, I thought his throat might burst. "You avail yourself unashamedly of all the advantages that come with your inherited title. Yet you defy the very strictures and norms that have elevated you to your position of privilege.

Why should you be celebrated for your knavishness? Why should your wrongs go unpunished?"

I turned and walked away from Burke in a crisp imitation of Archibald Knifing's military gait. I'd actually been somewhat worried about what he might able to do, but it was now clear that he was entirely helpless. I would not be subjected to the indignities my father had suffered at the hands of his creditors. I was a baron, while Mad Jack had only been the nephew of one.

Chapter 23

And, after all, what is a lie? 'Tis but
The truth in masquerade; and I defy
Historians, heroes, lawyers, priests, to put
A fact without some leaven of a lie.
The very shadow of true Truth would shut
Up annals, revelations, poesy,
And prophecy—except it should be dated
Some years before the incidents related.

—Lord Byron, Don Juan, *canto II*

To tell a lie is the most unnatural thing in the world. It's a contravention of human nature, a violation of the social contract. Most people can't do it, or at least they can't do it well. Language fails them when they try. Their twitchy eyes betray them. Their hands sweat. There aren't many people who can maintain a steady gaze and an authoritative tone while telling a lie.

I can. I've had a lot of practice.

For as long as I can remember, I've had a secret ritual, one I have concealed from even my mother, Joe Murray, and the Professor.

Late at night, while everyone else sleeps, I sit in front of a mirror, and I lie to myself.

"Your father loves you," I say. "He would never abandon you."

A gifted liar believes every word he says, even though he knows his statements misrepresent the facts. Such is his faith in his own narrative that he believes he can remake the world through the exercise of charisma, persuasion, and sheer force of will. Only falsehood can reconcile the world as it exists with the world as it should be. Or, at least, if there's another way, it requires a great deal more effort.

Alone, in my darkened bedroom, I stare into my own reflected visage and try not to blink.

"He is away, in the East. He has traveled beyond the horizon, beyond the sunrise, in search of secrets."

If there is doubt in my voice, I reproach myself for my faithlessness. How dare I slander the father who loves me so much that he has gone questing, like Odysseus, through the savage places of the world so that he may bring back the secret of immortality?

In any case, he had to leave; he was in my way. If he'd stayed, he'd be Lord Byron, and thus, he'd be keeping me from my special destiny. He forsook his own birthright, such was his love for me.

A lie is like a seduction, and the skillful liar knows a falsehood's recipient is a co-conspirator rather than a victim. If the lie is framed in a way that makes the listener want to believe it, he becomes a willing party to his own deception.

That's why I don't ask myself how Mad Jack knew that William's heirs would predecease him. I don't want to think about that. I don't want to examine the lie too closely. My rise was no accident; it was all designed, by Providence and by Mad Jack, my ever-vigilant benefactor.

To write a poem, it is said, is to tell the truth; poetry is worthless dross if it is not true. But the truth of poetry isn't the truth of the world observed. Poetic truth is the truth of the world imagined; a truth made true by artistry and artifice and the sheer certainty of the writer and his reader that the world can be this way, and that, if it can be this way, it must be this way.

So I sit in front of the mirror.

My hand is steady. My eye is steady.

My cup is full, and then empty, and then full again.

And I say to myself: "Your father is not dead. He cannot be dead.

"He searches, in the East, for the secret of eternal persistence.

"You are loved.

"Your father loves you. Your mother loves you. Your friends love you.

"You will never be alone.

"You are a special boy, meant for a special destiny.

"Death is not an inevitability. Where others falter and cease, you will endure.

"Empires will rise and fall, and cities will crumble to dust, and you will persist, unchanging, drinking and dancing and making love.

"Forever."

My hand is steady. My eyes do not falter. I sit in front of the mirror and I lie to myself.

My cup is full, and then empty, and then full again.

And I believe every word I say.

Chapter 24

But 'midst the crowd, the hum, the shock of men,
To hear, to see, to feel, and to possess,
And roam along, the world's tired denizen,
With none who bless us, none whom we can bless;
Minions of splendour shrinking from distress!

—Lord Byron, Childe Harold's
Pilgrimage, *canto 2*

Upon my return to the campus, I found the lawn at the center of the Great Court crowded with students. Old Beardy, the professor who was so concerned with my growth as a man, was speaking from a makeshift dais.

"The College has been beset by senseless tragedy," he was saying. "We have lost two beloved members of our faculty. This happened without warning, for no very good reason."

Of course, if there had been any response from the College to the murder of Felicity Whippleby, perhaps these killings might have been avoided. Perhaps, had Cambridge been alarmed after the first murder, volunteers could have patrolled the streets and kept the killer at bay. Violet Tower's maid might have been properly warned of the danger, and she would not have opened the door when the killer knocked.

But warnings probably would have done no good; Joe Murray had admitted three strangers to my quarters since Felicity's death; Frederick Burke, Archibald Knifing, and Fielding Dingle. He also let Leif Sedgewyck into the party. I would have to give him a stern lecture and, perhaps, dock his wages. I could not have him subjecting me to unreasonable risks as a result of his genial and trusting nature. But even I had not previously thought to warn him of this.

"It is the role of the academy to serve as a beacon of civilization in a world predominated by cruelty and brutishness, so this kind of disruption cuts to the quick in a place like Cambridge," Beardy said. He was impressive as a speaker. His voice swelled to a volume that overwhelmed the noise coming from the restive and nervous crowd, and his even, commanding tone seemed to calm the students. Though his esteemed colleagues were being torn to pieces in the streets, the men of Cambridge could not imagine a world where Beardy's authority was anything but absolute.

"We live in a nation in which there are vast inequalities of means among the elites and ordinary folk. All of us are the beneficiaries of these imbalances, at least to some extent, and in many cases, to a great extent." Here, he paused. Nobody laughed, so he continued: "But the desperation of the underclass produces ill effects that will bring sorrow and suffering to the more fortunate. A man who cannot buy bread will kill a well-dressed stranger for the coins in his purse. Every day, men and boys die in coal mines, crushed beneath the earth or asphyxiated by toxic fumes. Every day, women and children are mangled in textile factories. If the poor are desperate enough to do these things to themselves, think of what they'd do to us, given a chance. As long as we live in close proximity to the hungry and the hopeless, as long as we allow untreated lunatics to roam the streets, our walls will never be high enough, our locks will never be sturdy enough, and our guns will never have enough bullets to keep us safe."

The crowd grew noisier, and the students' collective murmur managed to drown out Beardy's stentorian oration. Someone jeered loudly. This kind of disrespect was not often shown to the faculty at Trinity, except by me. Knifing had been right when he told me that people crave certainty and normality. The students had come to hear the faculty's plan for rectifying the killer's intrusion into the College's bubble of safety. They did not want to hear that the entire social order that served as their lives' foundation was unstable, or perhaps illusory.

Beardy quelled the uproar with a wave of his hand and smoothly redirected his speech to address their concern: "The twin losses of Professor Cyrus Pendleton and Senior Fellow Jerome Tower are grievous and deeply felt injuries to this institution. Both these men were beloved here, and relied upon. They can never be fully replaced, and I fear the effort to find appropriate candidates to fill their professional capacities will be difficult as well."

Archibald Knifing had said that the killing of the Towers might have been some message to me. My affair with Violet had been sufficiently discreet to conceal our dalliances from her trusting husband, but it would not have been difficult to uncover. Anyone following me or watching her home could easily have noticed my arrivals and departures.

I considered what Knifing had said to me at the murder scene, tried to remember any revealing flickers of expression that might have crossed his nearly inscrutable features. He might have known of the affair, or he might have only suspected. Or he might have perfected the art of seeming to know things he didn't even suspect, as a technique for eliciting spontaneous confessions.

Whether he knew or not was less important than the possibility that he could have known, for if he might have known, the killer might also have known. I thought of Professor Tower, dead and faceless, sitting at his dinner table, which was so similar to my own.

"Students who were taking courses with Professors Pendleton and Tower will be able to finish their work under different instructors. I will be taking over Professor Pendleton's literature course; as some of you know, I taught that course until two years ago, and Professor Pendleton was using a modified version of my own syllabus, so we can resume without disruption. Similarly, since Professor Pendleton was to succeed me as faculty chair at the close of the calendar year, I have volunteered to stay on in my current capacity until such time as a qualified replacement can be identified. Professor Sharp and several of the other fellows will be taking charge of the remaining classes. I can assure each of you that, while our departed friends and colleagues will be sorely missed, the progress of your education will be unaffected, and the operation of the College will face no long-term interruption."

This was met with several angry shouts from the crowd, but Beardy raised his hand again to silence the students. It was amazing how much deference and respect he was afforded by this mob of tense and frightened young men.

"We will have a short-term cancellation of classes for the next ten days, however, and any absences will be deemed excused for an additional week after that. Quarterly examinations will be postponed, accordingly. I know many of you feel that the safest course of action is to leave Cambridge while these unpleasant events are unresolved, and the College will take no steps to prevent you from doing so. Two professional criminal investigators from London are already in Cambridge, searching for clues. I believe the killer will be caught before classes resume. For those of you who wish to leave, we have notified local stagecoach dispatchers that many of you will require their services. Messengers have been sent to London to hire more carriages. We wish you pleasant travels. For those of you unable to leave, I would emphasize that it is not my belief, nor is it the opinion of the faculty, that the College is unsafe. Personally, I will be staying in Cambridge to assist the investigators in any way I can."

I could hire a stagecoach and return to Newstead, leaving the murders and the faculty and Mr. Burke behind me; problems for other men and other days. So many of the students would be leaving Cambridge, out of fear or out of a desire to make use of the holiday. If I were among them, no one would think less of me.

Knifing had told me I should leave, and maybe he was right. It seemed like such good advice, in fact, that I wondered why he'd given it to me. Perhaps he told me to leave because he wanted me to stay, and he knew I would disregard his counsel. If I left, after all, I would spoil myself as a murder suspect, and he'd said he had nobody better to arrest. But if he truly wanted to frame me, why would he warn me of his intentions? Why would he try to drive me off?

I had my suspicions that a judge or jury's desire to restore certainty and order would be insufficient to win a conviction once Mr. Hanson got finished punching holes in Knifing's case, and I suspected that was the real reason he was hesitant to charge me with the crimes. Of course, if he accused anyone else, that suspect's lawyer would tell the jury about me and my odd and notorious reputation; about my skull-cup and the liberties I took with other men's wives. The mere proximity of a character such as I to the murder might create enough doubt to cause the acquittal of another suspect, even a guilty one. So Knifing had good reason to want me gone.

But I was stubborn, and I didn't want his convenience to dictate my actions. When he locked that dead white eye on me, it seemed like he could divine my secrets from the planes of my face and hear them whispered on my breath. He betrayed nothing to me; when his face closed, he became a complete cipher. He'd told me ten times at least that he was willing and prepared to arrest me for the murders. I knew absolutely that he was capable of it, and I also knew that I'd be completely surprised if he did it.

The worst thing about Archibald Knifing was that I could not help liking the man, despite his protean nature and his penchant for insulting me. He had evidently been a distinguished soldier, and he was obviously a brilliant investigator. Everything about him was admirably, aggravatingly capable, and his self-deprecating wit was both appealing and disarming. I liked his casual, smirking admissions of his own corruption. I liked his quickness and facility with language. I could see how witnesses and criminals might forget themselves in his presence. It was too easy to say too much to him. There was no question that I admired Archibald Knifing more than was safe. It would be advisable to admire him from a great distance.

Fielding Dingle was dangerous, too, even though he was dumb and I didn't like him. And I could not forget the killer, that as-yet-unidentified monster who had gutted a professor, bled two women, smothered a little girl, smashed a baby, and torn a man's face off. I had some reason to believe this ruthless butcher had entered my residence and noticed my dining room table, and I also suspected that he might be an indestructible monster of supernatural origins. So that was a fellow one might go out of one's way to avoid.

Under the circumstances, remaining in Cambridge was a phenomenally stupid thing to do; the only sane choice was to book the first stagecoach home. But I had always believed that rational behavior made life much less interesting. So, to hell with that.

I would stay in Cambridge, and I'd do it for ridiculous reasons. Non-reasons, really. I wanted vengeance for Violet, and for her baby. But I'd shirked more pressing responsibilities in the past. I could have accepted justice rendered by another man's hand; Archibald Knifing could probably dispatch a colder and more punishing retribution than I could ever begin to imagine. The only thing that prevented me from getting out of Knifing's way was the unshakable, irrational belief that the killings were related, in some way, to my father and the *vrykolakas*. It was a stupid, crazy thing to believe, and I knew it was stupid and crazy, which just made it stupider and crazier to continue to risk my life and freedom by involving myself in the investigation.

But, God help me, the lie I'd told myself so many times had taken root in my mind, and I couldn't walk away from even a very slim chance that I might learn the truth behind Mad Jack's disappearance. And, anyway, my mother was at Newstead, and if I went home, I'd have to see her. I felt that I'd prefer the vampire's company.

By the time Beardy's crowd dispersed, night was falling and my course was set. I would stay and I would see this thing through. And, as long as I was remaining steadfast, I figured I might as well try to fuck Olivia Wright.

Chapter 25

I am so changeable, being everything by turns and nothing long—I am such a strange mélange of good and evil, that it would be difficult to describe me.

—Lord Byron, *as recorded by Lady Blessington*

Men were not permitted into the women's rooming house after dusk, but I've found that if I behave as though rules do not apply to me, then they usually don't. So, I paid no mind to the feeble protestations of the house matron, who squawked without effect as I strode past her roost by the front door.

"Lord Byron, why have you returned to my residence?" Olivia asked when she answered her door.

"I have seen terrible things today. Mangled corpses and murdered children. I am distraught, and I am seeking solace," I said. "I believe I misplaced some between your bosoms."

I reached for her, but she pushed me away. "You're drunk, Lord Byron. I apologize if I confused you this morning, but I cannot yield to your advances."

"I think you are the one who is confused," I said. "You can give in to your impulses, and you should, whenever possible."

"I'll regret it later."

"Later might not come. Trading the pleasures of now for the possibilities of later is no way to live a life. There will always be a later to prepare for, but you will not always be young." I thought of Mad Jack, flinging china plates into the air. "And if later comes, and you regret your pleasures, so be it! A life without regrets is a life without texture. When now becomes later, you can make a new now; drown your regrets with drugs and strong spirits and do more regrettable things. Let's seize our opportunity to be scandalous together. Let's commit some spectacular folly."

Olivia was not persuaded. "I should guard my chastity, I think, until I can ensnare a proper suitor," she said.

I smiled and brushed my fingertips against her cheek. "That would not be an imprudent course of action."

"I am a prudent girl. I treasure my prudence," she said. "You could be a most excellent man, Byron, if only you would be less reckless."

"A poet mustn't live by the strictures that govern ordinary, conventional lives. Propriety is anathema. Art is about testing limits and reveling in the joy of unrestraint. I am not the man you want to face your regrets with later. I can only offer to share this moment with you."

She stretched her neck toward me, so my mouth was near to hers. I looked into her eyes and saw that they were full of tears. "Perhaps, for the right woman, you would change your rakish ways?"

I smiled. "Perhaps. For a month, or two, or even three. But before too long, I'd meet another right woman, and off I'd go, racing after her. A poet's heart is not a thing to be owned. A lover's love is too wild to be tethered in one place. I am fated to chase my desires, irrespective of other obligations. The world is full of beauty, and I want to taste all of it."

"Some things that look beautiful are poisonous, you know."

"I fear I shall not live a long life. But I would not live otherwise." I tried to kiss her, but she pulled back from me and retreated across the room, so her bed was between us.

"And what of faith and fidelity?"

"If you want those things, you oughtn't flirt with poets. Faith and fidelity are the province of the prudent man. Someday, you'll meet one of those, and perhaps you'll marry him. The prudent man is the most proper of suitors."

"You speak as if prudence is a distasteful thing."

"Not at all. Prudent men have the wisdom to resist the possibilities of now. A prudent man knows that the combination of two fortunes will yield greater comfort to both parties. A prudent man will understand that he desires children to carry his name. A prudent man will recognize that he wants companionship as he ages, that he wants tender hands to care for him as he grows infirm."

"He sounds like an honorable fellow."

"He is honorable, and it is upon a sturdy and honorable foundation that he builds his life and his future. And I, the poet, the lover, am most dishonorable. I don't build anything. I care only for pleasure, and I behave as though my actions have no consequences. I am profligate with money and amass debts wherever I go. I keep dangerous beasts as pets. I am lazy in my studies. And I am rumored to be incapable of sexual fidelity."

"You could be more prudent. You could be faithful, for a woman who understands you, for a woman who inspires you."

"I don't want to change," I said. "And I know that if I changed, you would cease to love me. Maybe you should preserve your virtue for the prudent man. He deserves it more than I. He shall remain by your side, and he'll always be faithful. If you grow ill, he shall hold vigil at your bedside. If you should predecease him, he shall weep at your funeral and bring fresh flowers to your grave. But you know what I know; love is not a lifetime of fidelity, and love is not a prudent combination of interests. Love is a single, sublime moment, transcendent but fleeting. You know there's a kind of love so intense that you can't look at it directly; so bright that you still see its shape when you close your eyes. And you know that a prudent man can't love like that, because he's too heavily invested in later to commit himself to now. He can commit for life, but I can only commit to right now. You may forsake true love for the fidelity of a prudent man. But you will recognize his faithfulness is dullness and his honor is weakness. You will know that he is boring."

"But why can't I have both the now and the later?"

"The very thing that makes me radiant and desirable will carry me away from you. I need to rove. I will sleep in castles on cliffsides and listen to the ocean crashing against rocky shores. I will watch the sun setting behind minarets. And I will carry my love for you to all the places I will go, but my love will never be yours alone. There will be many other women and probably a few boys, and I'll love each of them as fiercely and wholly as I love you right now."

"But if you really loved me, you would forestall your own selfish pleasure to protect me from pain." She stepped backward again, into the far corner of the room.

I shrugged. "If you really loved me, you would not wish to deny me any pleasure. The minute you're out of my sight, you're no longer part of my now. The first time desire tempts me, I will succumb to it. My heart is an insect, drawn to the nearest flower by forces beyond its comprehension."

"And as you flit to the next flower, I shall be left all alone to wilt and dry out and rot and die." She crossed her thin arms over her breasts. "You're not a poet or a lover or a drunk or a hero, Byron. You are none of the things you claim to be. You are a changeling. You are always playing a role. And you have assessed me frightfully well, preying upon my unspoken desires and stoking my romantic impulses while dismissing the solid virtues of Mr. Sedgewyck. It's funny, the choice between a good man and a bad one ought not be so wrenching."

I resisted the urge to tell her what I knew of Sedgewyck's virtues. "I would not go so far as to say Mr. Sedgewyck is a bad man."

She laughed. "You clown and jest, and you're so quick with your magnificent tongue. But I'm sure you know that you are not the good man in this scenario."

I circled around the bed and moved close to her. The wall was at her back, and she could retreat from me no farther. I touched her warm, pale cheek with my hand. "Why? Because I am imprudent? I am sure you know that a prudent man like Mr. Sedgewyck will never love you in a whole lifetime as much as I can in a single passionate embrace. It's not that he doesn't wish to; he is a sensible man, and loving you is a sensible thing to do. But he is incapable of my kind of ardor. He lacks the imagination to even realize such a thing could exist. You want me because passion is the opposite of prudence; its heat and its light attract you, though you know a thing so volatile can never endure."

Her face rubbed against my hand, and she closed her eyes. "Is that the poet's gift?"

"Yes, but not the only one."

"What else have you got?"

I moved my hand from her cheek and caressed her long, white neck, bringing my thumb to rest in the indentation at the base of her throat. "My magnificent tongue has uses beyond jest and clowning, and I can fuck you until your thighs shake and your toes curl up," I said.

"You have a high opinion of your abilities, Lord Byron."

"In a thousand years of tongues and fucking, there's never been anyone better."

She pinched her eyes shut again, and exhaled with some force, and her breast heaved beneath my persistent caress. "That might be true. But I think I must decline your offer."

"You think you must," I said. "But what do you really want?"

"I don't want to endure a lifetime of shame as penance for a single imprudent act, while you bask in your infamy and write mock-epic poems about your conquests."

"The present slips away while you fret about the future. You must choose, dear Olivia, to seize your now. I know what you want. I can give it to you. And it's better than you can possibly imagine. You need only to ask for it."

A lingering silence passed between us. I wanted to use this as an opportunity to gather her in my arms, but the moment seemed wrong. Even with my confidence bolstered by drink, I knew that her desire was not tilting my way, and conquest was not at hand.

"Mr. Sedgewyck—" Olivia began. Her voice was soft and husky, and tears welled in her eyes.

"No, that's not what you want," I said, uninterested in hearing whatever she might have to say about that unpleasant gentleman. "Turn me away if you feel like you have to, but don't ever lie to me."

"Please, Lord Byron, you must let me speak." Her tone was

insistent, but her voice was so soft, it was barely audible. "Last week Mr. Sedgewyck visited my father and asked for my hand. My father gave his blessing. Mr. Sedgewyck is known to be well situated, and this match may ensure the future fortunes of my family. He intends to propose."

"So, when he wandered into my home, uninvited, to insult me, he did so at your behest?"

"It was nothing so unkind as that. I think he was intimidated when he learned I was attending your party, and maybe he was trying to impress me."

"He came into my home at your behest and insulted me in front of my friends. I was humiliated." And then I realized something: "He asked your father for his blessing last week? Before the murder of Felicity Whippleby?"

"Yes. I don't see what the one thing has to do with the other."

"How long has Sedgewyck been courting you?"

"Several months."

"While he was purportedly betrothed to Felicity?"

I'd assumed Sedgewyck was merely a bachelor on the hunt for a smart match, and that his pursuit of Olivia had been his pragmatic contingency when the possibility of union with Felicity was extinguished. The fact that Sedgewyck had made secret plans to marry Olivia when Felicity was still ostensibly his intended bride changed my entire perspective on the events of the previous two days, as did the fact that Sedgewyck had apparently concealed his simultaneous courtship of two respectable young ladies from me and from the investigators.

"His engagement to Felicity was, as you said, merely a pragmatic arrangement," Olivia said. "It is not unusual to break off an engagement when an opportunity arises to make a smarter match."

"Why didn't he end things with her sooner, then?"

"His parents were infatuated with the idea of marrying into her good, old family. He was loath to disappoint them."

"So he found a way to get rid of her that didn't require him to spurn the bride his father had chosen for him."

"Leif didn't—he would never."

"Killing her was a prudent thing to do, and Leif Sedgewyck is ever so prudent," I said. "And you've chosen his prudence over my passion. The life he offers you is as cold and bloodless as the corpse of the last girl he was supposed to marry. You will never know what we could have had together."

She collapsed onto the bed and began to weep. "On some level, I may resent Mr. Sedgewyck and my father for making this arrangement," she said. "You're right that I don't love him, and you're right that he isn't passionate. I think that you have sensed within me some unspoken desire to undo the match, to wreck what's been built, and your insect heart can smell a flower ripe for plucking. Or perhaps I've committed some seductive act to draw you in; I cannot absolve myself of all blame. But I must stop before I embark upon your spectacular folly. I cannot forsake my duty to my family's interests merely to slake my own desire; not for something so fleeting as your limited promises of temporary passion."

If I consider it in retrospect, I must admit that this new information didn't connect Sedgewyck to Cyrus Pendleton or Violet Tower, and it didn't explain how he could have attended my party, walked Olivia to her doorstep, and still had time to commit all the murders of the previous night. But I was full of fury at the discovery of the Dutchman's duplicity.

Olivia, for her part, seemed to find nothing suspicious about her suitor's strategic maneuvers. In the world where she traveled, one's entire purpose was to pursue the optimal marriage. But she had deceived me nonetheless, and I wasn't about to do her any favors.

"That's fine," I said to her. "I don't really care. I'm moving on already, toward another carnal impulse."

"What impulse?"

"I want to beat Leif Sedgewyck until he shits blood, and it's a desire I've got every intention of indulging."

Chapter 26

First, I can hit with a pistol the keyhole of that door. Secondly, I can swim across that river to yonder point, and thirdly, I can give you a damned good thrashing.

—Lord Byron, *insulting John Polidori*

Insulting a man is a lot like seducing a woman. Both arts share similar linguistic structures and are, at their essence, tests of one's cleverness. The same kind of insight helps one spot a man's pride and a woman's longing. I'm good at insults. I can gently mock my friends, sting my rivals, and devastate my enemies. But there comes a point in any seduction when charm has run its course, and circumstances demand action. Insults, too, exhaust their function.

One of the first things you learn at Harrow is that one must never talk when one should be punching somebody. Past that barely perceptible threshold, language, no matter how quick or facile or magnificent one's tongue may be, is no longer appropriate. A man's skill at talking his way around violence is a good measure of his wits, but so is his ability to recognize the point when talking is of no further use. When diplomacy fails irreversibly, one must make a preemptive strike. Linger too long taunting or bargaining or cajoling, and you'll catch a mouthful of knuckles.

You don't give a warning. You don't make a threat. You don't tell a man you're about to hit him. He'll figure it out when his vision goes white and his brains slosh against the back of his skull and his nose smashes like a beam of rotten timber. You talk about fighting only to women. They tend to dampen their petticoats when somebody handsome regales them with tales of violent exploits. Among men, however, violence is its own vernacular, and it delivers its own messages.

So, when I found Leif Sedgewyck nursing a pint in the Modest Proposal, and I punched him in the side of the head, it meant: "I've learned of your schemes and depredations, and will have you punished for your sins, you blackguard." He twisted around and fell off his stool, which I took as a confirmation that my point was well received.

Another thing most boys learn quickly at Harrow is that one shouldn't wait for a response or a conversation after punching somebody. The ideal fight is more of a monologue than an exchange. While it may seem polite to wait for one's opponent to take his turn after drawing first blood, to do so is folly and, moreover, bad for one's complexion.

So, I let Sedgewyck get only halfway to his feet before I punched him again, full in the face. His head snapped backwards, and the rest of him followed it to the floor. I kicked him in the mouth, with my weak foot. It hurt, but I enjoyed the irony. I kicked him with it again and he gasped and spat blood.

"You rotten sod," I said. "These boots must be specially ordered, and now you've stained them with your putrid juices."

"Byron," he said.

"It is I. I came here all by myself, navigating the cobbled streets with surprising agility, considering my lameness." As a sort of punctuation, I aimed the toe of my boot at his belly and kicked him again. I think the sound he made was supposed to be a scream, but it was more like a rattling gasp.

I looked around the barroom. The place was emptier than usual; nighttime activity had slowed because of the murders, and people were avoiding the Modest Proposal specifically, because Professor Fat Cheeks had met his end there. Nonetheless, six or seven drinkers were present in the bar, as well as the barkeep, a delightful fellow named Richards. He had a fine case of Calvados in his cellar, which he'd acquired before the war with France, and he kept a bottle of it under the bar, even though nobody but me ever asked for it.

As I stood over the battered wreck of Leif Sedgewyck, though, Richards's expression was anything but friendly. The spate of recent violence was ruining his business, and I was contributing to it.

Apologetically, I grabbed a handful of Sedgewyck's white-blond hair and dragged my foe out the tavern's front entrance. In the better neighborhoods of London, the streets were illuminated at night by gaslights, but such luxuries had not yet come to Cambridge. A few of the buildings nearby had oil lamps hung next to their doors, but those weak, guttering flames barely cut into the darkness of the thoroughfare.

"What do you want with her?" Sedgwyck said. He still hadn't found a proper voice in his bruised throat, but he was managing to whisper. "Will you give her what I intend to? She deserves more than your passing fancy. I would make her my wife."

But this wasn't about Olivia anymore. She had deceived me

and played a role in my humiliation. My desire for her had been as furious and urgent as a summer storm, and it had passed just as quickly.

"Are you *vrykolakas*?" I asked him.

"I am Sedgewyck," he said.

"Are you *vrykolakas*?" I repeated. "Are you a vampire?" I grabbed him by the hair with my left hand, and punched his head again with my right.

He looked up at me with wide eyes. The white part of one of them was turning pink from the injury I'd inflicted upon it. "I don't know those words. Please, no woman is worth this trouble. I don't want to die. Stop hurting me, I beg you."

"What do you know about Mad Jack? Does he live?"

"Mad Jack?" he said. "I don't know who that is. I will admit I plan to propose marriage to Olivia." He fumbled in his waist-coat pocket and produced a gold betrothal ring. "I've made arrangements with her father and accepted her dowry only last week. I can tell you, her parents will be most disappointed if our promised nuptials do not occur."

I kicked him in the stomach again, and he curled up into a ball. "Why would you marry Olivia? Her father possesses no inherited title. A match with her confers no respectability upon your family."

Sedgewyck spat more of his blood onto my shoes. "The arrangement with Felicity was my parents' doing, not my own. I found the prospect of marriage to her untenable, and made other plans. My father's ideas of the social order are outdated—so are yours. There's no respectability left in moldy old titles granted by the ancestors of a king who can't even control his own colonists. The aristocracy is hollow. You people are a bunch of beggars. If I'd wed my fortune to the rotten Whippleby estate, Felicity's damned fool family would have spent my father's wealth on foppery and excess and valets and maids to powder their arses, and we'd all have a share of their noble poverty in half a generation. Money confers respectability in this new age, Lord Byron, and if you marry money to more money, you get a lot of respectability."

"So you hung Felicity by her feet and bled her like a sow."

"I swear to Christ, I never did. I only meant to jilt her, to break the engagement. And maybe have a roll with her first; I'm only a man, and you can surely understand the urge. But someone else has killed her. Truth be told, I thought it was you."

I believed him. Sedgewyck was not the monster I'd read about in my ancient vampire tomes, nor was he the sort of monster that could have slain Jerome Tower in hand-to-hand combat. This was a man who, despite an advantage of six inches of height and twenty-five pounds of mass, was groveling in the street before me, begging for mercy. He was a coward, and that was why he had been unable to end his engagement with Felicity even after he'd lost interest in her. His grief over her death had been false; a polite charade, since mourning was appropriate, given their arrangement. But he hadn't killed her. He lacked the capacity to solve his problems with violence.

Vampire or not, however, he was a most loathsome creature.

"I want you to leave town, Leif Sedgewyck."

"I will, I promise, at first light."

"There are plenty of stagecoaches available tonight. I see no reason you should wait."

He rose to his feet, wincing and clutching his injured belly. I squared my shoulders and raised my hands, in case he wanted to swing at me, but he didn't even seem to think about it. He was unmanned and pacified.

"What about Olivia?" he asked. "She deserves better than you."

"Perhaps she does," I said. "But you're worse than I, by birth and by merit. Moreover, you're useless in a fight. You're no solution to her problems."

He looked at the ring, and then he slipped it into the pocket of his waistcoat. "Very well," he said with a bitter laugh. "It seems you have beaten me." His eyes were turning dark where I had punched him, creating deep hollows against his pale skin, and there was blood in the spaces between his teeth. He looked exactly like a vampire ought to look.

He stalked back into the bar, and I heard him ask Richards to send for a driver. Thus, I had one fewer problem. I considered returning to Olivia, flush with victory over her suitor, to claim her as my own. But I doubted she'd approve of my disposition of Sedgewyck, and anyway, I was angry with her.

I went looking instead for sweet Noreen, Mr. Sedgewyck's pretty housemaid. He would likely no longer be in need of her services, so she was thus available to service me. I didn't love her, but she would do for the night.

Chapter 27

Now Hate rules a heart which in Love's easy chains
Once Passion's tumultuous blandishments knew;
Despair now inflames the dark tide of his veins;
He ponders in frenzy on Love's last adieu!

—Lord Byron, *"Love's Last Adieu"*

I first learned about love when I was eight years old, from a governess named May Gray. Her job in the daytime was to look after me. At night, she was a whore. As someone experienced with numerous practitioners of both professions, I can safely say she excelled at neither. She smelled like whisky, and her breasts tasted like old sweat, and she was as quick to raise the strap as she was to lift her skirt. My feelings about her have always been conflicted; though I was never passionate about her, she aroused and awoke my nascent passions for proper and liberal application elsewhere. I suppose I appreciate the education she provided.

Real love, though, would wait another two years, until I met Mary Chaworth. In the interim, my great-uncle, the fifth Lord

Byron, passed without surviving issue, and my mother and I moved into Newstead Abbey.

Mary was a distant cousin of some sort; the Chaworths lived near the Byron lands, on the edge of Sherwood Forest, and the convenience of proximity had been the seed of a number of love affairs and marriages between the two families. Mr. Hanson thought she was a fine girl, and he encouraged me to quickly betroth myself unto her. Together, he believed, we might build a productive and upright life. My mother agreed, and conspired to foment a match during the summer vacation after my first year at Harrow.

The day I met Mary, though, she was only really interested in one thing:

"Can I see the sword?"

"What sword?" I asked. We were eating a picnic lunch in a disused sheep-tract between Newstead and the Chaworth lands. We'd found a lovely little rise crowned with a diadem of trees, and we sat on the shaded grass to eat cold chicken and drink hock and soda-water. These pastoral environs, according to my mother's theories, were conducive to burgeoning romance. I still had seven months, at that time, until my eleventh birthday.

"The sword your dad used to murder my grandfather."

The aspersion against my father tensed my entire body and set my vision double. Blood roared to my ears. How dare this foolish child impugn the honor of one of Britain's greatest heroes, even as he undertook necessary and dangerous adventures abroad on the State's behalf, which kept him away from his devoted son?

"Take it back!" I yelped as I leapt to my feet. The audible creaking of the metal leg-brace beneath my trousers undercut the effect of my rage. "My dad never murdered anybody. He's a soldier and an honorable man."

"He ain't a soldier anymore," she said. "He's just dead."

"He's not dead," I said. "Only those without imagination ever die."

"The real Lord Byron—the old Lord Byron—is still alive?"

"Oh. No, he's dead. He wasn't my father. He was my great-uncle."

"Well, that still means your father is dead."

I was incensed. "How would you know that?"

"If he were alive, he'd have become the Lord Byron, and not you."

I tried to stammer something about vampires and the Gypsy legends of the East, but she just laughed at me.

"I can promise you that everyone dies," she said. "Your father told you a fanciful story."

I would say that was when I first loved Mary Chaworth. She represented, to me, the allure of adulthood; the stripping away of the pretty lies of childhood to perceive the world as it truly is, even if I had no intention of shedding my illusions.

Clergymen say the desire for knowledge is the Original Sin, and that was certainly the case for me. Like Adam's, my pursuit of Knowledge came at the behest of a woman. Ever since Mary Chaworth, the scent of perfumed flesh and the warm touch of it beneath my fingertips has reminded me of the fact that I would not endure forever. Awareness of death, I think, mingles passion with urgency.

"So, what about the sword?" asked Mary on that sun-dappled afternoon in my distant, formative past, sitting in the grass with her legs tucked coyly beneath her ruffled skirts.

"What sword?"

"You don't know much about Lord Byron, do you?"

"I am—"

"No, the real Lord Byron."

The sword, as it turned out, was part of a rather comical bit of family lore. My great-uncle had a neighborly dispute with Lord Chaworth, Mary's grandfather, on the subject of whose lands were more abundant with game. My uncle was determined to resolve this argument, and did so in a rather clever manner: He got roaring drunk and disemboweled Chaworth with a sword, in full view of a number of witnesses, at the Stars and Garters tavern in London.

As punishment for the murder, my uncle spent two years imprisoned in the Tower. Murder is a capital crime, of course. But in England, nobility is still respected. Only commoners get executed.

They say Lord Byron felt winning the argument was worth the two years. When he returned to Newstead, he hung the murder weapon above his bed as a trophy, and when my mother and I inherited the place, we left it up there to collect dust and cobwebs. Mary found some sort of macabre delight in looking at it.

"The Byron name has come to stand for cruelty and senseless, remorseless violence," she told me. "You've got a grand legacy to live up to."

How could I do anything but love her?

Three summers later, I was somewhat more mature, and I decided that Mary Chaworth was my muse and that I was destined to spend my life with her. I refused to return to Harrow, because I could not stand to be apart from my beloved. But, thanks to the peculiar acoustic qualities of some of the larger rooms at Newstead, I overheard her from some distance away, saying that she cared nothing for "that plump, lame, bashful boy lord." She was soon after engaged to a gentleman named Musters, a man known for his dubious morals and questionable finances.

This destroyed me utterly. I had given this girl a piece of my heart, and she took it and locked it away in a dusty cupboard. And throughout all my affairs and adventures that followed, I could never again give that piece of my heart to anyone else, for she had it and it was hers forever, though she cared nothing for it.

It was because I was unworthy of Mary Chaworth's love that I began swimming miles in icy waters in wintertime, and running great distances in layers of heavy clothing in hot weather.

I ought to drown you in the river.

It was because I was unworthy of Mary Chaworth's love that I stopped eating and started drinking. It was because I was unworthy of Mary's love that I began serially fornicating with near strangers.

Deformed. Useless.

It was because I was unworthy of Mary's love that I spent lavish sums, often borrowed, buying custom shoes that hid my clubfoot.

A physical manifestation of my failings and inadequacies.

So, if anyone ever wonders why it is that I am the way that I am, it's because Mary Chaworth couldn't love me.

Chapter 28

*I am buried in an abyss of Sensuality. I have re-
nounced* hazard *however, but I am given to Har-
lots, and live in a state of Concubinage.*

—Lord Byron, *from an 1808 letter to
John Hobhouse*

A woman's undergarment is an intimidating device to confront
when one is very drunk. After fumbling with Noreen's corset for
a few minutes, and finding my situation growing extremely urgent, I solved the problem with my knife. The taut laces popped
under only a little pressure, and the restraining mesh of quilted
linen came free. I threw it to the floor, where it fell in a sad little
heap. Mastery of the thing gave me a grim sense of satisfaction;
it reminded me of the torturous contraptions that quack doctors
inflicted upon my poor leg when I was a child.

"Byron," she protested, "those are quite expensive. Why must
you ruin everything?"

"Because I don't care about things," I said. "And it isn't ruined.
It merely needs relacing."

Her body smelled of powder and female excitement, and her skin was damp and flushed. I pulled her to me and kissed her hard upon the mouth as I pressed my hand beneath her skirts. She was fumbling with my trousers.

"You must remove your boots," she murmured.

"Of course," I said. But first, I blew out the lamp so she would not see my shriveled right foot.

I climbed on top of Noreen and moved to kiss her, but she pushed me away. I swore a nasty oath at her as I covered my leg with the blanket and reached down to the floor, feeling around in the darkness for a shoe.

"No, it's not that," she said, wrapping her arms around my neck and pulling me back onto the bed. "It's just that he's watching us."

I turned around and saw the hulking form of the bear, who had wandered into the room. He was nudging the girdle around on the floor with his nose.

"Darling, I assure you, the Professor's interest is purely academic."

But her protests continued, and so I climbed out of the bed, taking the blanket with me to hide my leg from her. I coaxed the bear out of the bedroom, down the hallway to his study. He grumbled with protest at his exclusion from the evening's recreation.

"I know," I said. "But the girl requires privacy."

He nodded, and rubbed his bristly haunches against my greatuncle's sinister black cabinet before retreating to his pile of bedding in the corner of the room.

"Thank you, Professor. That is a fine idea, and you are gracious to suggest it, under the circumstances."

I unlocked the cabinet. On the highest shelf was my green

absinthe bottle. In a hidden drawer, there was another bottle; a small gray one with a glass stopper. I knotted the blanket around my waist and carried both bottles back to the bedroom.

"I come bearing delectable treats, sure to expand the mind and excite the senses." I handed Noreen the bigger bottle.

She examined it and ran her fingers over it, peering at the opaque glass and the heavy cork jammed in the neck of it. "I've never tried absinthe," she said, looking at the peeling, yellowed label. "I wouldn't even know how to drink it."

I relit the lamp so she could appreciate summer-green color of the liqueur as I poured it into crystal glasses; glasses like the ones my father had smashed against the side of my mother's long-lost castle at Gight.

"It's very simple," I told her. "You drink it with laudanum."

The stopper extended into the little gray jar, serving as a long, thin implement for ladling out the precious fluid, one drop at a time. I let a fat, clear bead run down the glass arm and hang briefly on the end before falling onto a cube of sugar, which I held in the palm of my hand.

"When the Greeks spoke of the Muses, they must have been referring to opiates," I said. "Without drugs, I think there would be no poetry." I let seven drops of laudanum soak into the sugar, dispensing it like some pagan rite. I flourished the glass rod as if it were a magic wand.

She stretched her arms over her head and splayed her naked form before me. "Am I not inspiration enough for your poet's soul?"

"Of course you aren't," I said. "My flesh yearns for you, but my mind needs to get twisted." I placed the drugged sugar cube upon a slotted silver spoon and balanced the spoon over the rim of one of the glasses. I had a decanter of cool, fresh water, and I let it trickle over the cube so that the sugar and laudanum slowly dissolved and mixed with the absinthe.

This ritual, sacred to a certain, discerning sort of drunk, is called *la louche*. The water turns the emerald liqueur a pale, milky color, and it is said, as well, to release the mystical properties of the star anise and wormwood from which the absinthe is brewed. If one wishes merely to get drunk, absinthe served neat will oblige; its alcoholic content is nearly twice that of most other spirits. But absinthe, properly *louched*, is a different kind of experience. It fucks with your soul. Especially when you mix it with laudanum.

"Drink this, and you'll understand," I said as I gave her the glass.

"You are a wicked and dangerous man, if I may say so, Lord Byron, and I fear your influence will bring me unto ruin."

"Ruin comes whether we court it or whether we cower," I said. "We must sin while we can so that when ruin finds us, we deserve it." In my head, Mad Jack's voice: *Mortality is only for the foolish and the poor.*

I mixed a second glass, and we sat naked in the near dark, holding our green sacraments, staring at each other.

"To ruin, then, Lord Byron," Noreen said, and we partook. Then I kissed her. She tasted of sugar and of the anise in the absinthe; like licorice candy. Her lips quivered with some fevered urgency as she pressed them against mine. Her heart fluttered beneath my caressing hand. That much is clear in my memory, though the rest slips into haze.

Rationality, I think, is the enemy of romance. It grounds one in one's flesh and anchors one to the earth. This sad condition is inevitably fatal, and its devastating effects can be delayed only by the regular consumption of powerful intoxicants. I know writers who never partake; who put pen to paper in a state of stony sobriety. They're terrible. Banal.

Whatever would happen afterward, my dim and shifting memories of that night assure me that what transpired between us was transcendent; the kind of awed experience that language can merely describe, but can't fully communicate.

In that flickering lamplight with Noreen, I forgot about the murders and about my debts. I forgot my academic troubles and my clubfoot. I forgot about Olivia and about Sedgewyck and even about Violet. We tangled and disentangled, we merged and separated. Flowers bloomed from the wall and exploded into clouds of butterflies. But our idyll could not be prolonged: our elegiac now turned into a grim later; the echoes of Mad Jack's voice grew louder, until his fury was like thunder; a storm raging inside my skull: *Disappointment. Deformed. Vrykolakas. Ought to drown you in the river.*

Menacing shadows undulated just beyond the reach of the lamplight, and one of them took corporeal form and lunged at us.

I think I remember Noreen screaming, and I remember scrambling amongst the tangled sheets, my hands seeming to belong to some other person as they searched for my pistol. I remember kicking out at some unseen assailant with my desiccated right foot, and failing to find purchase. But my hands found what they sought, and I brandished the sidearm. I remember taking aim, squeezing. The gunshot reverberating. A sound like galloping hooves.

The room flashed white, and time slowed until everything hung still, a macabre tableau. The woman, pale and petrified with fear, and insensible from drugs. The monster looming. And between them, the poet, gnashing his teeth and firing his gun. The dull gray ball hung, spinning in midair, floated lazily past its target, and melted away. And then the frozen enemy became liquid, and moved with preternatural speed. My weapon was discharged and spent, and the thing was upon me.

Its face was blurry, and its form seemed to stretch and melt away as I swung my fists at it. For a moment, I was sure it bore my father's visage, but then the features distorted again and the attacker became unrecognizable to me.

Another pistol was somewhere nearby, but I couldn't remember where. I had a knife, but it was on the floor with Noreen's undergarments. So very, very far away. And the Professor was locked in his study. I could hear him bellowing and scratching at his door, but he couldn't help me.

My mind wasn't working, and the room had lost all sense of proportion. The nightmare engulfed me. I punched at it, but my arms seemed feeble, and its body was like stone. Something like a brick hit the back of my head, and I stopped resisting. My fingers wriggled, but they were limp and boneless; unable to grip. I could manage no further retaliation. Strong hands clamped around my neck, and I awaited the bite, but instead, the thing took hold of my head and covered my nose and mouth. I realized I was to be smothered like Violet Tower, and when I attempted to take air, a stink like that of some strong liquor filled my nostrils. I tried to open my mouth, but the thing held it shut. I couldn't get loose from the monster's grip and I couldn't escape the chemical scent.

I realized then that I'd forgotten to scream. Joe Murray might have heard the gunshot, but I'd drunkenly discharged pistols before in my rooms on several occasions. He would ignore the sound. I looked over at the girl and saw her pale, stunned, rubbing with druggy confusion at her eyes. I wanted to tell her to shout for help, but I couldn't speak.

Great waves of darkness surged around me, and I plunged into them.

As I fell, I could feel the *vrykolakas* all around me, long needle-fangs clacking together and leathery bat-wings beating in the darkness. I looked for Mad Jack among them, but I could not find him. He had abandoned me.

Chapter 29

The freshness of the face, and the wetness of the lip
with blood, are the never-failing signs of a Vampire.
The stories told in Hungary and Greece of these foul
feeders are singular, and some of them most incredibly
attested.

—Lord Byron, *from a footnote to* The Giaour

My mind condensed from its evaporated state a few minutes
before I managed to lift my eyelids. My mouth was cracked
and arid, and the thick ruin of my tongue was stuck to the inside of my cheek. The bedsheet was tangled around my legs,
but I felt unforgiving hardwood against my chest and stiffness
in my neck, and guessed I'd spent most of the night on the floor.
Blood throbbed in my temples. Beneath my face was something
metal that stank of burnt powder: the pistol. The air was heavy
and tasted like copper. I summoned all my strength and lifted
my swollen, preposterous head. It wobbled upon its narrow
stalk, and I let it slide back to the floor. I pressed a hand against
the back of my skull to stop the room from spinning. My fin-

gers came away sticky. I peeled my eyes open, and I was staring at a cheap pair of men's shoes with fat ankles sticking out of them.

"Lord Byron," said Fielding Dingle, "I am placing you under arrest for the murders of Felicity Whippleby, Cyrus Pendleton, Jerome and Violet Tower, their two minor children, Leif Sedgewyck, and Noreen Lime."

"Sedgewyck's not dead," I said, sitting up and leaning against the bed. "He left town."

"He did not. He was all over the street in front of the Modest Proposal. He left in a stagecoach after your fight, but somebody brought him back in a couple of burlap bags."

Dingle reached up into the pile of shredded flesh and meat that had been Noreen, and found a man's severed hand among the slimy coils of her unraveled guts. The thing was gray-white like the belly of a day-old fish, but the skin and fat had been flayed off the fourth finger, so that a familiar betrothal ring could be jammed down onto it.

"Somebody left a bit of him here as well," he added, holding the foul thing close to my face. "Mr. Sedgewyck, as you know, planned to propose marriage to Olivia Wright. I spoke to her, and she told me of your objection to their union."

"Yes," I said. "Sedgewyck intended to forsake his betrothed, Felicity Whippleby, to marry Olivia."

"In light of Mr. Sedgewyck's murder, I think we can eliminate him as a suspect in Felicity's death. Several witnesses saw you beating him last night."

"They also saw him return to the tavern after I left."

"Your whereabouts during the hours after the fight cannot be verified."

"I was here, making love to Noreen."

"That would be a convenient alibi, if only she were able to confirm it."

I could not even recognize her face in the mess that had been made of her; the vampire had bashed her head to mush with something heavy. Some part of me believed I'd seen my father in the opium haze of the previous night. Some part hoped to Christ I hadn't. And some part knew that Mad Jack could not have been the killer, because he was dead and buried in a pauper's grave, somewhere in France.

In fact, some part of me knew that my belief that Mad Jack might be involved meant that I was crazy. And if I was crazy, I myself might have committed the murders. My recent habits had not been conducive to clear-mindedness or reliable recollection. I'd starved my body of food, deprived it of sleep, and filled it with drugs and liquor. I had no illusions that my grasp upon reality was anything other than tenuous. This had always been my intent, for reality was something I viewed with a measure of disdain. But it was possible that my purifying regimen had dredged up something ugly from some deep, primordial place within me.

"I have learned the Towers had a second servant girl, a maid who survived the attack on their home," Dingle continued. "Were you aware of this fact?"

"I don't think so," I said.

"The girl has two young brothers in Wales, and she sends funds for their support. To earn their keep, she cleans for the Towers in the daytime and prostitutes herself at night."

"Oh yes. I know that one," I said, and my still-foggy brain forgot the grimness of the current situation long enough for me to smile at my recollection of the girl's thighs.

"She knows you as well. She saw you coming and going from

the Tower residence on multiple occasions. Why did you conceal your adultery with Violet Tower from me and Mr. Knifing?"

"I saw no need to share that private fact with you or anyone else."

"Surely you're aware that it seems pertinent in light of recent events?" Dingle gestured toward the remains of Noreen.

I didn't know what to say, which was fine, since Knifing chose that moment to enter the room. He marched up to me and grabbed my face with his hands. He pinched my eyelid between his thumb and forefinger and stretched it open. Then he leaned close, as if to kiss me or to bite my throat. Instead, he sniffed at my lips.

"Ether," he said. Then, to Dingle: "Someone drugged Byron. His servant, too."

"What of it?" said Dingle. "Byron probably dosed himself on that foul stuff. He consumes every other manner of intoxicant."

The laudanum and the absinthe were still sitting on the bedside table, and everyone was clearly aware of them. I wanted some of the laudanum, and I wondered if it was polite to offer it to my guests in these circumstances.

Instead, I asked: "Has Joe Murray been harmed?"

"He'll recover," said Knifing. He walked over to the bedroom window and examined it. "Dingle, this has been forced open from without."

"This murder occurred inside a fourth-floor apartment," said Dingle. "Is it your hypothesis that the killer flew in here?"

I thought of an inscription from one of my books; an image of the *vrykolakas* climbing the sheer wall of a castle, like a spider. I remembered certain legends that said the vampire could turn its body into mist and pass through the cracks beneath doors.

But I had to concede, a degenerate poet in a drug-frenzy seemed a likelier suspect.

"A man in good physical condition could scale the side of this building. The window-ledges are wide enough to stand upon, and the spaces between the bricks would serve as adequate handholds. I believe the killer gained access to Felicity Whippleby's residence in precisely such a manner." Knifing walked over to my bedroom window and threw it open. "Here upon the sill, there is a notch; a groove in the wood. I found similar damage to the window-frame at Felicity Whippleby's rooming house. This sort of damage is consistent with someone lowering a large chamberpot or a similar vessel out of the window on the end of a rope; it's how the killer took the blood."

"So?" Dingle asked, his face blank and uncomprehending.

"So, the killer left this place via the window. Unlike Lord Byron, who, of course, is still here. Surely you've noticed that Noreen Lime was drained of blood. Where do you suppose that went?"

"Byron could have taken the blood someplace and returned after he'd got rid of it," Dingle said.

"So you contend Byron killed the girl, drained her corpse, and lowered the blood out of his own window. Then he took the blood someplace and disposed of it, but left the disemboweled corpse in his bed. And afterward, he returned here, drugged himself with ether, hit himself over the head, and passed out on the floor. How does that make sense to you, Mr. Dingle?"

Dingle didn't seem to like what Knifing was implying. "I do not concern myself with trying to find sense in the conduct of madmen. Nor do I see any purpose to these deductive exercises you seem to enjoy so much. In my experience, when an investigator finds a practitioner of witchcraft in bed with a victim of a ritual murder, the difficult work is mostly done."

"Have you ever found a practitioner of witchcraft in bed with a victim of ritual murder before?" Knifing asked.

"Not as such."

"Then you have no experience to speak of, do you?"

"I don't practice witchcraft," I said.

"You have a cup made from a human skull," Dingle said.

"What of it?" I asked. "You've got folds of loose flesh around your neck, but that doesn't make you a turkey."

He leapt at me like an obese jungle cat, with his fat fingers clawed to scratch me, or something. But he was very slow, and even with my head still foggy, I was easily nimble enough to step to his side. As he propelled himself past me, I gently tapped his head with my fist. He toppled sideways, tripped over the end of the bed, and landed facedown in Noreen's uncoiled entrails, which broke open like overcooked sausages and filled the room with a horrific stink.

"Constable!" Dingle shouted as he floundered wetly in the remains of my paramour. Angus stepped into the room and looked with disapproval at Dingle, who was trying to climb up off the bed, making the mess there somewhat worse.

"Take Lord Byron into custody," Dingle ordered. "If he resists, you may use deadly force."

Angus didn't do anything; he was waiting for direction from Knifing.

"Fielding, if you have any respect for me, as an investigator or as a colleague, I think you should delay your decision to arrest Lord Byron," Knifing said. "There are too many facts that don't fit neatly into the picture. We cannot, for example, place Byron at the scene of any of the murders at the times they were committed, and Byron was hosting a party in his residence, among two dozen witnesses, at the time Cyrus Pendleton was most likely killed."

"Such esoteric points will hardly hold a court's attention once I have shared the grisly details of these slayings."

Some tiny change in Knifing's features, the deepening of some crease or a slight twitch of an eyebrow, was the only demonstration of his boundless contempt for Dingle. "Recognition of esoteric points and their significance is instrumental to the craft of criminal investigation," he said. "Any lay observer or volunteer watchman can document grisly details."

The casual insult seemed to deflate Angus, but Dingle was uninterested in lectures, and did not seem to perceive the menace beneath Knifing's gentle tone. "Will you throw public doubt upon my case?"

"Doing so would harm both our reputations," Knifing said.

"You have more to lose than I." Dingle seemed to realize, with some surprise, that he had the upper hand in this negotiation. He blinked with dumb astonishment.

"If you charge Lord Byron with the killings, I will not dispute your conclusions," Knifing said. "But I will not testify in support of them either. If you do this, you will do it alone. I'll have no part in such folly."

"If he is convicted, I'll have a place among the eminences of the field," Dingle said.

"Once I am acquitted, I'll see that you are stripped of your assets and your credibility, and that you die destitute and reviled," I told him.

"Perhaps you shall," said Fielding Dingle. "But first, you will wear shackles."

Chapter 30

All earth was but one thought—and that was death,
Immediate and inglorious; and the pang
Of famine fed upon all entrails—men
Died, and their bones were tombless as their flesh;
The meagre by the meagre were devour'd

—Lord Byron, *"Darkness"*

Two secure carriages were parked on the thoroughfare in front of the Great Gate to the Great Court. Joe Murray had hired one of them to carry the Professor home to Newstead, where his calm demeanor and steadfast resolve would make him a fine companion for my mother during the difficult months that were surely ahead of us as I faced trial for murder.

Fielding Dingle had procured the second from a gentleman several towns over who was an acquaintance of Angus the Constable; a prison carriage, specially built for use in transporting criminals to remote courts to stand trial. It was a solid box constructed from thick planks of lumber, with only narrow slits near the roof to let in a little light and even less air. It was quite unlike other stagecoaches I'd hired, which usually had big open windows that offered riders access to cooling zephyrs and fine views of the countryside.

"What in seven hells do you think you're doing?" Archibald Knifing asked Dingle, who was half-dragging me out of the student residence building and toward this monstrous conveyance.

"I am delivering this suspect to the magistrate's office in London," said the fat investigator.

"Your stupidity continues to astonish me," Knifing said. "The trial must be held in Cambridge. The witnesses are all here. The physical evidence is all here. You ought to sequester Byron in his rooms and send for a prosecutor and a traveling judge."

"I'll not give him a chance to commit more atrocities, nor will I give you a chance to undermine my case. I'm taking him to London."

"I'll stand guard over him in his apartment, if you like, Mr. Dingle," said Angus. "I can batten things down tight. He won't get loose."

"If you take him away from here, you'll have no case," Knifing said. "Who in London will testify to the events you allege? What can you produce there in support of your theories? This is a baron you're accusing, and he'll mount a vigorous defense."

"I've always collected my bounties from the office in London, and I see no reason to deviate from my custom," said Dingle, unmoved by Knifing's logic. "You have your way of doing things, and I have mine."

"The habits of a penny-ante thieftaker are ill-suited to the work of a professional criminal investigator," said Knifing. "There are established procedures, and you aren't following them."

"You said you'd have no part in my folly," Dingle said. "That's fine with me, but I'd appreciate it if you'd take no part in a quieter fashion."

"You twit," said Knifing. "You simpering imbecile."

"Bugger off," said Dingle.

The seats in the prison coach left much to be desired; they were hard wood benches bolted securely to the walls and floor. Iron rings protruded from the back of the bench, so the chains on my shackles could be looped through them, immobilizing my arms and legs.

I thought it unwise to risk giving Dingle a reason to attempt to use lethal force, but neither did I cooperate with his attempt to load me into the stagecoach. I just sort of let my body hang limp, so the fat man had to physically haul me into the vehicle. Momentarily, I regretted my weight-loss, but that sentiment was short-lived. The only thing worse than being forced to stand trial for horrific crimes is being forced to do so while also being fat.

Angus and Knifing watched as Dingle and the carriage driver lifted me into the cab. They made no attempt to help. Angus sucked on his mustache and shifted on his feet; I knew he didn't think I'd done the killings, but he revered the investigators. The idea that someone like Dingle could be so confidently and decisively wrong shook the foundation of the constable's worldview. Knifing's features remained, as ever, sour and in-scrutable.

Only steadfast Joe Murray seemed unconcerned. He'd been through this same procedure with my great-uncle William, the fifth Lord Byron. Twice, actually. In addition to stabbing poor Lord Chaworth, my predecessor also killed his chauffer for driving too slowly. As the servants at Newstead told the story, William shot the man in the back and threw the corpse into the

Lady Byron's lap so he could climb up onto the driver's seat and whip the horses. Due to the difference in social standing between the killer and the victim, William never stood trial for that one. His wife left him soon after, however.

It took Dingle fifteen minutes of monumental effort to get me chained to the bench inside the carriage, and when he finished, he was wheezing and drenched with sweat.

"You look awful," I said. "Are you feeling ill?"

"I hope you're this droll on the day you hang," he said, and he pulled the door of the carriage shut. Outside, the driver secured the padlock. The inner door had no handle, to prevent escape.

Dingle heaved himself onto the bench opposite me and leaned forward on his hammy haunches. Up above, the driver whipped the horses, and the coach lurched into motion.

"Old Knifing makes a great show of his supposed skill at tracking and detection," he said. "But I figure there's a reason the red Indians and the African blacks who showed him his trade never built themselves anything like a society. I don't think foreign races that sleep in the dirt have anything useful to teach civilized folk."

"Vampires sleep in dirt," I said. "And they live forever."

Dingle pounded the wall of the carriage with a meaty fist. The wood seemed to yield a bit under the force of the blow, which made me wonder if the carriage had some rot in it. I wriggled in my chains to see if I could force myself loose from the bench, but my restraints held. "You never seem to stop mocking me," he said. "You think you're so clever and I'm so dim. But you're at my mercy now, boy."

"We will see who is where, when Archibald Knifing catches the real killer."

Dingle reached out and grabbed my shirt, yanking me forward and pulling my chains tight, so they cut into my wrists. "Archibald Knifing is daft. He can tell you how the crime was done, but he can't tell you who did it. What's the point of that? The man is nothing but a fine suit stuffed with urbane banter and horseshit. You leered at Felicity Whippleby, feuded with Sedgewyck and Pendleton, and fornicated with Violet Tower. And you were found unconscious in bed with the mangled corpse of Noreen Lime," Dingle said. "You're a monster."

"At least I'm not ugly and stupid."

"No, but you're a clear murder suspect to anyone who looks at the facts. And if Knifing can't see that, then I've no respect at all for his vaunted skills."

"You've made an awful mistake," I said to Dingle, leaning forward and jangling my restraints. "Despite your fat, foolish certitude, I am innocent of these crimes and will be vindicated."

"You'll be convicted, on the strength of your confession," Dingle said, his broad, dumb mouth turning up at the corners.

"I will give no confession," I said.

Dingle lifted his bulk from his seat, placed his stumpy left paw on my shoulder, and punched me twice in the gut with his right fist.

"I believe I can persuade you to change your mind, Lord Byron," he said. "It's hours to London, and I've got nothing else to do."

Chapter 31

But I, being fond of true philosophy,
Say very often to myself, "Alas!
All things that have been born were born to die,
And flesh (which Death mows down to hay) is grass;
You've pass'd your youth not so unpleasantly,
And if you had it o'er again—'t would pass—
So thank your stars that matters are no worse,
And read your Bible, sir, and mind your purse."

—Lord Byron, Don Juan, *canto 1*

As it turns out, my preconceptions about Fielding Dingle's capabilities had not served me well. He lacked the conversational or observational talents of Archibald Knifing, but when it came to violence, he was both well trained and naturally gifted. I have had few beatings in my life that were so symmetrically organized or so thematically coherent. He rolled my body to the side with a deft strike from his left forearm, so he could poke at my kidneys with his knuckles of his right hand, and when I cringed or writhed from the pain, I stretched and twisted my shackled limbs.

Probing fists roamed across me, alighting upon my solar plexus, exploring my armpits and the joints of my elbow, digging into every place I was soft. My body had, in the past, endured similar abuses, but never while I was so unpleasantly sober. Dingle was smart enough to avoid striking my head or my face so that the magistrate in London would not have his sensibilities offended by the presentation of a battered suspect, but that small mercy was little consolation as my vision went red with agony.

"You can end this with the truth," Dingle said.

But defiance was second nature to me. "You'll tire before I will." The back of my throat tasted like blood, and the words hurt coming out.

He put his weight behind a fat, dimpled knee and aimed it at my crotch. I squirmed in my seat, and he caught me on the hip instead. It still hurt.

I'd resolved to die before I'd confess to anything, but I had a habit of falling short of my ideals and aspirations, and this situation was no different from previous occasions in which I'd disappointed myself. It wasn't very long before I started begging.

It made no difference. Hanson would rescue me from custody, hire a physician to document my injuries, and use the evidence of coercion to throw doubt upon my confession. Perhaps I'd even get hold of some powerful painkilling drugs. Dingle's victory would be short-lived.

I was trying to suck in enough breath to admit to killing Felicity Whippleby, and Dingle was winding up another punch, when I heard a cracking noise, like a champagne cork popping, and then the whole carriage seemed to jump. I could feel the horses break into a mad lope, and the wheels began weaving, jerking my arms in their chains and bouncing Dingle off the walls.

"What in bloody hell is that maniac driver doing?" Dingle

shouted. He didn't seem to be asking this question of me; he was just the sort of man who made a habit of spontaneously vocalizing his thoughts for no particular reason.

I decided to answer him anyway, since I was a cooperative witness. "You hired him, you fat simpleton," I said.

Dingle clawed at the iron mesh over the slit of a window near the ceiling of the cab, which allowed passengers to speak to the coachman.

"Slow it down, up there," he said, pressing his fishy mouth against the grate. "I want to reach London alive."

The driver responded by collapsing on his seat, so the liquefied contents of his smashed skull poured through the window.

"My God," Dingle said as he squirmed away from the mess. Outside, there was a dull thump as the corpse slid off the roof of the carriage and landed hard in the dust.

Under other circumstances, I would have come up with something clever to say about the series of events that had just transpired, but the coppery stink of blood and brains was filling my nose and lungs, and the violent motion of the runaway stagecoach was threatening to yank my arms from their shoulder-sockets. The pain was so distracting that I could do little more than state the obvious. "We must get to the driver's seat and rein in the horses."

"This is a prison vehicle," Dingle said. "We cannot get out. It unlocks only from the outside."

I twisted my body on the hard bench and began kicking my legs at the door. "Let us hope its purported security is exaggerated." My weak leg did little damage to the wood, but I felt the boards creaking and bending beneath my stronger foot's assault.

"That is useless," Dingle said.

The stagecoach nearly ran off the road, and my persecutor fell forward, into my lap. I considered trying to wrap my manacle chain around his throat, but I knew that doing so would neither resolve my current peril nor help me to prove my innocence later, should I somehow survive the journey to London. "Do you have a better idea?" I asked. I did not expect him to; he was, after all, a bit of a brick.

"We are doomed," he sobbed. "Doomed!"

If I'd had time to reflect on the situation, I might have been slightly amazed by Mr. Dingle. Every time I found myself believing I might have underestimated the man, he found some way to reinforce my preconceived notions. "Perhaps, then, while you await your demise, you might employ your considerable mass upon the task of helping me smash this door open," I suggested.

He nodded. His eyes were wide and dumb and full of terror, quite like one might imagine a cow's would look at the moment it realizes it has arrived at the abattoir. He began throwing his shoulder against the wooden door, though, to his credit. In that particular enterprise, his bovinity proved an asset. He had to throw himself against the side of the carriage only four or five times before the nails that held in the hinges ripped loose. Unable to withstand such violence, the vaunted external lock snapped off and the door flew open and broke away, smashing to bits as it hit the ground behind us.

"That was much flimsier than I was led to believe," Dingle remarked. He seemed quite surprised that he'd been lied to. For a professional criminal investigator, he was an absurdly credulous man.

"I shall remember that the next time I need to escape from prison," I said. "Now, if you enjoy being alive, kindly unlock my shackles so I can climb up there and rein in the horses."

"I must not," he said. "You are a prisoner, and will remain in your bonds until I deliver you to the court. I will take care of this myself."

Dingle hoisted himself out through the open doorway and perched on the running board along the carriage's lower chassis. Dangling precariously over the road, he reached out for one of the ladder rungs that were bolted to the side of the cab, and he began to grunt as he tried to lift himself up onto the roof. I had about five seconds to admire his bravery before I heard a second shot, and Dingle's head came apart. I saw him hanging, ever so briefly, in midair. The top of his skull and one of his eyes were gone, and part of his nose as well. Whatever struck him had done so with unbelievable force. The thick, wet lips hung loose and sort of flapped in the wind. What remained of his face wore an expression of confusion and incomprehension; he was as dumb in death as he had been in life.

The corpse pitched off the side, fell beneath the wheels, and burst like an overfilled meat-pie when the carriage rolled over it. The force of the impact bounced the whole vehicle into the air.

"He was right," I said, vocalizing my thoughts to no one and for no particular reason, as I hung in space, tethered to my bench by chains, "about being doomed."

And then, the stagecoach crashed.

Chapter 32

And there lay the steed with his nostrils all wide,
But through it there roll'd not the breath of his pride:
And the foam of his gasping lay white on the turf,
And cold as the spray of the rock-beating surf.

—Lord Byron, *"The Destruction of Sennacherib"*

The floor became the ceiling and the ceiling became the floor, and then things righted themselves briefly before the carriage rolled again. I didn't know up from down; I lost track of the world and forgot my place in it. Then everything fell to earth, and splintered and broke apart.

Angry hunks of wood slashed the thigh of my weak leg and raked my back and pounded my side hard enough to knock the breath from my lungs. When the stagecoach finally flipped sideways and skidded to a halt someplace off the side of the highway, I assessed my injuries. My ribs were bruised, but they had not caved in. The manacles had cut into my wrists, but my arms were not broken or dislocated. My head felt as if it might have been concussed, but it was in considerably better repair than the skull of Fielding Dingle. My cuts were seeping rather than gushing or pumping blood, which meant my wounds would not be mortal unless some putrefying infection set in.

I suppose I must consider myself lucky to have come through that ordeal largely intact, though perhaps I was less lucky than the millions of people who have never found themselves injured in the wreckage of a stagecoach someplace between Cambridge and London.

And I had other problems. I was still chained to my bench, and I didn't know where the keys to my shackles had gone. Either Dingle or the driver had been carrying them, and both their corpses had fallen off the vehicle, someplace back down the road.

I wrenched my arms so I could peer out through the kicked-out door, but I didn't see anything but the field I'd crashed in and the road, away in the distance. The keys could be miles back, lost in thick underbrush. And even if they were nearby, I had no way of finding them.

One of the four horses that pulled the carriage had snapped its leg. It was lying in the grass fifty yards away and bleating in agony. The other horses had broken free of the harness and bolted off.

I tried to take an optimistic view of what seemed a dire situation. If I were stuck in the wreck for longer than a day or two, I was bound to die of thirst or exposure. But before that happened, somebody would probably find the corpses on the road, or else someone would hear the dying horse and come to investigate. Until then, I could only wait.

My head throbbed and my body ached. I suppose I dozed intermittently. Several hours must have passed, though I had no sense of it, for when Angus the Constable found me, night had fallen.

I heard him before I saw him. More precisely, I heard a gunshot when he put down the injured horse. His first attempt didn't do the job, so I heard the loud crack of it, and then the animal's muted whimpering turned into a terrified, high-pitched scream, which it sustained for the entirety of the two minutes it took Angus to reload. I remember thinking it was strange that a brute animal's howl of pain and terror could sound so familiar and so human, and I thought of poor Violet and her children, who never got a chance to scream. The noise ceased only when the constable shot the horse a second time.

Then, Angus's flinty black eyes and round red nose appeared in the splintered doorframe of the stagecoach. He looked ashen and somewhat discombobulated, but he gurgled with relief when he saw I was alive. "You seem to have encountered a nasty bit of business, Lord Byron," he said.

"I hope it is evident to you that I did not kill Dingle," I said, jangling my shackles and showing him that I was still bound to the bench. "I have been indisposed since I last saw you in Cambridge, and have, since, endured some injury. What are you doing here?"

"I patrol the highways most nights," Angus said. "Someone has to keep the lookout for road agents and bandits." He proudly brandished the musket he'd used to kill the horse, and I wondered if he could have used that to shoot Dingle off the side of the carriage. He'd have needed preternatural luck to make a shot like that; and even the luckiest man alive couldn't have done it twice. But somebody had shot both Dingle and the driver, a feat of marksmanship that seemed beyond the capacity of any human skill.

A musket's barrel is quite a bit wider than its bullet, a necessity for fast reloading through the muzzle. As a result, the ball has a tendency to bounce around in the tube on the way out, which makes it impossible to control the direction of the shot with any degree of finesse. Muskets are effective when a lot of them are fired simultaneously in the general direction of a large group of enemies, but a single musketeer facing a single enemy would make himself an immeasurably greater threat by affixing his bayonet, or simply drawing his saber.

I didn't think Angus could have killed both men with only two shots, or even with twenty. Maybe he could have if he were a vampire; some of my texts said the undead possessed monstrous strength and extraordinary reflexes.

"Ever find any road agents?" I asked the constable.

"No," he said. "They strike sometimes on the highways around Cambridge, but I've never arrived at the scene of a robbery in time to apprehend the bastards."

"What will you do if you find them?" I asked.

"Kill them," he said. "I'll kill every last one." This was a ridiculous proposition, and if I'd been in my usual state of boozy levity, I might have laughed right in Angus's thick, earnest face. But there was something distinctly unfunny about his tone, a strain or a hitch, as if he was trying to flatten some swell of emotion.

"You think road agents waylaid this carriage?" I asked.

"Wouldn't reckon so," Angus said. "Little profit to be had from robbing jailers or prisoners. And when I found the bodies up the road, nobody seemed to have rummaged them. I think the gunman is the killer from Cambridge."

He began to climb down into the wreck, but I shooed him off with a roll of my shoulder. "It's no use. I'm chained in here quite securely, and I've no idea where the keys went."

"I've got them," he said. "Had to dig them out of Mr. Dingle's waistcoat pocket, but I knew you might be trapped someplace."

He worked the key in the heavy iron padlock, and I was free. With his assistance, I climbed out of the overturned vehicle, and sprawled my body out upon the grass.

"Are you in much pain?" Angus asked.

"I can only hope that no one has confiscated my laudanum," I said.

"It's good to see you've maintained your humor."

"I've got no other solace in these dire circumstances."

"Well, it could have been a good deal worse for you, I daresay," said Angus. "This carriage is only tipped on its side. If it had collided with something at speed, like a tree or a house, it would have been smashed to bits. You're lucky the horse broke free of the harness when its leg went, or else it would have got tangled in the wheels."

"From inside, it seemed as though the stage rolled end over end before it stopped," I said.

"It didn't. There are no gouges in the earth to indicate such, nor is there dirt or grass on the roof of the vehicle."

He reached down with his meaty hand and pulled me to my feet.

"You can see the track here, where the stage veered off the road," he said, pointing to the thick wheel-ruts that the carriage had cut into the earth. "The carriage just sort of ran into the grass, bounced around a bit, lost speed, and fell over. Laid you down quite gentle, I'd say."

"It certainly didn't feel gentle."

"Well, you just rest for a bit and get your bearings. After I found the driver, I hired a boy from the first farmhouse I saw to ride back to Cambridge and fetch Mr. Knifing. He should be along shortly to examine the bodies. Hopefully he'll arrive in a stagecoach. I don't suspect you're fit to walk back to town, nor would you want to sit horseback in your condition."

I didn't really care one way or the other about Knifing or the bodies right then, though I was possessed by a rather fearsome desire to be carried to my bed, where I could ensconce myself snugly with my bear and consume lots of drugs. "Have you got any whisky?" I asked. The fine red webbing etched upon Angus's face gave me reason to hope he might.

"I've been known to carry a little nip to gird meself against the wind," he said, confirming my suspicions. He handed me a dented flask, and I drank from it without even bothering to wipe his spittle off the mouth of it. It was cheap stuff, and it tasted like the wormy grain it was made of and the old, rotten barrels it was fermented in. But I could barely taste it, as my nostrils were filled, anyway, with the stink of blood; the horse's or maybe my own. And sometimes, a man needs a drink.

Chapter 33

If solitude succeed to grief,
Release from pain is slight relief;
The vacant bosom's wilderness
Might thank the pang that made it less.
We loathe what none are left to share:
Even bliss—'t were woe alone to bear;
The heart once left thus desolate
Must fly at last for ease—to hate.

—Lord Byron, The Giaour

"Do you suppose that, just before he died, Mr. Dingle's life passed before his eyes, and he realized, in that ultimate moment, what a terrible bore he was?" I asked Angus.

"Who can say what any of us will see, afore we pass beyond that threshold."

"At least his departure was interesting."

Angus chuckled. "That it was, though I don't know that he appreciated it."

"Of course he wouldn't," I said. "He lacked refined sensibilities."

"Not all of us have the time or the resources to devote ourselves to being interesting or refined, you know," Angus said. He pushed out his stout chest as he spoke.

"I apologize. I meant you no offense."

"If I may ask, what passed through your mind, Lord Byron, as the stagecoach crashed? Did you regret your sins?"

"Only the ones I hadn't yet got around to committing," I said, and I drank again and peered at Angus over the lip of the flask. "What brings a man to volunteer himself as a constable, and to spend his evenings patrolling country roads, hunting for bandits?"

Angus took the whisky back from me and swallowed some of it. "What are those creatures called that you collect books about?"

I supposed my archive of dark lore was no longer much of a secret. "Vampires," I said.

"Yes, vampires. I hunt for bandits, and you hunt for vampires."

I pictured Knifing hacking with an ax at the locked doors of my black bookcase. I couldn't quite visualize it; the investigator's tight-fitting suits left him with an insufficient range of motion to undertake such a task. I blinked, took the flask back, and had another drink. Then I pictured Angus breaking open the cabinet while Knifing watched. "You searched my rooms, I gather?"

"In fact, we did not," Angus said. "Knifing said you were innocent, so he wasn't interested at all in the contents of your residence. Dingle didn't look around much either, though Knifing said he should have, if he believed you to be guilty."

"How did you know about the vampire books, then?"

"Violet Tower kept a diary. She thought about you quite a bit, and I have to say, she was concerned by your fixations. Mr. Knifing and I know all about the vampires. And about your father."

"Of course you do. Remind me never again to share a confidence with a woman."

"I haven't caught any bandits," he said. "Do you suppose you'll catch a vampire?"

He gave me his flask again, and I had another drink. "It's not the catching that matters," I said. "Only the hunting."

"But do you really believe in such creatures?"

"I don't know," I said. "I try to. I like being the man who believes."

He let a long silence pass between us, and then he sighed loudly. "I had a daughter—I mean, I still have a daughter, but I had another daughter, Iris. My oldest," he said. "She was lovely to look at, and I don't just say that as her father. Everyone thought so." When he spoke, his eyes did not meet mine, for his attention was focused someplace beyond me, off toward the horizon, or into the past.

I looked critically at his rough, leathery features; at his round and ample gut. His misshapen nose and lumpy cheeks reminded me of the bulges and protuberances one might find on a large, strange potato.

"You seem surprised my daughter was beautiful," Angus said. "But I was quite handsome before I ruined my face with drink and my body with food and sloth. You'll not keep your own fine features for long if you continue to live the way you live."

"The way I live, I don't expect to need them for long," I said, and since I was still holding the flask, I drank from it again. He gestured toward me, and I handed it back to him.

"As I said, my daughter was very beautiful, and the men from the College started noticing her once she was around thirteen or fourteen. Of course, the rarefied university sort would never marry a girl with a father like me, no matter how pretty she was."

I rubbed gingerly at my bruised wrists. "What is your trade, Angus, when you aren't hunting bandits or guarding murder scenes?"

"I'm a carpenter," he said.

"So, you build houses and things?"

"No, I'm more of a craftsman. I make furniture. Chairs and bed-frames and tables. Plain ones, mostly, for ordinary folk. But I've got a bit of a talent for delicate carving. My hand is quite steady when I'm sober, and I've been known to make some fine pieces. The university commissioned some chairs from me a few years ago. In fact, I saw one of them in your parlor. How did it end up there?"

"Did you make my dining room table?" I asked, ignoring his question.

"I did. You came into my workshop yourself and bought it, when you first moved to Cambridge. You told me who you were and where to send it, and you said Mr. Hanson out of London would see to my payment, though the bill remained in arrears for quite some time."

If he'd made my table, he'd certainly made the identical one at which the corpse of Jerome Tower had been seated. Angus had probably also carved the bedpost we'd found Violet's corpse hanging from. This was, at the very least, a strange coincidence. Knifing had hinted that the table was significant, and he'd joked that he might arrest the constable. Maybe he knew something I didn't.

Angus spent his nights patrolling the streets of Cambridge. He was obsessed, apparently, with his lovely daughter, of whom he spoke in the past tense. Maybe I was sitting in the dirt, drinking with a lunatic; a man driven to madness and violence by grief over some past loss. It did not seem far-fetched at all to me, after the bloody events of that evening, to think that Angus might have murdered Felicity.

He'd been the first to happen upon the corpses of Dingle and the carriage driver, and he'd figured out where to look for the coach. If he wasn't the one who'd shot them, it was a stroke of excellent luck that he'd chosen this night to patrol this highway; there were several roads heading out of Cambridge in different directions. The buffoonish constable had, just by happenstance, wandered down the right road, and discovered the corpses of two murder victims, who some mysterious marksman had cut down with two impossible shots.

I feared the whisky he'd given me was poison, but he'd drunk from the flask himself, so that seemed unlikely. It could be that he intended to strangle or smother or beat me to death, and then claim he'd found me dead in the wreckage when Knifing arrived. Under normal circumstances, I could have fought him off, for though he was heavier than I, he was quite unfit. But I was hurt, and I didn't know how much my wounds might impair me if I had to defend myself. I tried to rise, and found my limbs unsteady.

"Are you going somewhere?" Angus asked.

"I'm in quite a bit of pain," I said, slumping back to the ground.

"Have this for it," Angus said, and handed me the flask again. I hesitated for a moment, and then I drained the last of the warm backwash. It was thin and tasted metallic. I returned the empty vessel to its owner.

"Tell me about your daughter," I said. It seemed best to keep him talking, since I was in no condition to fight or flee.

"Oh, Iris. Yes, quite pretty, she was. Caught a lot of lecherous glances from the undergraduates, and a few from the Fellows as well. I was worried for her. I protected her as best I could, but those men had seen a lot of the world, and that made them alluring to a young girl. There was one, though, a lad called Mr. Quincy Hawthorne, who was kind enough. He saw that Iris was from a family of decent people, and ceased his lewd advances. Acted real proper. Of course, like I said, the College men are all destined for better matches than town girls. Mr. Hawthorne was the younger child of Lord Teddington, which made him the next in line until his brother's wife birthed a son. So he was obliged to marry a proper lady. But he had a friend in London he thought might be a smart match for my daughter, a fellow named Chester Marigold. Marigold was common folk, but his father was a merchant of some sort, who'd been in business with Teddington, and the children had played together from a young age. Young Mr. Hawthorne wrote Chester a letter and drew a picture of Iris. A real likeness; quite a talented young man, that Mr. Hawthorne was. Anyway, Chester wrote back from London, and shortly thereafter, I exchanged correspondence with his father. The Marigolds seemed to be nice people, and Chester was awfully keen on the drawing, so we began to make arrangements. My wife, Maisey, was so pleased. The Marigolds weren't wellborn, you understand, but they'd made good. They moved in a better circle. The marriage would have been a step up for my daughter. A rosy future."

"I've got an idea of where this is going," I said.

"Yes, but just let me tell it," said Angus.

"All right."

"Maisey hired a carriage and set out for London. The driver was an older gent. He seemed amiable enough, but a bit infirm. He had one guard who rode along with him. Portly fellow, as I remember."

"They never got there, did they?"

"I didn't know nothing had gone wrong until eight days later, when I received a message from Mr. Marigold inquiring as to why they'd not arrived. I organized a search party and scouted the highway. We didn't have nobody like Mr. Knifing helping us, but I was touched that Mr. Quincy Hawthorne and some of the other young men from the College volunteered. On the third day of looking, I made inquiries at a house twenty-odd miles out of town. The farmer there had spotted smoke rising from a disused tract of land. We looked around there, and found the wheel-tracks in the grass, leading off the road. The wreck of the carriage was hidden in the woods."

He shook the flask, and then remembered it was empty.

"I should have known from the smell, but when I first saw them, I didn't even realize I was looking at bodies," Angus whispered. "The driver. The guard. My wife. She had lain there unburied four or five days, and this was in the peak of summer. Her face was unrecognizable because the whole corpse was covered in an undulating carpet of black."

"Black?" I asked.

"Flies," he said. There was a quaver in his voice. "And maggots in the flesh. I recognized her only by her wedding ring. It was so unimpressive, I guess her killers didn't bother to chop off her finger to get at it."

"My God."

"Deeper in the woods, we found Iris. Because of the decomposition, we couldn't know for sure, but old Mr. Bartholomew, the undertaker, said there were ligatures and wounds that suggested they'd done things, that they'd—" Here, he broke down into sobs.

"I'm sorry, Angus," I said. "I had no idea."

"I'd have killed myself, I think, if it weren't for Crystal, my younger one. In a few more years, she'll be married, I suppose, and I'll have nothing left to live for."

"Oh, don't say that," I said. I leaned forward and patted him on the knee. "You'll still have whisky."

"I hope it don't offend you to hear me say it, but you and I aren't so different," Angus said.

"How do you mean?" I asked.

"I didn't fully realize it until Mr. Knifing found Mrs. Tower's diary, but I reckon I knew all along why you couldn't stay away from the murder scene. It's the same reason I volunteered to be constable. The same reason I patrol these lonesome highways with my musket. You're looking for revenge."

"I'm looking for answers."

"Call it what you will."

I thought about that for a minute. Then I asked: "What's your surname, Angus the Constable?"

"Buford. I'm Angus Buford."

I smiled. "Well, I'm pleased to know you, Angus Buford."

"Likewise, I suppose, Lord Byron."

Chapter 34

For me, *degenerate modern wretch,*
Though in the genial month of May,
My dripping limbs I faintly stretch,
And think I've done a feat to-day.

But since he cross'd the rapid tide,
According to the doubtful story,
To woo,—and—Lord knows what beside,
And swam for Love, as I for Glory

—Lord Byron, *"Written After Swimming*
from Sestos to Abydos"

There's a great old legend about a boy from Abydos named Leander who fell in love with a priestess of Aphrodite named Hero. Hero dwelt in a tower in Sestos, and between Sestos and Abydos lay the Hellespont.

The Hellespont is one of the most treacherous straits ever documented by cartography or mythology, and Leander swam across it every night to rendezvous with his lover. Hero hung a lamp in the window of her tower, and its light guided him to her.

I remember my mother telling me about Leander and Hero as she tucked me beneath my tattered blanket in the rooms where we lived in Aberdeen, before I inherited Newstead. Mad Jack had already been gone a year, but my mother told me he was coming back, and I believed her. She told me love is a beacon, like Hero's lantern, and just as Poseidon's rage couldn't keep Leander from his beloved, my father's affection for us was mightier than any force in nature, and it would bring him inexorably home to us.

This is how boys are shaped into the men they are to be. When I was small, my mother told me bedtime stories, and when I grew older, I spent my sleepless nights drinking and lying to myself.

But here is the truth: On the third of May in 1810, I visited the place where Hero's tower stood, and I looked into the treacherous strait between the Aegean and the Propontis. It was mostly white-capped churn slamming against jagged rocks, and from my perspective, there was only one rational thing to do. I stripped my clothing off, and I walked into the water.

In my youthful imaginings, Leander was propelled by his ardor the way a strong headwind and a full sail drive a boat. I pictured him skimming across the waves like a lusty porpoise; his engorged ventral appendage slicing through the surf, and the pale-green sea froth lapping at his swollen purple bollocks.

The actual experience of swimming the Hellespont is somewhat different. The waters are swift and treacherous and black, even when the sun is high. The surface current and the undertow run in opposite directions, so if you push too deep trying to cut through the ten-foot swells, the undercurrent will drag you into the depths, and hold you there, and squeeze the breath from your lungs. The distance from the European side to the Asiatic is only about a mile, straight across, but the current is so powerful that I traveled a distance of between three and four miles on a diagonal to make it from one shore to the other. If you aren't a very strong swimmer, the Hellespont is an easy place to die. Trying to swim across it is an insane thing to do; nobody with any sense of prudence or moderation would ever even attempt it. My aim was to prove such a feat was possible, a thesis that was subject to some doubt until I accomplished it.

It took me an hour and ten minutes to make the crossing. Though the weather was warm, the fast-moving water was frigid, and I lost feeling in my extremities halfway through the swim, when I was quite far from either shore. Finishing the journey sapped me of my strength, and, unlike Leander, when I dragged myself onto the beach, I was in no condition to express any amorous urges. I just sprawled on the gray sand and vomited seawater for a while, and I was quite ill for several weeks afterward.

When I was a child, my mother told me the story of Leander and Hero, but she didn't tell me all of it. It wasn't until I got to Harrow that I learned how it ended; how all the legendary love stories end.

Leander made his swim each night throughout the summer, but when the seasons changed, the waters grew more violent and unendurably cold. I swam the strait in the daytime, and I could clearly see my destination on the European shore. Leander swam at night, when the sunless sky melted into the dark water. With the waves tossing him upward and the current sucking him down, he had only Hero's guttering lantern to show him which way was up, and which way to swim. When the raging winds blew her light out, he lost the shore, lost his equilibrium. He lost hope. And the sea swallowed him.

Hero saw his drowned body wash up on the beach, and full of grief, she threw herself from her window and smashed against the rocks.

Mad Jack said that death is only for fools, and maybe it's foolish to die for love like Leander and Hero. But maybe it's also foolish not to dive into black waters if there's a perfect girl waiting on the other side. Maybe it's better to die for her than to live without her.

And maybe it's foolish not to dive into black waters if there's a chance to explore the sparkling shore on the other side of them. Maybe it's foolish not to run and swim as far as one can, to push oneself to the limits of one's physical capabilities, to make a grasp for the horizon.

Vampires must shun the light and cower in their crypts. Where's the fun in that? What good is eternity if you can't spend it dashing after the rising sun? I'd rather my candle burn briefly but brightly than dwell eternally in darkness.

Chapter 35

Where there is mystery, it is generally supposed that there must also be evil.

—Lord Byron, *"Fragment of a Novel"*

I must have drifted to sleep on the grass, for when Knifing's singsong greeting roused me, the stars had changed.

"My congratulations, Lord Byron!" the investigator shouted at me across the heath as he approached.

I lifted myself into a sitting position, which caused me no small amount of pain. "For what?"

"For your deliverance," he said. "For your vindication. For your exoneration."

I squinted to see the thin, dark form approaching from the highway, some two hundred yards distant. Knifing had come in a black carriage pulled by black horses, and driven by a rather severe-looking gentleman clad, predictably, in black. I thought this was a fitting conveyance for the wraithlike investigator, because it looked like a hearse. Then I realized it actually was a hearse; Knifing had come out with the undertaker to collect the remains of Fielding Dingle and his driver. I was unhappy about having to ride back to town in the same vehicle as those ripening corpses, but it was better than riding in the prison-carriage, so I decided not to complain.

Instead, I asked: "Am I no longer suspected of murder?"

Knifing jauntily adjusted his bush hat. "My God, no. That preposterous proposition perished with its ponderous proponent."

I was nursing a rattled skull and a belly full of rotgut whisky, so it took some calculation on my part to figure out that he was talking about Dingle. Knifing seemed bizarrely chipper for a man who had been summoned from bed in the dark hours of the morning to examine the corpse of a colleague who'd been shot in the face and crushed beneath a stagecoach.

"You said you'd march me to the gallows, regardless of my guilt or innocence, to assuage your clients' uncertainty."

The investigator let out a peal of his singular, unpleasant laughter, and I realized why the carriage-horse's death-wail had sounded so familiar. "That's certainly something I'd say, but it's not something I'd do. I've got standards, you see, and you've got lawyers. Such threats were only a ploy; a stratagem designed to intimidate you into disclosing facts, and to scare you away from my crime scenes. Arresting you is something only Dingle would be fool enough to do, and in fact, it's something Dingle did, before Dingle died." The alliteration set him off into his disconcerting giggles again.

Though it caused some pain in my sore neck, I turned my head to see how Angus was reacting to his hero's strange behavior. The constable's eyes were bulging and his mouth hung slightly open. I wouldn't describe his expression as one of astonishment, however; Angus just always looked like that. "Are you drunk, Mr. Knifing?" I asked.

"That's quite a thing for you to ask me," Knifing said, and then he made his horse-scream noise, because he was so amused with himself.

"Have you seen the corpses, sir?" Angus asked.

"What was left of them," said Knifing, who had closed the distance between the road and the wreck of the prison-coach, and was looming unpleasantly over me as I lay sprawled in the dirt. "Quite a mess it was. I was greatly entertained to watch Bartholomew scraping Mr. Dingle off the road." He pointed with his thumb back at the hunched figure on top of the corpse-wagon.

"That's a queer thing to derive pleasure from," I said.

"I'll defer on that question to your experience, Lord Byron. You're our reigning authority on the subject of queer pleasures." He poked me in my bruised ribs with the end of his umbrella. "I will say that I like to see a bad man get what he deserves. That's part of why I do this job."

Angus scratched his jowls. "If you think Dingle's death establishes Byron's innocence, does that mean that you believe the Cambridge killer shot Dingle?"

"It's not likely that there are two killers about, is it?" Knifing asked.

"I don't suppose I know whether that's likely or not," Angus said. "Why would the killer rescue Byron from Dingle?"

"I don't think he meant for me to be rescued," I said. "How was he able to shoot them both? I've never met a man who could hit a fast-moving target at any great range with a musket."

"He didn't use a musket," Knifing said. "He used a rifle."

"I've heard of those," Angus said with a touch of awe. "Never seen one."

"They're supposed to be hard to load," I said.

I must confess I'd been as confused by the killer's uncanny

marksmanship as Angus was, but I probably should not have been. Forgetting that the alley gate at the Modest Proposal was open at night was an egregious observational failure, but my inability to recognize a rifle shot was nearly as embarrassing.

I was quite familiar with the Baker infantry rifle because I'd tried on several occasions to purchase one. In every case, the seller had either refused to part with his weapon or had demanded an exorbitant price. It was a remarkable toy and a difficult one to obtain, and so I lusted after it with a fervor that was, in other circumstances, reserved exclusively for beautiful women.

Unlike the wide, smooth barrel of a musket, a rifle's was narrow and grooved inside; when the gun fired, the grooved track caused the bullet to come out spinning, which allowed it to maintain a straight trajectory over a great distance. Because the rifle bullet fit so tightly into this special barrel, it took more than twice as long to load as a standard-issue Brown Bess musket.

Muskets were an excellent weapon for infantry who marched in formations, since, though the accuracy of any single shot was poor, a volley from an infantry line could cut through an opposing force. But even a skilled soldier armed with a musket would miss a target at fifty paces twice as often as he'd hit it. A good rifleman could put a chunk of lead through a man's eyeball at two hundred yards.

Since the Baker took so long to reload, it was an unsuitable weapon for infantry; a slower-firing weapon couldn't lay down the devastating hailstorm of bullets that was the specialization of the British Army. So, riflemen fought as skirmishers, either running out ahead of the advancing line to pick off targets before the main forces engaged each other or taking positions near the battlefield to shoot officers from the side or the rear.

Two years after the events in Cambridge, the Baker rifle would become famous when a sharpshooter named Thomas Plunket used one to kill a French general from a distance of six hundred yards. Then he reloaded and killed a second officer at the same range, just to prove he could do it twice. The killing of Fielding Dingle never garnered the same level of publicity, but it required similar prowess; though the range was likely closer, the targets were moving.

Knifing and Angus had both been soldiers, so either of them could conceivably have the expertise to make such a shot, but it was unlikely that either of them did. Angus's service predated the use of rifles by British forces by a number of years, so it seemed unlikely he'd been trained to use one. Also, he'd needed two tries to kill a fallen horse at point-blank range with his musket.

Knifing probably could have obtained a rifle without much difficulty, but his infantry days were long past and he had no professional reason to have made the effort required to become a master marksman with a new kind of weapon. And he only had one eye. Even with a tool as precise as the Baker rifle, it's difficult to shoot with accuracy from great range when one lacks the ability to perceive depth. It seemed a folly, however, to underestimate Archibald Knifing. He was diligent and blessed with a monstrous intellect. Perhaps with skill and practice, even a one-eyed man could calculate distance and hit his target. And if there was a potential hobby he might take up that would make him one of the deadliest men in the world, it seemed like the sort of project Knifing might find appealing.

"There cannot be more than a few men in Cambridge with access to a Baker rifle and the skill to shoot two men off a moving carriage from great range," I said. "The killer has finally made a fatal error. We need only identify those men who are likely to possess the rifles, and we can begin to interrogate them."

Angus looked shocked for a moment, and then he got quite excited. "I'll begin canvassing at once."

He started to climb to his feet, but Knifing settled him with a wave of his gnarled hand. "That's a better thought than any you've had with regard to hunting this killer. Better than anything that passed through the head of Fielding Dingle in the entirety of his career, excepting the bullet that killed him, which was quite impressive. But it's a futile pursuit."

I clenched my fists. "Why?"

"This perpetrator isn't from Cambridge."

"How can you possibly know that?" Angus asked.

Knifing braced his weight on his umbrella and carefully sat on the grass. He reached into his snug jacket and produced a slim silver flask. This one was polished and sleek in the same way that the constable's was battered and scuffed, but both were welcome in my company, so long as they were full of whisky.

He took a drink from it, and passed it to Angus.

"Why would a Cambridge resident with no criminal history decide one day to start butchering professors in alleyways, or climbing into high windows to murder women? I don't think one would. And how would such a person become an expert rifle marksman? I don't think one could. So, rather than narrowing the focus of our inquiry, the use of the Baker rifle eliminates any chance of tracing the crimes back to any Cambridge resident with a cognizable motive."

"But someone has killed these people, and the perpetrator must be caught," I said.

"What good will that do? Do you think the revelation of the killer's identity will explain anything? Do you think whatever you might discover will help you to cope with the fact that a slew of people died horribly at his whim? He'll be a stupid person, who did these things for stupid reasons."

"How can you know that, if you don't know who has committed the killings?"

"But I do know who has done them, at least in general terms," Knifing said. "And I know that nothing we can do here is likely to further our attempts to identify him, specifically."

"How do you mean?" I asked.

Knifing took his flask back and drank again. "The hostility with Napoleon has gone on for too long. Some able-bodied soldiers are mentally ill-suited for combat. War breaks men's minds, and long wars test the limits of even the steadfast. The killer is probably a former soldier turned lunatic vagrant, an unreasoning monster trained to kill by the military."

"After all this, you think the murders are just the work of some stranger, with no motivation behind them?" I said.

"What do you expect?" Knifing replied. "Do you want to finish this with some confrontation or catharsis? Do you want to learn that this violence was motivated by some comprehensible rationale? I've solved a lot of mysterious crimes, Lord Byron, and I shall save you the suspense. Mystery seduces, but solutions disappoint. The perpetrator of every crime inevitably turns out to be somebody unspeakably banal. He'll be dumber than you'd expect him to be, given the great deductive and observational effort required to identify him, for brutality is the special gift of stupid men. And he'll be crazy and delusional. Murderers are great monsters in the imagination, but the reality of them would be pathetic if it weren't so loathsome."

"So what are we to do?" Angus asked.

Knifing shrugged. "I will stay here until the killings cease, on the slim and unlikely hope that the killer's identity will be revealed by some lucky happenstance. Maybe when our quarry drains the next victim, he'll leave a trail of bloody drippings that will lead me back to his lair. I am not optimistic, however."

"You said you'd deliver certainty to your clients, even if you had to manufacture false evidence against an innocent," I said. Though he always sounded convincing when he spoke, Knifing seemed to constantly contradict his earlier statements. Every time I saw him, he was a different person, and it had begun to annoy me. He didn't even seem to be drunk anymore.

"My investigation won't end when I leave Cambridge. When I return to London, I'll press my military contacts to provide me with the discharge records for any trained rifle marksmen the army deemed mentally unfit for combat. Hopefully, when the killings begin again someplace else, I'll have better information."

Angus reached his hand out, and Knifing gave him back the flask. "What about us?"

Knifing took the flask back and slipped it back into his jacket. Then he rose to his feet, wincing slightly as his knees bent. "Your service has been appreciated, Angus, but I've no further need of it. You may return to your ordinary occupation. Lord Byron, you have sustained more than enough injury and humiliation in your pursuit of this killer, and it's time for you to stop. You should arrange immediate transport to your home at Newstead."

I climbed to my feet so he couldn't look down at me. The process of standing was painful, but not unbearably so. I rolled my shoulders and flexed my fingers, and found their condition much improved. "That is unacceptable, Mr. Knifing. These killings are not arbitrary. They are related, in some way, to me. I must find out how and why."

"I can promise you the perpetrator is not your dead father,

nor are the killings the work of some mythical creature," Knifing said. If his tone had been compassionate a moment before, it wasn't any longer. Now he was cold and contemptuous again. The man changed his skin like a tropical lizard.

"Jerome Tower's corpse was posed at his dining table, a piece of furniture identical to the one I own," I said.

"A table crafted by Angus, who sees no need to perceive himself as the fulcrum of recent events," Knifing countered. He'd always seemed to regard the volunteer constable with a sort of indifference, so I was surprised he'd taken the time to learn about Angus's trade.

"You said the tableau might be a message to me."

He shrugged. "I was only having a joke at your expense. Angus tells me there are at least two dozen similar tables in Cambridge. I've been quite diligent in running down every possible clue. Since I haven't found anything yet, I feel certain there's nothing to find."

"I sell lots of nice furniture to the dons and fellows, and to the better-off students," Angus said. "Buying a table from me is a good deal cheaper than hauling one in from London."

Knifing made a quick slicing gesture with the heel of his hand that was sufficient to silence the constable: "Nobody cares about that."

"But most of the victims are people I know," I said. "Cyrus Pendleton wanted to kick me out of the College. I was engaged in an affair with Violet Tower. Leif Sedgewyck was my rival for the affections of Olivia Wright. Noreen Lime was my paramour. For God's sake, he broke into my rooms and killed her, while leaving me alive. You can't truly believe this has got nothing to do with me."

"I believe any connection the killer has to you is arbitrary and incidental," Knifing said. "Though you've many character defects, you're a fairly clever lad. If the killer were someone you knew, you'd already be suspicious of him. Homicidal lunatics are not adept at disguising their predilections. You're something of a celebrity, though. He may know you, even if you don't know him. The criminally insane are prone to obsession, and the weak-minded fixate on magnetic personalities, and upon famous figures."

"Unless he is my father."

Knifing turned his back and started walking toward the hearse. "Your father is dead, Lord Byron. He's not coming back for you. I've really had enough of this. I'm trying to catch a killer, and you're telling fairy stories." He stopped and turned toward me. "You might be in danger. It might be that the killer's proximity to you aggravates his mania, and if that's the case, your continued presence in Cambridge may be putting others in harm's way. In the morning, you must return to Newstead. That's really all I have to say to you on this subject."

I tried to object, but Angus placed a firm hand on my arm to quiet me. We followed Knifing to Bartholomew's black carriage and rode back to town in silence.

Chapter 36

But in that instant o'er his soul
Winters of Memory seem'd to roll,
And gather in that drop of time
A life of pain, an age of crime.

—Lord Byron, The Giaour

Angus lived on the outskirts of Cambridge, so we let him off first. His house was not made of stone, but rather, from old wooden slats that had turned dark with rot. The roof was tarred paper. A yellow-haired girl, twelve or thirteen years old, sat waiting and watching out the window, her pale face almost ghostly in the dim light from a small oil lamp. When Angus opened the door, she ran to him and threw her arms around his neck.

Knifing let me out in front of the Great Gate. The lawn was empty, the windows in the College buildings were mostly dark, and the streets were eerily silent; many of the undergraduates had fled Cambridge, and the taverns had all stopped serving after the events at the Modest Proposal.

My own rooms were similarly dark and vacant. I checked my

bedroom and found that the mattress, blankets, and feather beds had been removed, along with the corpse of Noreen Lime. I called for my manservant, and when he did not answer, I lit a few candles and fetched a bottle of whisky and a crystal glass. The laudanum bottle was, to my relief, intact, and I made some use of it.

In the parlor, I found a note written in Joe Murray's blocky, hesitant penmanship, explaining that he had returned to Newstead with the Professor. As he saw it, there was no need for him to remain in Cambridge if I was to be absent, and my mother might find his presence comforting. He promised to meet me in London once I secured my release.

There was also a somewhat lengthier letter from my attorney. I sat down at the fine table Angus had made for me, and read it as I drank:

My dearest Byron,

Joe Murray has sent me news of your various recent difficulties, and I am writing you to offer my assistance, as always.

Foremost among my concerns is your visitation by Mr. Frederick Burke, who holds himself out as counsel for the Banque Crédit Française. I would urge you to engage in no further communication with Mr. Burke, and to refer him to me if he attempts to speak to you. It is of utmost importance that you refuse to agree to anything he proposes, either verbally or in writing, and that you make no statement admitting any fact he alleges until I've had an opportunity to review the matter.

Joe Murray informs me that Mr. Burke claimed I talked to him in London and invited him to deal directly with you in

Cambridge. He is lying. I have never been in contact with this man. I suspect that the bar association will not be pleased to hear that he misled you in order to deny you the benefit of counsel's assistance, and his misconduct may harm his client's interests, to our substantial benefit.

For the present time, you should pay Mr. Burke no mind, except to avoid him. I will handle this problem for you. The songs they'll sing of our vengeance will be rollicking, bloody ones, I promise.

Sometime soon, however, we really must have a serious talk about your finances. Your assets should allow you to live out your life richly and idly, if your holdings are well-managed, but if you continue to accrue debts, your future incomes will be lost to interest upon those notes. I know you are cavalier about disregarding my advice, but you ought to pay heed to this warning. Your temperament is not well-suited for poverty.

As to the matter of your recent upbraiding by the faculty, I'm sure you've realized that the Fellows are wholly impotent to punish you for your indifference to your studies. Utter disregard for academics is a privilege of and a tradition among men of your class. If you wish, I will draft a sternly-worded missive reminding them of this, but perhaps the prudent course would be to let the matter rest.

That being said, given your literary aspirations, you might do well to avail yourself of the resources at your disposal in Cambridge. I know you view yourself as a wholly-formed master poet, but I still think of you as the child I knew only a few years ago. I know you have suffered from your father's neglect of his duties toward you, and my occasional attempts to provide helpful guidance are sorry compensation, but I hope you will listen to me.

When we grow older, we regret the arrogance of our younger selves. We regret the opportunities we disdained; the possibilities we rejected. You may think it beneath yourself to take instruction from these bewhiskered dons who wear drab clothing and lead dull, cloistered lives, but they seek only to bestow upon you the benefit of their years of study, and if you neglect your coursework, you'll find the knowledge readily available to you now may be harder to accrue in the future. I hope you will not allow vanity to impede your progress, or prevent you from realizing your great potential.

Finally, on the matter of these dreadful killings in Cambridge, I have made arrangements for your transportation home to Newstead until that unpleasant matter is resolved. Joe Murray has reported to me that you were visited by thieftakers from London named Fielding Dingle and Archibald Knifing. I have made inquiries regarding these gentlemen; indeed, I expended great effort to deploy messengers to a number of colleagues so that I might find out everything I could about these purported criminal investigators you have gotten mixed up with. What I've learned has been quite upsetting. I shall not rest easy until I receive Joe Murray's confirmation that you are safely en route.

Fielding Dingle is the vilest form of human trash, a man so detested that even the most reprehensible criminals and ruffians refer to him as a "rat." He's been twice convicted of burglary, but he finally realized he was too clumsy and stupid to earn a living at that line of work. He now holds himself out as a trained private constable, but I am told that he has little real investigative talent. Instead, he claims to be able to track down criminals and stolen property by maintaining a network of "informants" in the London underworld.

In my experience, scoundrels of the lower orders enjoy stealing and rape above all other things, but, excepting those endeavors, informing upon one another is their favored activity, especially when there is a reward for doing so. Unfortunately for them, such men are often unable to collect the bounties on the heads of their friends because they are, themselves, wanted for various offenses. This creates an opportunity for Dingle.

By refraining from the criminal behavior that is his natural predisposition, he maintains the bare minimum of reputability required to be able to walk into a magistrate's office without being arrested. As such, he's able to purchase information from street hoods, and then sell it profitably to London's rather sorry policing apparatus. Dingle has also been known to accept payment for assisting victims of theft in ransoming their property, a task that is difficult to bungle when he is colluding with the thieves. However, his deductive skills are not held in much esteem; those who know him laughed at the prospect of him hunting a killer.

I have no idea where Lord Whippleby would encounter the likes of Fielding Dingle, but the presence of such an unsavory character indicates some corruption surrounding the Cambridge investigation in much the same way that the presence of maggots indicates that a haunch of meat has gone rotten.

Archibald Knifing inspires more confidence at first glance, but he is the subject of my greatest concern. I forwarded enquiries about both men to various constables, magistrates and barristers who are regularly involved in criminal investigations and prosecutions. While Dingle is a relatively obscure figure, scraping a living at the fringes of society, Knifing is an eminence in his field.

I was particularly interested to learn of a case Knifing famously solved; a series of killings in which female victims were hung by their feet and drained of blood, in much the same manner that I understand the first Cambridge victim was killed. I asked my contacts for more information about the matter, and they provided me with accounts that differed on significant facts.

First of all, there was some dispute as to the location of the events in question. A lawyer I know who defends violent criminals with some regularity believed that the killings occurred in Grimsby, but a traveling magistrate who often hears criminal matters recalled such a trial being held in Chelmsford. There was also some disagreement as to whether the man convicted of the crimes was a miller or a bricklayer.

My colleagues are fastidious, even with their gossip, and they are not likely to get their details mistaken, so I began to suspect that the differences between their accounts of the blood-draining case Knifing was renowned for solving suggested there were, in fact, two distinct events with similar facts.

I was able to contact the judge who presided over the Grimsby case at his home in London. While he could not confirm that there had been a second, similar incident involving Mr. Knifing, he assured me of the location of the trial; there could be no mistake, since he'd never visited Chelmsford.

However, my friend who was certain that the killings had, indeed, occurred in Chelmsford gave me the name of the lawyer who had unsuccessfully represented the accused in that case. It turned out he'd perished from fever some six months ago, but his law partner was able to find notes on the case, and shared with me a few details that were not protected by privilege.

Those records confirm that Archibald Knifing arrested and testified against a miller in Chelmsford in relation to the killings of three local girls there whose corpses were drained of blood. The defense lawyer had unsuccessfully tried to introduce as proof of his client's innocence the facts of a similar case in the town of Blackpool, two years before, involving killings with a similar method, and in which Knifing had also arrested a commoner with a previously unsullied reputation in the community, and with no known violent tendencies.

The judge in Chelmsford refused to consider this evidence, deeming the Blackpool matter settled and unrelated, since a man had already been convicted and executed there.

I find it deeply peculiar and suspicious that Archibald Knifing has orchestrated the arrest and prosecution of three different killers in separate cases involving identical crimes of a peculiar and specific nature. The investigator is the only common thread I can identify among those disparate incidents, and the conclusion I must draw from the facts I've collected is that Archibald Knifing is the killer, and he has used his reputation and expertise as an investigator to manufacture false evidence that suggests the guilt of other men.

I urge you most vehemently to disentangle yourself from this unsavory affair and flee at once for the safety of Newstead Abbey. If you wish me to, I will present the information I have uncovered to a magistrate here in London, once you have made your escape from Cambridge.

I await your further instructions.

Faithfully,

John Hanson, Esq.

Chapter 37

Though like a demon of the night
He pass'd, and vanish'd from my sight,
His aspect and his air impress'd
A troubled memory on my breast

—Lord Byron, The Giaour

All the houses in Angus's ramshackle section of Cambridge looked the same, so I banged urgently on a few wrong doors before I found the right one, and I severely frightened several townsfolk in the process. It was two in the morning, my clothes were soaked through with sweat, and I was so drunk, I could barely feel the aches in my wrists or my ribs or my shoulders anymore.

My face was swollen and bruised, my hair was quite disheveled, and I'd left my greatcoat on the floor in my parlor, so I had nothing covering the two pistols harnessed to my back. If anyone had been out to see me, they might have been quite shocked by my appearance.

When, at last, I found the right place, Angus answered his

door holding a lantern in one hand and his musket in the other. I could see his young daughter standing in the doorway behind him, and the constable took great care to physically interpose himself between me and the girl.

"What the hell are you doing here?"

I thrust the letter at him, and he set down the gun to take it. He read slowly, and moved his lips as he sounded the words out in his head. After a couple of minutes, I seized the papers from his hand and read Hanson's news to him aloud.

"The only thing I don't understand is how he could have hit Dingle with that rifle," I said. "He's got only one eye."

"I think you only need one eye to sight a rifle," Dingle said. "You aim down the barrel."

This fact seemed familiar to me; I didn't know why I had failed to remember it previously. Knifing had accused me of having a deficiency of observational skill. But Knifing was a deranged murderer, so his opinions were of little relevance. "We have to go get him before he kills again."

"Why don't you go home and let me handle this?" Angus said. "You're very drunk, and you've had a lot of excitement today."

"Absolutely not," I said. "I must be on hand to take him into custody. It was my discovery that established his guilt."

"It was your lawyer's discovery."

"Exactly. My lawyer, acting on my behalf. So it's my discovery."

"You're wounded and manic and intoxicated. You're in no condition to confront a killer right now."

I thought about this. "You're right. We shall wait until morning. They're weaker in the daylight."

I pushed past him into the house, ignoring his stammered protests. He shooed the girl into the back room, keeping his body between me and her until the door was bolted. I found a comfortable-looking cushioned chair positioned against the wall, and I wondered as I sat down in it where Angus could have obtained such a fine thing. Just before I fell asleep, I realized he had made it with his hands.

Angus roused me an hour before sunup. I ached from my wounds and from the after-effects of the liquor and laudanum I'd had, but my head was clear, or at least, clearer.

Angus was already prepared for battle. He was dressed in a clean blue military-style uniform shirt that his daughter must have made for him. His hair was damp and combed neatly. He had a pistol on his side, and his musket slung over his shoulder.

"It's time to go ask Mr. Knifing some questions," he said.

"I can only hope he's committed no more murders while we rested," I said.

Angus knew, from previous conversations with Mr. Knifing, that the investigator was lodged at the Burning Tyger Inn; at the junction of Emmanuel Street and Elm Street, so we journeyed back east, and past Trinity College. Here, Angus remarked that I could have slept in my rooms instead of passing the night, uninvited, in his home. I did not speak to disagree with him, but the truth was that I was hesitant to return to my empty residence. I didn't want to be alone with my recollections of the horrific events that had recently occurred there.

The sky was turning from black to gray as we passed Christ's College. We followed a narrow path called Milton's Walk that cut across the disused pastures that some clever students long ago had named Christ's Pieces. In short order, we arrived at the inn. Our knocks raised no response, but we found the door unlocked. The innkeeper's desk was vacant, and nobody answered the little bell when we rang it. The proprietor was likely back in his quarters, asleep. Or maybe his corpse was hanging from a meathook someplace; I don't think I ever bothered to find out what had happened to him.

In any case, Angus rummaged the desk drawers and found the master key. The inn was a large one; three stories high with eleven guest rooms, but the innkeeper's ledger revealed that Mr. Knifing was in room number 4. All the other rooms were inhabited, but I recognized none of the other names.

I thought it odd that the inn had no vacancies; most Cambridge innkeepers earned their year's keep during the few weeks when students' families packed the town: Fall student enrollment and for the graduation ceremonies in Winter and Spring. The rest of the year, there was a surplus of rooms to let, and that situation had been exacerbated by the murders, which had caused most travelers to conclude or cancel their business in town.

At least, however, this odd bit of fortune might have explained the innkeeper's absence. With his rooms all rented, he had no need to be on hand to receive new guests.

I found a pencil and copied the names in the ledger onto a scrap of paper; collecting such data seemed like something Archibald Knifing might have done in similar circumstances and, thus, the sort of thing the world's greatest criminal investigator should do as well. I also checked the book for Dingle's mark, but he must have found his lodgings elsewhere.

I produced a brimming whisky flask from my waistcoat, and Angus and I drained it before proceeding up the narrow, creaking stairs to confront Knifing.

"The smell of death is heavy in this place," the constable whispered.

I didn't smell much of anything, since my own nostrils were stuffed and scabbed as a result of my various recent injuries and indulgences, but I saw no reason to disagree with him.

The inner hallway was dark; barely lit by a couple of lamps, and I tensed myself as Angus worked the key in the lock. The door squeaked, and we stepped into Knifing's room, and found it empty.

"He hasn't been here," Angus said. "Perhaps he's slipped out of town."

"If he did, he left his things," I said. We paused for a moment to examine the heavy trunk at the foot of the bed. It was framed in iron and secured with a sturdy padlock. Breaking it open would require some uncommon skill or specialized tools, and neither was immediately at our disposal.

But something was wrong about the bed itself. I ran my hands over the blankets. They were tucked under the thin mattress and pulled tight and smooth.

"I've used the accommodations of various Cambridge inns when consorting with lovers whom I would not allow to be seen entering my campus residence," I said. "I often find the bed-clothes rumpled in these places and I'm lucky if the linens appear to have been recently laundered. I've never known an innkeeper to make a bed like this."

"You're right," Angus said. "That's how we square a rack in the army. Knifing did this himself." He peeled back the bedclothes and ran his hands over them. "The sheets are cool, but just slightly damp. He's slept here tonight, but he left some time ago."

In the wardrobe, we found the Baker rifle. Angus stuck his little finger down the barrel, and it came out black with powder.

"It's been fired very recently, unless Knifing's the sort to leave his weapon dirty." Neither of us thought Knifing was that sort. "But if Knifing is the killer, why would he stop Dingle from arresting you?"

"I'd have mounted a vigorous defense against the charges, and uncovered his misbehavior in the course of clearing my own name," I said. "He needs to pin the crimes on someone who can't effectively rebut them."

"But if he's fled, how do we find him?"

"Most likely, we don't," I said. Angus and I were employing techniques to track Knifing's whereabouts that the investigator himself had taught us. It was no wonder he had escaped ahead of our discovery; he probably had a number of deductive skills he hadn't shared with us. Maybe he had some way of knowing about Hanson's missive to me, and if he was adept in the tracking techniques of the bushman and the red Indian, he was probably capable of covering his trail as well. He'd have no trouble escaping to safety on the Continent before we ever got close to him.

"What a disappointing resolution," I said. "There were no vampires for me to discover, and no bandits for you to rain vengeance upon. Just a mad one-eyed butcher who outflanked and outsmarted us."

"Maybe when we crack open his luggage, we'll find some clue."

"I don't think he's the sort who'd leave us one. We didn't find anything useful at any of the murder scenes."

I looked around the room. Everything was clean; far cleaner than any room I'd ever seen in any English inn. He must have wiped the dust from all the furniture and moldings, and swept the floor, either as an expression of his fastidious nature or as a means of destroying some evidence of his guilt. I wondered what he'd done with all the blood he'd taken from the victims.

Angus shook his head. "I suppose it will be me who will have to go to London to tell poor Lord Whippleby his daughter's killer slipped away from us."

"I'll do it, if I can keep the rifle," I said.

"That's a murder weapon. You want no association with that."
We stepped back into the hallway and Angus locked the room.

"It's such a nice murder weapon, though."

Angus stuck the keys in his pocket; he didn't seem to think
the disposition of Knifing's rifle was a matter open for discussion.
"I could do with some breakfast," he said as he started back
downstairs.

"I could do with a drink," I said. But I stopped; a thought had
occurred to me. "When you said the stink of death was in this
place, did you mean that in a metaphorical sense?" I asked.

Angus turned, smushing his ample belly against the walls of
the narrow stairwell as he did so. "No. It smells in here."

The blood was concealed someplace nearby.

"We're not done searching," I said.

Chapter 38

For the Angel of Death spread his wings on the blast,
And breathed in the face of the foe as he pass'd;
And the eyes of the sleepers wax'd deadly and chill,
And their hearts but once heaved, and for ever grew
* still!*

—Lord Byron, *"The Destruction of Sennacherib"*

Angus paced up and down the hallway and decided the scent was strongest right by Knifing's door, so we searched the room again. We tugged on the floorboards, tapped on the walls, and moved the furniture around. There wasn't anything in there. We stepped back into the hallway and locked the door again.

"The smell is stronger in the hallway than it is in the room," the constable said.

I turned slightly, and regarded the door opposite Knifing's; room number 5. According to the paper I'd copied from the innkeeper's ledger, the occupant was one Colin Underhill. The name meant nothing to me.

Angus turned his key in the lock and pressed the door slightly open. I hadn't been able to smell it before, but I was buffeted now by a thick, meaty, rotten stink; the sheer power of it made both of us take a step backward.

"We should flee from this place," Angus whispered. "We should send for soldiers, or a magistrate."

"If we leave, whatever is in there may be gone by the time help arrives," I said. "We must summon the fortitude to investigate now."

Angus let out a soft, strained laugh. "I will say, in this situation, I am deeply sorry that we are not accompanied by your Professor."

"He'd never be so foolish as to step into that room."

"Remind me, then, why we act with less wisdom than a dumb beast."

"I'm a foolish drunk, and you're foolishly honorable."

"That's true, I suppose. So, our path is set."

Angus pressed on the door. Its hinges groaned in protest, and we lost any hope of surprising any enemies lurking inside the room. I peered through the opening, but saw nothing stirring. Indeed, I saw nothing at all; though it was a bright morning, the room's occupant had drawn heavy curtains over the room's one small window, and the dim light from the lamps mounted on the walls of the interior hallway didn't penetrate far past the doorway. Only a sliver of sun cut through the space between the curtains, giving us barely enough illumination to discern the outlines of the room's furniture; a chair, a low cot, and a large chest or wardrobe against the back wall, by the window. From the corner of the room farthest from both the door and the window, there was a strange sound; a discordant, toneless hum like the sound of a dozen violins playing out of tune and out of time, and muffled beneath a feather bed. In the darkness, I could not identify the source.

"What is that sound?" I asked.

"I've heard it once before; the day I found my wife and daughter in the woods. It's flies."

"But to make such noise, there must thousands."

A single tear rolled down Angus's rough cheek. "If we're going to undertake this plan, let's stop discussing it, and rise to action," he said. He unslung his musket and kicked the door all the way open. Leading with his gun, he barreled toward the room's darkest corner, where the awful noise originated.

I cleared the distance to the window in four strides and drew open the curtain, flooding the room with daylight. Angus was pointing the musket at a large wooden bathing-tub. It stank like Hell's breath, and insects crawled all over it, and across the puckered, congealed surface of the viscous liquid that filled it.

Angus turned toward me. "Here is all the blood he took," he said. "Oh my God, there is so much blood."

And then a figure rose from the bathtub; a tall, lanky man-shape, slick with gore. And as he rose, the putrid blood slopped over the edges of the foul vessel and poured onto the floor. The flies rose up in a black cloud, surrounding the monster and swarming outward, away from his movement. As they took to the air, their muffled buzzing turned into the high-pitched whine of ten thousand pairs of tiny wings beating in unison.

I shouted a warning to Angus, but he was too slow on his feet, and the bloody creature grabbed hold of the musket before the constable could take aim. The weapon discharged uselessly into the wall. The wraith had a knife, and he slid it into Angus just below the rib cage and then drew it down sharply, opening the constable's torso along his right side. Angus tried to scream, but he had no voice. I heard a wheezing sound coming from the chest wound, and knew that the knife-point had found his lungs. The blood-fiend gave the blade a cruel twist, and Angus's eyes rolled upward and his legs gave out. He hit his head on the edge of the tub as he fell, and his body collapsed to the floor like an inanimate thing, a sack of flour or a discarded doll.

The killer turned toward me; mad yellow eyes and sharp white teeth flashing in the light from the window. In the East, my father said, there are men, or things like men; things that have conquered death and feed on the blood of the innocent.

"I always knew you'd come back for me one day," I said to the vampire.

"For you?" it said. "Why must everything always be about you?"

I peered at the naked figure, the long face and neck, and the high peak of his forehead, and the limp, blood-matted strands of hair slicked against the sides of his skull. It was a familiar face, but it was not Mad Jack's.

"Mr. Frederick Burke," I said. "Does this mean that I need not fear litigious action from the Banque Crédit Française?"

"That should be the least of your worries," he said. "And Burke is not my name."

He leapt at me, and I pointed my pistol at him and discharged it. I should have hit him without difficulty, but my hand was shaking and the reek of fetid blood was so overwhelming that my eyes were full of tears. I missed; the ball whizzed past his head. He did not even flinch at the sound of the shot. And then my weapon was spent and useless, and he was upon me.

I braced myself against my strong leg; hugged his torso as he hit me, and I twisted in the direction of his momentum; hurling him to the ground. He wrapped an arm around my neck, and I gulped air, choking on the coppery stink. My weak ankle buckled beneath me, and I collapsed on top of him. As I fell, I bent my knee and aimed it at his body. I needed to hurt him. I needed to cripple him. But he was wet and slippery, and I couldn't hold him in place. He wriggled out of the way, and my knee hit the floor with the force of my weight behind it.

I howled in pain, and he saw in my misfortune an opportunity to wrench himself from my grasp. I recovered my senses as he was trying to get to his feet, so I gripped my spent pistol by the barrel and swung my arm in an arc, aiming to smash his skull with the hardwood grip. Burke attempted to dodge it, but I caught him high on the cheekbone, and he grunted and fell flat on his back. I heaved my body up into a kneeling position, ignoring the shooting pain in my bad leg, and I raised the gun again. If I could hit him hard enough at the spot behind the eye, where the skull was thin, the bone would give way. But he kicked out one of his long legs and struck me in the shoulder. I cried out, and lost my grip on the weapon.

Burke used the moment's respite this gave him to roll out from underneath me, and I staggered to my feet. He seemed to consider lunging at me again, but instead, he retreated toward the stinking vat; toward Angus and, I realized, toward the unused pistol the constable had been carrying.

Against the wall next to me was a wooden wardrobe, like the one we'd searched in Knifing's room. I threw my body against it, and it crashed to the floor. I dove behind it for cover. I drew my own second, loaded pistol from its holster at the base of my spine.

Angus was lying on his belly, trying, without much success, to keep his guts inside him. Burke grasped him roughly by the collar of his uniform shirt, and the constable put a hand in the killer's face to try to stop him. But Angus had little strength to resist; his life was draining out of him, and he could barely draw breath. His wound was making a wet sucking noise now.

Burke managed to roll Angus's body over, but the pistol had

fallen into a puddle of blood, and Angus had lain upon it as he bled. I peeked over my makeshift barricade and saw blood streaming out of the muzzle as Burke lifted it.

So I rose from my cover and the killer pointed his weapon at me; he squeezed the trigger. Nothing happened, of course; the powder was soaked.

"Mine's dry," I said.

"Twice you've missed me." Burke's voice was ragged from the exertion, but betrayed no fear; no emotion at all. "Miss once more, and I shall own you."

He was straddling Angus and eyeing the hilt of his knife sticking out of the dying man's belly. If I fired and didn't kill him, he'd need a second and a half to pull the blade loose, and two seconds more to run the length of the room. If I was very lucky, the dirk might stick a bit in Angus's flesh and buy me an extra few seconds.

Burke was strong, and he was bigger and taller than I. While he held the blade, I'd be unable to attempt to neutralize his reach by grappling with him. If I could not kill him with my pistol, I probably would not prevail in the struggle that would follow.

"Stay very still," I said.

He laughed.

Maybe I was about to shoot him; I certainly remember that I tried to steady my aim. And maybe he was about to pounce upon me; he appeared to be coiled to do so. But then, Archibald Knifing appeared in the doorway, holding a gun.

Chapter 39

A little tumult, now and then, is an agreeable quickener of sensation; such as a revolution, a battle, or an adventure of any lively description.

—Lord Byron, *from an 1813 journal entry*

"I see you've found the killer, Lord Byron," said Knifing. "I'm impressed. However did you figure it out?"

"I thought it was you," I said. "We came here to search your room, and stumbled onto Mr. Burke."

"My name is not Burke," said Burke.

"Whoever he is, I am just about to shoot him." My wrist, battered from the shackles and the stagecoach crash, was feeling sore and kind of shaky. I tried to steady my aim.

"When Lord Byron misses, I will stab him," said Not-Burke.

"Let's relax," said Knifing. "We can all still walk away. We don't want to commit some irreversible and ruinous act here."

"It's already too late," I said. "Angus Buford is mortally wounded by Burke's hand."

"The constable's death is convenient for all of us," said Knifing.

"He's got carpentry tools that can break open most locks in town, so he possessed a means of ingress to the private residences where the killings took place. He's former infantry, so he could have fired the rifle that killed Fielding Dingle. We can all claim to be witnesses to the depravity he committed in these rooms. We can walk away from this."

Angus could no longer speak, but the sound of his rasping quickened.

"He's owed dignity, if nothing else."

"What use have the dead for dignity?" Knifing asked.

"What else have the dead got?" I said.

"The dead have nothing," Knifing said. "That's why the prudent course is the one in which all of us live."

I waved my gun at him. "While I hold this, nobody gets to live without my permission."

"You can't kill us both with your one gun," said Not-Burke. "And once it's spent, you're at the mercy of whichever of us is left standing."

"Well, I've got it aimed at you now. So stop grinning at me."

"I don't fear you or your toys," Not-Burke said. "You are a coward. If you were man enough to fire, you would have already." He knelt down and pulled his knife out of Angus's gut. As the blade slid out of the wound, it brought with it a ruptured coil of purple viscera. Angus's whole body seemed to clench, and his back arched, and he sucked in a long rattling gasp. After that, he did not move again. His chest was still and his unblinking eyes stared fixedly into the middle distance; toward something imperceptible to the living. And then, the flies settled upon him.

"Who is this lunatic, Knifing? And why are you protecting him?" I asked.

"I serve the King," Knifing said. "I am here in Cambridge on His Majesty's orders."

I looked at Not-Burke, red and wet and naked, with insects crawling all over him. He looked like the very portrait of the Devil.

"Why would the King want this maniac protected? Why would His Majesty send you to cover up these crimes?"

"How much do you know about all this?" Knifing asked.

"I know about Blackpool," I said. "I know about Chelmsford and Grimsby. I know there were sprees of brutal killings in each of those places, and corpses drained of blood. I know that you investigated each event, and that, each time, you arrested and executed some local laborer. I know, now, that Burke was the perpetrator of all those crimes, and you bore false witness against innocent people to protect him."

"My name is not Burke," said Not-Burke. "And you know almost nothing; only enough to make your death convenient."

"My counsel in London, Mr. Hanson, collected that information, at my behest. He retains copies of all relevant documents, and knows what to do if harm befalls me."

"I'm sure we can make some sort of a deal," Knifing said. "Your discretion in this matter is of crucial importance to the security of England."

"All I see is a madman bathing in human blood. England will be well served by his destruction." I was tense, unsure whether to take my gun off Not-Burke to point it at Knifing. Both men were exceedingly dangerous.

Knifing kept his voice calm and soothing, and made no move toward me. "Let me ask, Byron, are you a loyal subject of the King?"

I shuffled my weight back and forth on my feet. My arm was starting to hurt. Not-Burke was standing as still as statuary, or as still as a predatory cat waiting for unsuspecting prey to wander within pouncing distance. "I'll not have you cast aspersions against my honor," I said to Knifing. "My family has a long military tradition, and my fealty is not subject to dispute."

"So I can assume, then, that you love your King and accept his rule?" Knifing asked.

"Of course." I took a step back and pressed my back against the far wall of the room, by the window. Neither Not-Burke nor Knifing moved toward me. I allowed my arm to bend a little, which relieved some discomfort but made me feel less safe.

Knifing leaned forward, casting a long, sinister shadow that rippled across the bloody hardwood floor of the room. "Why?" he asked. It was like he was prodding me with a rapier.

"Why do I love the King?"

"Yes."

I studied his face for clues and found none. He was impassive and inscrutable. I couldn't tell if the long pink scar robbed his face of expressiveness, or if it was the only thing that kept him from being completely blank. "I don't understand the question," I said.

He asked: "Have you ever met the King?"

"I've seen him, but never spoken to him at any length." I'd appeared at court during the previous London season. His Majesty had seemed aged and unwell. After a brief introduction, I had kept my distance and focused my attentions on various available women.

"And yet you love him. You must not love him for any personal quality he possesses, for you do not know him. So, we may say that you love the King solely because he is the King. Would you love him if he were not King?"

I could not understand why Knifing was playing rhetorical games. I was trapped; the two of them stood between me and the door, which was the only route of egress from the cramped room. I didn't say anything. The gun was starting to feel heavy. Knifing turned and regarded me with his white eye. I wondered if it was really dead, or if it still had some kind of sight, despite its discoloration.

When I did not speak, Knifing continued: "His Majesty's periodic affliction of the mind is well known, and was publicized during the regency crisis some years back. But while the populace is convinced His Majesty has recovered, the possibility of permanent incapacity is real. The severity of his illness is a closely held secret."

"But if the King is too infirm to fulfill his duties, the Prince of Wales may rule in his stead under a Regency Act, can he not?"

Knifing shrugged. "It has not been so long, relatively, since the American colonies rejected the Crown, and the French royalty was deposed shortly thereafter. The state of monarchy in Europe has, perhaps, never been more tenuous. The rule of a prince, even a crown prince, is not rule of a king. And if England undergoes a period of prolonged rule by something other than a king, even if it is a king-in-waiting, the Throne shall never regain its power. It has long been held that the King's rule is his Divine Right; that the King is appointed by God. How can George be the divinely chosen King, and yet be unfit to sit the Throne? The very idea of a regency punctures the essential premise of the monarchy, and would forever erode the legitimacy of the King's claim; of any king's claim. Parliament is staging a coup, Lord Byron."

I began to suspect Knifing was trying to keep me talking until my arm dropped. I braced my right hand with my left and squinted down the barrel at Burke, or whoever he was. "I see very little relation between these esoteric political concerns and Mr. Not-Burke and his vat of putrid blood."

Knifing kept talking. "There are influential members of the House of Lords who want to see the monarchy weakened. They are agitating for a new Regency Act, a law that will frame the King as a madman and strip away the powers of the Crown without His Majesty's consent. A few powerful Peers command legislative constituencies that can block the bill. These men wield tremendous influence over how the Empire will be ruled in the future, and this gentleman's father is among them."

I tried to think of a marquess or a powerful earl who physically resembled Not-Burke. I didn't think he could be a duke's son; most of them were relatives of the Royal family and not predisposed to betray the Crown.

"So this influential father will help to hide the King's madness, and protect the Throne from action by Parliament, in return for the King's assistance in covering up the son's killings," I said.

"My father is a swine," Not-Burke said, and he filled the room with manic giggles. "I'd cut him up like your silly constable, if he would ever come home to see me. But I am undeserving of his attention, it seems."

"His father has promised to keep him sequestered in the countryside, where the harm he does can be contained," Knifing said. "But it is unseemly for a gentleman to turn his manor house into a prison, and propriety must trump security on certain matters. The young master escapes sometimes. The father will not allow his son to be recaptured by force; someone of his line must not have lesser hands laid upon him. So, His Majesty has tasked me with retrieving the lad when he gets loose, gently remanding him to his father's custody and containing the damage he's caused. My charge finds great delight in watching me scramble to cover up his crimes."

"But surely you realize that protecting this man is reckless and immoral. The amusement he derives from forcing you to conceal his crimes is probably the only reason he has not yet stabbed you while you sleep."

"I do not fear death," Knifing said.

"Perhaps not, but I am sure you would prefer to receive it from more honorable hands."

Knifing frowned. "There is no greater honor than death in His Majesty's service."

Not-Burke laughed again. He was still standing over Angus, who had been a better man, by far, than any of the three of us. I felt sordid, making conversation with the constable's killer while his still-warm corpse lay supine on the floor.

"Why has he been killing people I know?" I asked. "Why did he impersonate a debt collector to hound me? Why did he come into my window to kill Noreen Lime? What's this got to do with me?"

"Men like you and my father wander arrogantly about, taking whatever you want, while I am stuck in my house and consigned to the margins of society for my predilections." Not-Burke gripped the knife so hard, his knuckles turned white and the cords of his forearm bulged beneath the skin of his wrist. "Why should you walk among men and cavort with girls, while I am locked away? Why should your excesses be tolerated, while mine are condemned? Who says you're better than I?"

Knifing pointed a contemptuous finger at Not-Burke. "I told you; unstable minds are drawn to celebrities and magnetic personalities. Lord Whippleby is a friend of his father, and he came here after Felicity, but you certainly got his attention when you showed up drunk at the murder scene, demanding entrance. He's fascinated with your notoriety. He would have gone to Harrow or Eton, but after he dismembered a chambermaid, his father kept him home. I told him when I followed him here that he must not get up to his mischief in such close proximity to you, but my warnings seemed only to encourage him to do everything possible to force your continued involvement in this business. For that you have my sincere apologies."

I raised the gun again, ignoring the pain in my shoulder. "You're the one who supplied him with the information about my dealings with Banque Crédit Française. He used that as a pretense to enter my home. How did you even discover the details of my private business?"

"I'm an investigator, and I am very thorough in my inquiries. But I should not have disclosed that information to my charge. In retrospect, I see it was an error in judgment."

The knowledge that the bank itself, lacking Knifing's thoroughness, might not yet know of my misconduct was a source of some relief, and the revelation would have been quite welcome under other circumstances.

"That apology would be accepted with appreciation if you weren't holding a gun on me," I said.

Knifing shook his head. "It's the best I can offer. But I mean it sincerely."

"Mr. Dingle arrested me," I said. "I could have been hanged for Burke's crimes."

"No." Knifing gestured emphatically with his pistol, and, startled, I nearly threw myself to the floor. "I never would have allowed you to be tried. Your lawyers would have investigated my records, discovered the other murders, and unraveled the conspiracy. I hope you appreciate my decision to extricate you from Mr. Dingle's clutches."

"Your actions and your omissions put me in that situation, and I could have been killed in the stagecoach crash. You were willing to tolerate that risk, though, weren't you?" I looked at the bayonet scar that bisected his face, and considered his square-shouldered military bearing. "You've got quite an aim with the Baker rifle, especially for a one-eyed man," I said. Rage surged in my chest, and I felt my face and neck flush.

"The continuity of the monarchy is worth more than either of our lives."

"Not to me, it isn't. I've no desire to die protecting a mad killer so that his corrupt father will shield a mad king."

"Watch your tongue, boy," Knifing said, his scar crinkling around his twisted features. "You come dangerously close to treason when you speak that way."

"Look at this room, Knifing," I said, pointing at the blood splattered on the walls and pooled on the floor, and at the corpse of the constable. "All this death to protect a King who can no longer protect himself, a King who must bargain with extortionists."

"We can find an agreement," said Knifing. "We can all walk away from this. A man like you is always wanting things. Money and women and drugs. The King has many resources, and some could be made available for your benefit."

"There will be no deal," said Not-Burke. "I've no reason to negotiate with you, Byron, because you have uncovered no secrets I care to protect. Your information can connect those killings only to Archibald Knifing. Your representative knows nothing of me, and once you're dead, he never will. If he publicizes what little he's uncovered, only Knifing will be incriminated, and this loyal servant will accept the blame for my crimes to protect his beloved King. He'll hang by his neck, and he'll be thankful for the opportunity to be of service. I will be rid of both of you, and I'll be free to resume my activities. You and your representative do not even know my name."

"Perhaps I don't," I conceded. "But I know how to learn it."

"I'm curious to hear how you propose to obtain that crucial fact."

"I shall read it in your obituary," I said, and I discharged my pistol.

The ball struck his long throat, bursting his Adam's apple like a fat pimple and ripping his neck open. Not-Burke made several wet, gasping noises and then collapsed to his knees. He retched, and blood poured from his mouth, and from his gaping injury as well. He tried, once, to stand, but the trauma had rendered him feeble, and he pitched forward and struck his head upon the wood floor with a sharp crack. He clawed with his fingers at the ragged wound in his throat as if trying to clear his windpipe of some obstruction. He opened his mouth and tried to scream, but no sound came out. His cheeks had turned blue, and his lolling tongue was thick and purple.

He collapsed and bashed his head against the floor a second time, and then his body began to shake violently. When he spastically rolled onto his back, I could see that his skull was misshapen; he'd beaten his own brains out.

Not-Burke did not rise again; he only twitched a few times, and then he was still. His blood sprayed out of his neck in great spurts at first, but the pulses quickly grew weaker, and then slowed to a trickle, and a black shroud of flies settled upon his body, as they had upon Angus.

"My God. You've killed him," said Knifing.

"Of course I did," I said. "You saw the atrocities he committed against Violet Tower and her children." I threw my spent weapon on the floor. "In this circumstance, prudence and passion counseled the same response. I could not have done otherwise."

Chapter 40

He, who grown aged in this world of woe,
In deeds, not years, piercing the depths of life,
So that no wonder waits him; nor below
Can love, or sorrow, fame, ambition, strife,
Cut to his heart again with the keen knife
Of silent, sharp endurance: he can tell
Why thought seeks refuge in lone caves, yet rife
With airy images, and shapes which dwell
Still unimpair'd, though old, in the soul's haunted
    cell.

—Lord Byron, Childe Harold's
Pilgrimage, *canto 3*

I was unarmed and cornered. Knifing was still standing in the doorway, legs spread shoulder-width, holding a pistol on me.

I believed I had better-than-even odds of beating him in a fistfight, though I was hurt and exhausted. He was a tough man and a trained soldier, but he was old and slight. Still, I didn't see how I could get close enough to lay hands on him; he'd shoot me down. I had no hope he might miss. He'd made two impossible shots with the Baker rifle to kill Dingle and the coachman; it would be for him a triviality to hit me with a pistol from three paces away. I probably should have used my shot to take down the investigator, and taken my chances in hand-to-hand combat with Not-Burke and his knife.

"So, what's going to happen now? Are you going to shoot me?" I asked.

Knifing thought about it for a moment, and then lowered the gun. "I hope I won't have to."

"Are you angry I've killed your little friend?"

"Quite the opposite. The world's no worse off for his loss. My honor would not permit me to disobey orders and get rid of him myself, but I am not displeased by this resolution."

"But you are undone now," I said. "Surely the father will be wroth, and he'll cease to aid the King in Parliament."

"He will not," Knifing said. "I have planned for this contingency. Hoped for it, even. This could have happened the other night when Jerome Tower almost got the better of him, or any night that little shit went slithering into someone's residence with ill intent. The father can still be controlled; he still has a secret that needs keeping. He doesn't want the world to know what his son was, and how he abetted the lad's gruesome deeds."

"But surely all that will come out now. How can it possibly be concealed?"

"I already bought the innkeeper's discretion. The undertaker's, too."

"What about the other tenants here in the inn? They must have heard the shot."

"There are no other tenants. I rented all the rooms when I arrived, and signed for them with false names. As far as anyone is concerned, this man never came to Cambridge. He died on his father's estate, mortally injured in a tragic accident. There is nobody around to say otherwise."

I raised an eyebrow. "There's me."

"Yes," Knifing said.

"So your charade depends on my acquiescence. It seems I find myself in a position of considerable power over you, Mr. Knifing," I said.

He brandished the pistol. "Only if I decide not to shoot you."

"If you shoot me, Mr. Hanson will publicize what he knows about you. To protect the King then, you'll have to admit to the crimes and hang for them. I'm sure you'd prefer not to."

"I'd rather have your complicity," Knifing conceded.

"You mentioned money, girls, and drugs?"

He nodded.

"I'd like all those things, please." This dire situation was beginning to look more agreeable. "I have amassed considerable debts, as you've evidently uncovered in your research. I'll need them settled, including my account with Banque Crédit Française."

Knifing nodded again. I decided to press for more.

"A number of properties I inherited from my great-uncle were burdened with improper leases and other encumbrances. As his interest in those assets was only a life-estate, he had no right to let those assets for any duration beyond his death. However, litigation with his tenants is ongoing. He gave away the lands on unconscionably one-sided terms to spite his heirs, and the present occupants cling to them tenaciously. I'd like to see these matters resolved in my favor."

"I'm not sure I can interfere with the process of the courts,"

Knifing said. "The legal system's independence from politics is fiercely guarded, and judges hate being told what to do."

This was expected. "Then I want more money," I said. "The market value of leases on those properties, retroactively and prospectively, made available to me on deposit."

"I'm sure we can offer you a tidy sum," Knifing said. "A reward that will satisfactorily convey the King's gratitude for your discretion in this matter. But I will warn you not to attempt to use this secret to extort more money from the Crown when you waste what we give you. While the King rains indulgences upon his friends, he does not capitulate to his enemies."

"His Majesty rolled over and offered his royal ass to Burke's father, didn't he?"

"Lord Byron, you will mind your tongue. I am content to shower generosity upon you if we may settle this matter now, but if you persist in being a loose end, you will get tied up."

"You will blame all the murders on poor Angus?"

"He was a decent chap, but he's dead. No slight on his reputation can cause him further harm."

"He has a daughter. This will be disastrous for her. She'll have no prospects, and she has no one left to look after her."

Knifing nodded gravely. "His Majesty's generosity will be extended to her as well. I'll get her out of town, away from her father's name and its history, and set her up in the country with a nice income and some property. She'll be cared for by chaperones until she's of age, and then she'll be a fine match for any eligible lad who happens to be interested in wealth."

I searched his face for dishonesty. He was, as always, inscrutable, and I knew he was untrustworthy. But I wanted badly to believe him, so I decided he was telling the truth. "The

Treasury is laying out a great deal of coin to keep this matter quiet," I said.

"These funds are the King's to dispose of as he sees fit," said Knifing. "And the King sees fit to keep his Throne."

"The man I shot is neither Frederick Burke nor Colin Underhill. Who is he?"

"On my honor, I'll never tell you his name, nor are you likely to learn any more about this matter. You'll certainly get no more from me. None of this ever happened." He put away his pistol.

I hesitated for as long as the noble facets of my nature could hold me at bay; not longer than a few seconds. Then, I succumbed to temptation. "Of course it didn't," I said, and I shook his thin, bony hand.

Chapter 41

Such are the men who learning's treasures guard!
Such is their practice, such is their reward!
This much, at least, we may presume to say—
The premium can't exceed the price they pay.

—Lord Byron, *"Thoughts Suggested by a*
College Examination"

I left Knifing and his friend Bartholomew the undertaker to clean up the hideous mess in the inn. I went straight to the brothel, where I let the whores draw me a bath, and then I drank and fucked until I slid into a state of dreamless unconsciousness. Despite all my recent excitement, I'd slept more in the three days since I'd begun investigating the murder of Felicity Whippleby than I had in the previous three weeks.

I awoke late in the afternoon and had another tumble with one of the girls. When I was finished, I added the services I'd consumed to the line of credit the establishment had kindly extended me and headed back toward the College.

I found Old Beardy in his office. The sun was only just

beginning the downward part of its daily arc, but he had his curtains pulled closed and was working by the light of an oil lamp; writing furiously in some kind of ledger. He looked up as I entered.

"Hello, Professor Brady."

"Lord Byron," he said. "I'm pleased by the news that you've been exonerated, as I understand it, of all those nasty accusations. I was somewhat aggrieved, however, to learn that kindly Mr. Buford was responsible for the killings. I knew him a little bit, and never would have suspected. I commissioned quite a bit of carpentry from him; a number of lecterns and desks and chairs for the College. Perhaps I shall have to replace them now. Regardless, I'm pleased to see you back in Cambridge."

"I don't intend to stay here for long," I said.

"As I've told you, I'd consider it a grievous error in judgment for you to abandon your studies."

I spoke without waiting for him to ramble out another disorganized thought. "Nothing will be abandoned. My studies will be finished in top form, and I'll earn all the most prestigious prizes and Latin honors your department is empowered to confer upon me. I just won't be spending any more time in Cambridge."

"I don't understand," Beardy said.

"Let me explain it simply, then," I said. "If you'd like, you may consider this my thesis project: It would have been difficult if not impossible for Angus Buford to kill Cyrus Pendleton on the same night he massacred the Tower family. The massacre, you see, would have been quite a time-consuming enterprise. The killer needed to drag the corpse of Professor Tower from the bedroom to the dining room, and pose it at the dinner table. He had to drain the blood from Mrs. Tower's corpse, and then he had to carry a sloshing bucket of the stuff to the foul vat he had concealed in a rented room all the way across the city, at the Burning Tyger Inn. Pendleton was seen inside the Modest Proposal alive at half past ten. The Towers' housemaid opened the door to Buford. She would not have been awake much past eleven. The tavern closed at midnight. The timing of the murders is confusing."

"What are you suggesting?"

"Angus Buford did not kill Cyrus Pendleton," I said.

"This is really absurd."

"Pendleton had pushed you out of the College, hadn't he? He'd taken over your position. You were to be sent off to your pension and your dotage. A just reward for a long and distinguished career."

"I don't think I like what you're insinuating."

"I'm only saying that, in the wake of this sudden and unfortunate tragedy, it's quite noble of you to delay your well-earned retirement and stay on as the head of the department."

"Can you prove these incredible allegations?"

"Proof is a malleable thing, Professor. You show people a set of facts that makes sense, and they're apt to believe it," I said.

"This is slander. This is entirely baseless. This is—"

I interrupted him again: "This is ruinous, once the allegations are uttered in public, and I'm sure you understand that."

"You're a monster."

"We've both killed men this week, Professor Brady. Let's not go putting ugly labels on things, though. My silence in this matter has a price you can afford."

"Diplomas. Prizes. Latin honors," he said.

"And a fellowship for my bear. It doesn't need to have a teaching component. Just a sheepskin denoting the honor, and a reasonable stipend to fund his studies."

"You're depraved," said Old Beardy.

"Well, I learned from the best," I said. "Or, at least, the best outside of Oxford."

"Blackguard. Extortionist. Mad, lame, drunken thief."

"I'm pleased you find my terms acceptable. My lawyer will be contacting you to handle the details. Good day," I said. And I stood and strode out the door, keeping my gait as smooth as my weak leg could manage. Blood was singing in my ears as I burst through the front door of the building and out onto the manicured carpet of the College's Great Lawn.

My body was bruised and my head was concussed and I was sick to my stomach, but nonetheless, I felt liberated. My finances were now in better repair than they'd ever been, my education was complete, with top marks, and my future was spread before me. I turned my face toward the late afternoon sun and closed my eyes. I could go wherever I wanted.

A few weeks later, I went East.

Chapter 42

I have a personal dislike to Vampires, and the little acquaintance I have with them would by no means induce me to reveal their secrets.

—Lord Byron, *from an 1819 letter to the editor of* Galignani's Messenger

Archibald Knifing delivered the money he promised, and that run of fortune paid for my adventures in the Levant, which inspired me to write *Childe Harold's Pilgrimage,* a work of enormous and incontrovertible literary import.

However, I searched the London papers for reports about tragedy in the family of some earl or viscount, and I found no death-notice that could possibly have described the man whose name was not Frederick Burke. This seemed strange, but the wealth of those close to the Crown could buy a lot of discretion, and it was not unheard of for a shameful death in a well-heeled family to go unheralded in the press.

So I listened for gossip. While Knifing would not tell me whether Not-Burke was an heir or a younger son, the death of anyone in line to inherit an important title was always much discussed among certain social circles. Wild fluctuations in the marriage market would necessarily ensue in the wake of such a tragedy. Various players would have to reconsider their strategies. Some younger brother or close cousin would be a step closer to inheriting, and the prospects of all eligible relations to the decedent would need to be recalculated. But I heard no discussion of any death that could possibly be Not-Burke's. Perhaps, if Not-Burke had been formally disinherited, he could have died and been buried without much fanfare or outside interest, and such an act by his father may, indeed, have been the fount of Not-Burke's rage.

But still, the mad, disgraced son of an earl would be of implicit interest to gossips, and the death of such a figure would ordinarily be, at the least, fodder for much idle conversation. The silence surrounding these events was suspicious.

But I had sworn myself to secrecy and could, thus, undertake no further inquiry into the matter. Asking questions would break my promise to Knifing. So I set out for the Continent and left my thoughts about the man I'd killed behind, along with my mother and the Professor.

It was years later, as my fortunes and my marriage and my reputation came unspooled that I began to reconsider everything that had occurred in Cambridge. I had recently vacated Newstead after separating from my wife, and I discovered William Byron's big black wardrobe among the effects Annabella had sent to my new lodgings in London. I still had a key to the sturdy padlock, and I found my arcane texts undisturbed inside.

As I had lapsed into solitude and melancholia, I found myself with ample time to consider the Cambridge murders, the vampires, and the fate of my father. Breaking, for the first time, the promise I'd made to Knifing, I began recording my narrative of those dark events.

Among my collection of vampire lore were certain tracts that discussed the habit among vampires to employ weak-willed men as thralls or familiars; hypnotized slaves tasked with seeing to the monster's interests while it slumbers. These men gradually lose their minds as their wills are broken by the vampire's influence, and they are known to subsist on insects and rodents and the festering remains of drained victims.

As I sat amidst the detritus of my ruined life, I reconsidered these materials and convinced myself that the wild-eyed Mr. Not-Burke, bathing in sour blood and covered in flies, may not have been the monster he seemed, but rather, merely an ordinary man under the power of such a nefarious spell.

The thrall, according to texts, will lure or force victims into the vampire's lair, and bleed them so the master may feed at its leisure. If circumstances require it, this wretched mortal servant will happily die to protect the monster. This revelation made it clear to me that Knifing was a vampire after all, and that he'd fabricated the story about the killer and the King, and had sacrificed his minion in furtherance of the lie.

If this supposition was correct, poor, innocent Angus had been a scapegoat for a scapegoat, and my lies about his death had insulated and protected the deeper lies that Knifing told me.

I spent a lot of time thinking about vampires' supposed allergy to sunlight, and about how Knifing had carried an umbrella when the sky bore no signs warning of rain, and how he shaded his pale skin with his wide-brimmed bush hat when he went about in the daytime. And I began to make certain inquiries.

According to public records, which my attorney, Mr. Hanson, assisted me in researching, Archibald Knifing disappeared in

1809. His house was found empty, and he had apparently informed no one of his whereabouts. After a reasonable time, it was assumed he had died while traveling abroad, and his affairs were disposed of according to the law. Since Mr. Knifing left no will and the court could find no heirs, the property reverted to the Crown and was sold at auction.

I will protect the current inhabitants by not revealing their names or the address of the house, but I visited the place. It was a relatively ordinary country estate, well constructed and appointed, but of modest size. I was convinced that some secret to Knifing's true nature was concealed within. Fortunately, the owners had read my poems and were flattered to receive the attention of a celebrity. They indulged my investigation, which must have seemed strange to them, and allowed me to search their home for clues.

First, I counted the house's exterior windows and verified that their number corresponded to the number of interior rooms, as they ought to have; an extra window would have signified a secret chamber. I measured hallways to see if there was a geometric inconsistency that might indicate the presence of a false wall. I tapped on baseboards, looking for hollow places, and I tugged every molding, fixture, and candelabra, in hopes of finding a concealed lever. There was nothing of the sort.

The house's only feature of note was a small cellar with earthen walls. While it wasn't extraordinary for a house to have an unfinished underground space to store wines or vegetables, a cellar would ordinarily have an outdoor entrance, or would be accessed through the kitchen. The entryway to Knifing's cellar was in the master bedroom, which I thought was a most unusual place for it. The door to it was also very heavy and sturdy, and could be locked from the inside.

I consulted an architect about this strangeness, and he told me that it was not so uncommon a feature as I might have imagined; it was even fashionable among some well-off bachelors to build a small wine cellar accessible from their bedrooms so that fine beverages might be easily available without having to interrupt an intimate liaison by summoning a servant to fetch wine.

The architect also posited that the addition of the secure door might allow the cellar to function as a sort of modern castle-keep; a fortified room into which the occupant could flee and take shelter if brigands invaded the house. In fact, many finer homes throughout England had been outfitted with such burrows after Louis and his queen were dragged from Versailles by a mob of common folk.

But it seemed to me that such an earthen cellar would also be an ideal place for a vampire to keep his coffin; much of the vampire lore held that the creatures needed to return to the soil to rest. And, anyway, how could a man like Archibald Knifing, a war hero and a confidant of the King, simply disappear? If he was dead, why was there no news of his demise?

I laid the whole story out for Hanson, and he felt it more sensible to ascribe ordinary explanations to the various events that aroused my suspicions. Disappearance, he said, was not uncommon among wanderers. Many people did not carry forwarding addresses for their relatives among their effects while journeying abroad, and when tragedy struck, such people were routinely remanded to local undertakers and ended up buried anonymously in churchyards. As for the cellar, Hanson was happy to accept the architect's explanation. And, he said, lots of men carry umbrellas when there's no rain, especially older gentlemen who are too proud to admit they need walking-sticks to lean upon.

I always listen patiently to Hanson's advice, but I frequently disregard it. So, I'm not yet done with this. When I return to the Continent, I will distract myself from the shambles I've made of my life and my marriage by attempting to pick up Knifing's trail. There are rumors that the King of Prussia has a one-eyed military advisor. I've heard talk, as well, of a doomed caravan lost in the Austrian Alps. Only one man is said to have made it out alive. The vague descriptions of the lone survivor don't seem to match Knifing's features, but they might describe my father's.

The Alps, I think, are close to Prussia. I find it all very suspicious. There must be more to this; there must be some meaning to it.

A poet must have a keen eye for details and for feelings; for subtext and for innuendo. This same set of skills is also essential if one hopes to have any success at the pursuit of vampires and the settling of accounts with absentee fathers. My investigation is ongoing, and I am eminently well suited to the task.

Epilogue

I am too well avenged!—but 't was my right;
Whate'er my sins might be, thou *wert not sent*
To be the Nemesis who should requite—
Nor did heaven choose so near an instrument.
Mercy is for the merciful!—if thou
Hast been of such, 't will be accorded now.
Thy nights are banish'd from the realms of sleep!—
Yes! they may flatter thee, but thou shalt feel
A hollow agony which will not heal,
For thou art pillow'd on a curse too deep;
Thou hast sown in my sorrow, and must reap
The bitter harvest in a woe as real!

—Lord Byron, *"Lines, On Hearing*
That Lady Byron Was Ill"

I saw Olivia Wright once more, when I visited her during the course of preparing this account of the 1807 Cambridge murders. During the nine years since I'd last spoken to her, she had taken over her father's business interests and, through clever maneuverings, improved them. But she never married.

The first thing I noticed when I visited her London home was the size of the staff she employed. I counted a house steward, several domestic maids, and two footmen as I waited in the parlor for her to receive me. The presence of the footmen implied that the house employed several cooks, and Olivia must have had at least one more maid to care for her wardrobe and chambers. There was probably a housekeeper someplace to supervise this extensive retinue.

Even the more lavish London homes were much smaller than sprawling, drafty country estates like Newstead Abbey, but I had let entire wings of my house fall into disuse and disrepair, and despite my larger space, I'd never employed this many domestic servants. I'd never had enough money to support so many people, even in the flush years after I accepted Knifing's bribe.

That a commoner's house should be grander and better kept than a nobleman's was increasingly the fashion. Many old families had nothing but unalienable land holdings, the incomes from which were often insufficient even to combat the rot and dilapidation of the properties themselves.

Britain had become, therefore, a nation of pimps, as the new rich, like Sedgewyck's family, awash with cash but lacking respectability, sought to wed their daughters and their fortunes to hereditary titles. The old aristocracy, meanwhile, bartered its sons for the funds to continue in the lifestyles its members considered their birthrights.

My own marriage had been untainted by parental depredations; my wife's darling mother hated me so much that she had written the Prince Regent for a special permission to prevent her

daughter from taking my name. Her dislike was entirely unjusti-
fied, as I was quite the ideal husband, unless one was so crass as
to take issue with my state of financial disarray or my constant
drunkenness or my habitual adultery.

But my trespasses were entirely forgivable, given my wife's
coldness, her obnoxious rectitude, and her inability to sate my
lusts. Our attraction had been based, on both sides, upon a myth
of romantic transformation; she thought she could redeem me,
and I believed I could corrupt her. We'd both been wrong.

Olivia's steward guided me through the entryway, down a
short hallway, through a well-appointed library, and to a set of
glass doors that opened upon a lush interior courtyard. Though
the little garden was probably shaded for much of the day, the
area was evenly carpeted by healthy grass, and the cascading
flower beds along the perimeter of the space were remarkable for
the color and variety of their foliage. Many of these plants, I
knew, were quite fragile and challenging to cultivate, and I added
a master gardener to my mental tally of the house staff.

At the center of this idyllic space sat a small wicker table and
two chairs; furniture light enough that it would not bruise the sod.
A lady's silk scarf lay on the grass, and a book rested on the table,
open, with the spine up. I smiled; Olivia had been sitting out
here when I arrived, and she fled inside when she'd heard I was at
the door. I wondered if she had gone to put her face together, or if
she'd merely left so I'd have to wait for her to receive me.

I picked up the novel. It was a recent bestseller, beloved by
women; one I hadn't had the time or inclination to read. It was
called *Pride and Prejudice,* and the author was named only as "a
lady." I flipped to the front, intentionally losing Olivia's place in
it, and I perused the first page:

It is a truth universally acknowledged, that a single man in possession of a good fortune, must be in want of a wife.

"Perhaps he'll take mine," I said to myself.

"Do you need something, sir?" asked the steward, who had overheard me.

"I was only reading." I pitched the novel onto the ground. "Where is Olivia?"

"She'll be out presently. I'm sure she apologizes most sincerely for the delay. May I offer you a cup of tea?"

"I'll take whisky, if you've got any," I said.

But she left me sitting for nearly half an hour, long enough for me to drink three generous glasses of well-aged Scotch and start on a fourth. At some point, I retrieved *Pride and Prejudice* from the grass and leafed through it. Olivia appeared, eventually, looking quite radiant, though, at the age of twenty-six, the flower of her youth had long since withered.

"Lord Byron," she said. "It has been some time since I've seen you."

I rose from my seat. "Nine years."

"I apologize for making you wait. It was quite unavoidable," she said without actually seeming the least bit sorry.

"It's quite all right. I've found something to read."

"Oh, that." She took the book from me, gently brushed the dirt from its cover, and set it back on the little table. "It's been very popular in London, though I suppose it's hardly the equal of *Childe Harold's Pilgrimage*."

"You didn't write it, did you?"

"Hardly. Though the author is a friend of my family. A sweet, sweet woman. What is your expert's literary assessment of its merits?"

"There's nothing wrong with that woman that I couldn't fix in ten minutes, with my prick," I said. I suppose I'd meant to shock or offend her, for I was annoyed by the long delay, though her courtyard was a nice enough place to sit.

She merely laughed at me. "Perhaps your reparative efforts would be better directed toward Lady Byron."

"I fear, alas, that what's broken in that one is hopelessly unsalvageable."

Olivia leaned toward me and touched my knee with her fingertips. "I've heard rumors about you. Are they true?"

I pulled myself away from her touch and, piqued, swept the book back onto the ground with my forearm. "Some of them are. And the rest of them might as well be, once they've been whispered in every ear in London. What drugs and promiscuity and rampant spending could never do to me, marriage has done in but a single year. I am ruined. I'm fleeing England, forever."

"So why have you come here?"

"I am writing a memoir; my account of the Cambridge murders. I'd like to ask about your recollection of those events."

"I don't really know much," she said. "I'd heard you were arrested, but then you weren't anymore. And then Mr. Knifing announced the killer was that horrible carpenter, and you left Cambridge shortly after. I thought you'd come calling, after Mr. Sedgewyck's death. Though I grieved for him, I was, in a way, relieved that I didn't have to marry him."

"He probably would have made a fine husband," I said. "I'm sure he would have tenderly loved your family's money."

"How romantic of him."

"He wasn't a romantic. I'm a romantic. He was a prudent man. I warned you about prudent men."

"And I have approached such sensible suitors with caution ever since."

"Sedgewyck's death was perhaps the least tragic of the Cambridge killings, though I had little affection for Professor Pendleton or Fielding Dingle."

"His manner of dealing was heartless and cowardly. But you left me, as well," said Olivia.

"I did not. You spurned me, and chose Mr. Sedgewyck."

"You said you loved me, but you never returned, not even to say good-bye."

"I was arrested."

"Only briefly."

"Is that why you never married? Out of devotion to me?"

She laughed again. "I wouldn't call it devotion, though being perceived as Byron's leavings has been no great help to my prospects. However, the chief reason I have never married was that I never found anyone suitable."

"Surely you've had many proposals." I knew a number of eligible barons and at least one marquess who would have thought Olivia's countenance entirely acceptable, despite her age, and they'd have found her wealth quite compelling.

"The last time I saw you, you presented me with a dichotomy, a choice between the passionate lover and the prudent suitor. You and Mr. Sedgewyck gave me an object lesson in the failings of both sorts of men. I do not like being viewed the way Sedgewyck saw me; as a chattel—as a piece in some game. But you gave me little reason to hold out hope for romantic love, Lord Byron. You turned so cold, so fast, and you abandoned me."

I didn't need to tell her that I was abandoned first. I said, "I was never dishonest about what I had to offer you."

"You'd carry your love in your insect heart, to cliffsides

and mountains and minarets. I remember what you offered. You weren't dishonest. You were only selfish. I have never married because I require an unselfish man, and I have yet to meet one."

"You must be very lonely."

Her brow knit: "Men of inadequate character make for poor company. I am quite content with my business and my books."

"But surely you desire a legacy. Who will look after all you've built, when you're gone?"

She shrugged indifferently. "I've a handful of nieces and nephews, and some cousins. When the time comes, I may divide it among them, or bequeath it all to the worthiest. Or I might birth a bastard. No law exists anymore that would prevent such a child from inheriting. The world is changing, Lord Byron. Thirty years ago, a lady could not have survived on her own, but men have lately become quite superfluous."

What I was thinking was that, if she no longer sought a prudent husband, she no longer had any reason to guard her chastity. "We remain necessary in at least one respect," I said, and I rose from my seat and moved toward her.

"You'd be quite surprised," she said. "There are techniques. And devices."

"I'll wager a thousand pounds that my techniques are better than your techniques."

"You haven't got a thousand pounds, Lord Byron."

But when I reached out to touch her face, she let me. "I rather doubt you're entirely satisfied by your solitary life," I said, brushing my fingers through her hair.

She smiled. "Are you offering to fix what's wrong with me?"

"I wouldn't want to leave again, without giving you a proper good-bye."

"Very well," she said. "I've no other plans for the next ten minutes."

She stood with a smooth motion, and I drew my hand back. The steward held the glass door open as she walked back into her house. Her stride was long and supple and imperious.

I finished my drink, and then I followed her.